Exposed Ink

USA TODAY BESTSELLING AUTHOR

NIKKI ASH

Little by little, we let go of loss, but never of love.
—Unknown

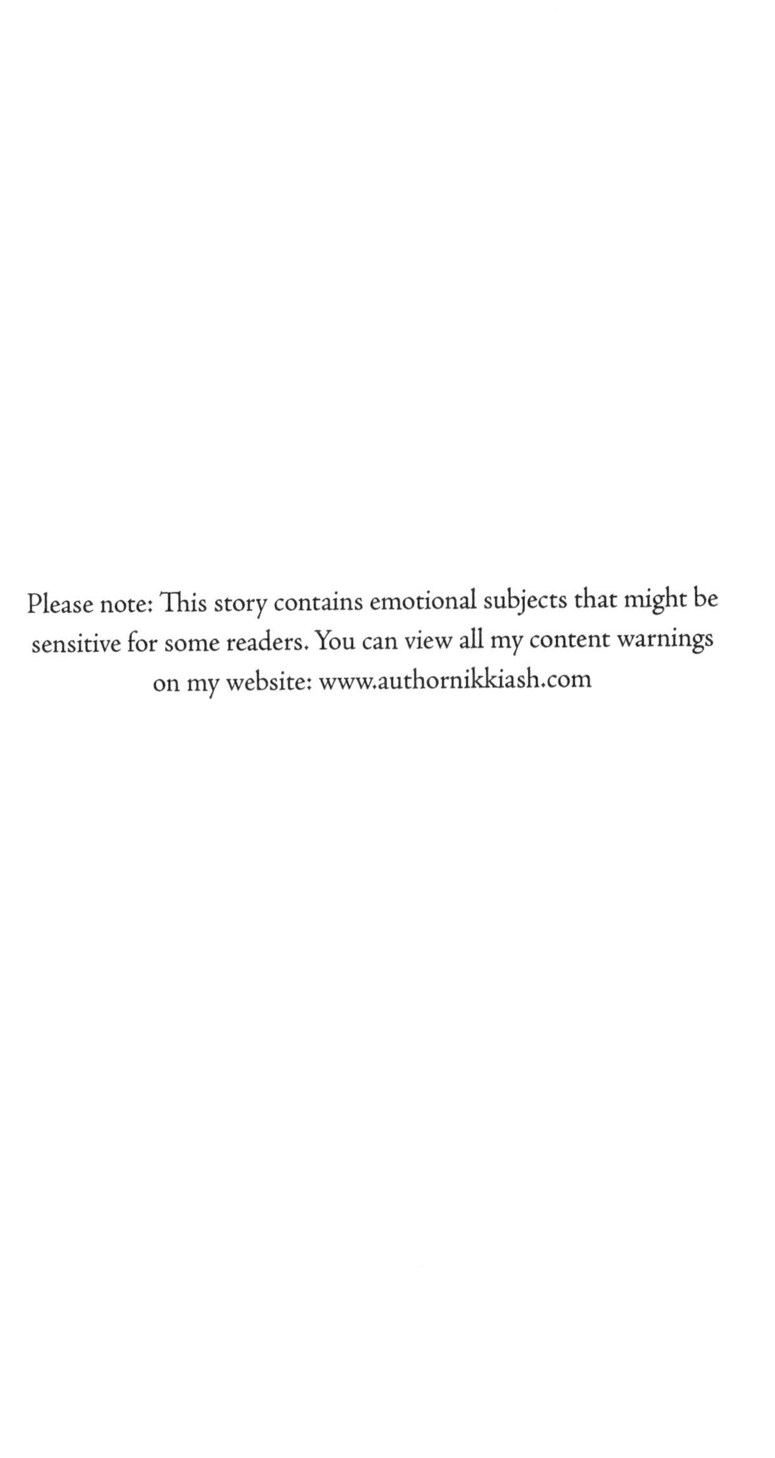

Please note: This story contains emotional subjects that might be sensitive for some readers. You can view all my content warnings on my website: www.authornikkiash.com

Exposed Ink Playlist

24/7, 365 – elijah woods
Tie Me Down – Gryffin & Elley Duhé
Cold Water (feat. Justin Bieber & MØ) – Major Lazer
10,000 Hours – Dan + Shay & Justin Bieber
Anyone – Justin Bieber
Message in a Bottle (Taylor's Version) – Taylor Swift
H.O.L.Y. – Florida Georgia Line
Speechless – Dan + Shay
Stay With Me – Sam Smith
What Ifs (feat. Lauren Alaina) – Kane Brown
To a T – Ryan Hurd
Take Your Time – Sam Hunt
Something Just Like This – The Chainsmokers & Coldplay
Fearless (Taylor's Version) – Taylor Swift

One

Kinsley
The Present

"Girl, this looks amazing," my cousin Natalia says as she stands in front of the floor-length mirror, admiring her new tattoo.

She's twenty-eight, the same age as me, but unlike me, it's her first time getting inked. She's tried over the years to get me to ink her, but I have a rule—the tattoo must be meaningful. If it's not, I'm not permanently putting it on your body.

I don't give a shit if that means I lose business. If you want me to do the work, you'd better be prepared to explain why you want the design you're getting, or you won't be getting it from me.

Because Natalia's a fashion designer, following in her mom's and older sister's footsteps, I designed a custom piece for her—a hanger that loops into a needle and thread and then morphs into a tape measure that connects to a pair of scissors. It's chaotic and beautiful, just like my best friend, and it's on her hip, where no one can see it unless she wants them to.

"Seriously, Kins, I love it."

She turns around, her shiny black hair whooshing around her heart-shaped face, and cuts across the room with her mile-long legs that many are envious of.

"Thank you!" She dramatically throws her arms around my neck while I stand in my spot, not wanting to touch anything with my gloves since I still need to do her aftercare.

When she hugs me tighter, I can't help but stiffen under her touch. It's not often I allow people to get this close to me, so when they do, it hits me hard. Years of avoiding affection will do that to a person.

"You're welcome," I choke out, stepping out of her embrace. "Make sure you take care of it, so it stays looking good."

She gives me a *duh* look while she quickly snaps a picture, no doubt to post on her social media, which is fine with me since she has, like, a gazillion followers, and she'll tag me, which will ultimately lead to new business—something every business can use.

I grab the ointment, apply a thin layer over the tattoo, then cover it with a bandage.

"Here are your aftercare instructions," I say, handing her the printout we provide at Exposed Ink, not needing to go into detail since her dad—my uncle Jase—is a retired tattoo artist, who co-owns Forbidden Ink, one of the biggest tattoo shops in New York City.

"How'd it go?" Scott, the front-end manager, asks when we walk up to the desk.

When he's not answering the phones or handling the schedule, he's apprenticing with my dad, who works here part-time.

My dad retired from tattooing several years ago when our family moved to Brookside, a small town just outside of New York City. But a couple of years ago, when I was struggling, he decided to open a new tattoo shop in town, insisting that we do it together.

"So good." Natalia thrusts her phone into his face. "Kinsley is the best."

"Damn right she is," Dad says, walking to the front. "She learned from her old man."

While my dad has red hair and green eyes, looking every bit like the Irish heritage he comes from—the same hair and eye color my younger sister and brother inherited—I have brown hair and blue eyes. We look nothing alike, which makes sense since Lachlan Bryson isn't my biological dad, but he's the only man I'd ever consider calling Dad, genetics be damned.

"Looks great," Dad says when he leans over Scott and looks at the picture Natalia is holding up.

"Thanks." She grins, putting her phone away and taking her card out to pay.

"You're not paying me," I scoff.

"Of course I am," she insists, handing the card to Scott. "If you keep doing everyone's ink for free, you'll never make a profit."

My dad nods in agreement even though he knows damn well that we don't need the money. Exposed Ink brings in plenty of revenue, and on top of that, I own it free and clear, thanks to my dad, who covered all the expenses to get it up and running and refused to let me pay him back. He claims we're partners, yet he never takes a dime the shop brings in.

"So, what are you girls up to tonight?" Dad asks, snapping me from my thoughts.

"We're meeting my sisters at Neptune's," Natalia answers. "They're in town."

"Who's *we*?" I ask, glaring her way.

"You agreed!" Natalia huffs. "It's Galentine's Day, a day to celebrate friendship, and as my best friend, I'm insisting that you come out and celebrate with me. And before you even try to come up with an excuse, Scott has already confirmed I was your last appointment tonight and you're free to leave."

I sigh, knowing there's no way I'm getting out of this, at least not without Natalia throwing a fit, and since she's only in town for the week—she lives in the city since that's where Leblanc, her mom's fashion company, is run—the least I can do is plaster on a smile and have a drink with my cousins. They've been here for me through every up and down, and I owe them more than I'll ever be able to pay back. My family is the best, and I don't deserve any of them.

"All right," I agree. "One drink …"

"Two," she counters.

"Fine. But I'm not changing."

I'm dressed in my black Exposed Ink shirt and ripped jeans, paired with my black Chucks, and if she thinks I'm going to change …

"Fine," she parrots. "Let's go."

She hooks her arm with mine and pulls me out the door, waving behind her to my dad and Scott.

"Have fun!" Dad yells as the door shuts behind us.

"Did you drive?" I ask once we're outside, the cool breeze wrapping around me and sending a shiver up my spine.

"Nope. I knew you wouldn't agree to that," she says as we walk down the sidewalk toward Neptune's, one of the more popular bars in town.

Since I was older when my parents moved here, I stayed in the city, not moving back until three years ago, when my entire life changed and staying in the city was no longer an option.

It's been an adjustment, to say the least, going from the hustle and bustle of the city to the quiet of a small town. But it's been *less* hard, having zero memories or reminders of the past everywhere I look, like I would if I still lived in the city.

I don't have to drive anywhere since everything is pretty much in walking distance, and whatever isn't is reachable with the town's public transportation—i.e., the one bus that goes around town, picking up and dropping people off.

"I have to go to Milan for Fashion Week," she says, glancing at me. "You know, if you wanted to join me …"

"As much as I appreciate the invite, I promise I'm doing okay. I'm working and keeping busy. I have the shop, and I recently joined the health club in town."

"Oh! I heard it's nice. My mom and Skyla said they've been doing yoga and Pilates there."

Skyla is her older sister, but since she's twenty years older, married with kids, and busy running Leblanc with their mom, they're not as close as Natalia is with her other two sisters, who are only two years older than her.

"I haven't checked out the classes yet," I tell her, "but I've been making use of their treadmill and steam room. And … I've started thinking about moving out of my parents' place. This year will be easier. I'll be okay."

"All right," Natalia concedes. "But if you aren't …"

Her eyes meet mine briefly, and despite her being over-the-top zealous, I'm thankful for my best friend. We might be opposites, but I love her with every fiber in my being, and I can't imagine I'd have gotten through everything without her—and the rest of my family.

"You'll be the first person I call," I promise.

Before she can argue, we arrive at Neptune's, the bass from the music drowning everything else out. The second we step foot into the bar, our names are called, followed by Natalia's twin sisters, Melanie and Melina, waving us over.

"Hey, you!" I give Melanie a quick hug. "I can't believe you're out."

Melanie is married with two kids—one of who is only a couple of months old—and lives in Brookside, where she owns a cute clothing boutique that sells Leblanc as well as other high-end brands.

"Hector practically pushed me out the door after Nat told him she wanted to do a Galentine's Day girls' night out," Melanie says with a laugh.

"As he should," Natalia says. "You've been stuck in that house for months."

"I haven't been stuck." Melanie rolls her eyes. "I've been recuperating after giving birth."

"Yeah, yeah." Natalia waves her off.

"And look at you," I say to Melina, changing the subject. "You look amazing!"

Melina has been gone for months, traveling for Leblanc. The last time I saw her, she was a mess over her breakup from her fiancé, who she'd caught cheating. She left with black hair and a broken heart, but the woman in front of me looks refreshed and happy. With beautiful blonde hair and a smile, it's clear she's past her breakup—or doing a damn good job of hiding it.

"Life's too short to dwell on the past," she says, making me flinch. I hope she didn't catch it, but it's clear she did when she smiles sadly. "I didn't mean—"

"Hey, stop." I wave her off. "You know I hate when you guys filter your thoughts around me. I know what you meant, and I'm glad you've moved forward."

"Thank you … because I met someone. His name is James, and I brought him home to meet my parents. I'm hoping we can do a barbecue with everyone."

"That sounds like fun," I tell her, as we walk up to the bar.

I glance at the rows of liquor bottles, trying to decide what I'm going to order. I rarely drink, but if I'm going to get through this girls' night, I'm going to need some liquid courage.

"What can I get for you?" the bartender asks with a grin.

His name is Patrick, and he's asked me out no less than a dozen times over the past three years despite me telling him I have no desire to date.

"White Russian," I tell him with a smile I hope conveys friendly, but doesn't lead him on since he apparently can't seem to take a hint. "Bryson Black Label."

If I'm going to drink, it'll always be my family's liquor.

"I'll have an old-fashioned," Melanie says.

"Old-fashioned for me too," Melina adds.

"I'll take a lychee sour," Natalia tells him.

"You got it," Patrick says.

While he makes our drinks, we catch up on what everyone has been up to.

My uncle Jase and aunt Celeste are flying out to Paris the week after next for Fashion Week, and my mom will be going to LA for a photo shoot.

She didn't travel often when we were growing up, but once my brother and sister left for college and I was living on my own, she started traveling more. After I returned home, she took some time off work to be with me—despite me telling her she didn't need to—but she's slowly been traveling again, and since I know how much she enjoys it, I'm happy she's doing it again.

Now, I just need to convince my dad that I can run the shop without him, so he can join her—or more so that I'm emotionally stable enough for him to leave me.

"To family, who make the best friends," Natalia says, raising her drink.

"To family," Melina, Melanie, and I all agree.

We take a sip of our drinks, and then Natalia drags me onto

the dance floor. With the music pumping, I get lost in the moment, letting the alcohol take over temporarily.

As one song rolls into another and then another, for the first time in a long time, I feel almost happy. It feels good to let go for a little while—to set aside the anger and resentment and raw emotions.

With the liquor flowing through my veins, I'm so buzzed that I'm not paying attention when Patrick sets the wrong drink in front of me, and I down it in one go.

At first, it hits me that it's not my drink, that it has a fruity note to it, but it's not until I'm back on the dance floor and having trouble breathing that I realize the drink must've contained raw fruit. And since I'm allergic to raw fruit, I'm about to have a big problem.

"What's wrong?" Natalia asks, immediately noticing the change in my demeanor.

"I drank the wrong drink!" I yell over the music, reaching over my shoulder to grab my … "Oh shit! I left my purse at the shop."

My purse … which holds my EpiPen … which means—

"I'm calling 911!" Natalia shouts, already knowing what to do.

This isn't the first time I've mistakenly consumed something I'm allergic to, but it's been years since I've had an allergic reaction and not had an EpiPen on me.

She pulls me off the dance floor and finds a manager, explaining that I'm having an allergic reaction. He takes us into his office while we wait for the ambulance to come—during which time, my symptoms increase by the second.

My hands itch, my skin burns, and every breath I take becomes more labored than the last. I can't see my face, but based on the way my arms are swelling in various places, I'd bet it's swelling up as well.

I'd suggest we go to the shop to get my EpiPen, but the raw fruit must've been potent because my symptoms are hitting me quickly.

By the time the paramedics arrive, I'm so scared that I can barely make out what they're saying. Realistically, I know I'm going to be okay, but there's always a chance an allergic reaction can be deadly.

There are two guys. One is checking my vitals, and the other is asking Natalia questions. They help me onto a gurney and wheel me outside, and that's when I see the ambulance.

"No!" I choke out. "Please don't put me in there. Just … just help me here. I just need an EpiPen."

"Ma'am," one of the paramedics says patiently, "you're having an allergic reaction, and we need to—"

"No, please!" I cut him off, shaking my head and begging him not to put me in the ambulance. "I can't go there."

"Go where?" he asks, his warm brown eyes filled with confusion because only a crazy person would beg not to be brought to the place that would help heal them.

My gaze locks with his. "To the hospital."

Two

Kinsley
The Past

"HELL YEAH, BABE. THIS LOOKS PERFECT." BRANDON steps away from the mirror and leans down to give me a kiss. "I can't wait to finish this sleeve when we get back from our baby trip."

"Baby*moon*," I say with a laugh. "And I'm so jealous. As much as I love carrying this little one, I miss getting tatted."

"Soon," he says, rubbing my very pregnant belly. "She's only got a few more months in there. And the first tattoo you get will be something to symbolize her arrival into this world."

I grin up at him. "I already know what I want."

I pull out the drawing I sketched when I couldn't sleep the other night and hand it to him. "I think I want it on my left shoulder blade or maybe along my rib cage. I'm not sure yet."

It's a drawing of her heartbeat—the first one we heard at the doctor's office, which I recorded using a special app—that morphs into her name, Brenna.

The moment I saw it in a baby name book, I knew it was perfect for her. It reminds me of Brandon and sounds sweet.

"That's awesome," Brandon says. "And it's going to look beautiful on you. Does this mean you'll finally let me tattoo something on you?" he asks with a smirk.

"Maybe," I say with a grin.

When Brandon first started working at Forbidden Ink eight years ago, he wasn't licensed, and I refused to let him ink me. Unlike most tattooists I know, I'm not inked all over, and I'm very particular about what I do get inked. That shit's permanent—unless you want to go through the immense pain and expense of getting it removed—so whatever I get needs to be meaningful and something I want on my body forever.

Because of how picky I am, I've only let a few people ink me. My dad, of course, since he's the person who taught me everything I know. My uncle Jase and uncle Jax, who opened the tattoo shop I work at. And my aunt Willow because she's the most badass female tattoo artist I know.

At first, I wouldn't let Brandon tattoo me because he was new and inexperienced, but even after he proved to be a good tattoo artist and us dating for two years and being married for another two, he has yet to ink me. I guess it's turned into a running joke between us, one that will come to an end once our little girl is born.

"There's no one I would want inking this on me but you," I tell him, tugging on his shirt to pull him toward me. I give him a kiss that starts to get heated but is quickly tamped down when the sound of my dad's voice is heard.

"Coming!" I yell, confused as to why my dad is here when he retired last year after my brother, Barrett, graduated and they moved to Brookside, a small town outside of the city.

I finish applying the ointment and bandage to Brandon's tattoo, and then we walk up to the front to see what my dad is doing here. Since it's still early and the shop is open, I'm expecting to see people getting inked in the rooms, so I'm thrown off by every room being empty until we get to the front and everyone is standing there, smiling at us.

"Surprise!" my mom says, coming over and giving us a hug. "Welcome to your baby shower."

"What?" I glance around at our family and friends.

There are pink and green balloons everywhere, along with a pink cake and what smells like Antonio's, my favorite Italian restaurant that's located right down the street.

"This is amazing. Thank you!"

They must've put it all together while I was tattooing Brandon.

"I can't believe my little girl is going to have a baby girl of her own," my mom says with tears in her eyes. "I'm so proud of the woman you've become, and I know you'll be an amazing mom."

"Thank you," I whisper, hugging my mom again.

The next couple of hours are filled with delicious food, conversation, and lots of laughter. Everyone insists we open the gifts, and once the baby shower is over, we pile everything into Brandon's car since he insists on owning one despite living in the city. I guess it now makes sense why he pushed to drive us here this morning—he was in on the baby shower.

"What time do you guys leave?" Dad asks once all the gifts are loaded into Brandon's trunk.

"Six a.m. I'll text you guys before the flight takes off."

We're heading to Florida to enjoy the warm weather and beaches since it's March and in the high eighties there, unlike New York, which is a chilly forty degrees.

Because I'm pregnant, we can't really enjoy the theme parks, so we're going to Miami Beach to lounge at a resort that looks to have a beautiful pool and is located right on the water.

"Sounds good." Dad gives me a hug and kiss on my forehead. "I love you, Kins."

"I love you too, Dad."

After I give my mom a hug, Brandon and I take off to our townhouse in Brooklyn Heights. It was once my uncle Jax's, passed down to my mom, who gifted it to Brandon and me when my parents made the decision to move out of the city.

"Should we bring everything in tonight or in the morning?" I ask when we arrive at home.

"Tonight, but you're not lifting a finger," Brandon says. "Go take a shower, and I'll meet you in bed once I unload everything."

"You're too good to me," I say, leaning over and giving him a kiss.

"No, I'm the right amount of good to you," he argues. "I love you. You're my family, Kinsley, and I meant what I said when we got married—I will do everything in my power to show you every day how much you mean to me."

Brandon's parents were addicts who lost their rights to their son. He grew up in foster care, and once he turned eighteen and aged out, he took off on his own. He apprenticed with some shady shops, and when he came to us, my dad got him on the right path. Now, eight years later, he's a damn good, licensed tattoo artist.

"You do show me," I tell him, palming his cheek. "Every single day."

"Can we stay here forever?" I ask, glancing over at my husband, who smiles softly at me, knowing I'm full of shit.

As much as I'm loving lounging by the pool, swimming in the

ocean, and checking out the different restaurants on the strip, I could never live anywhere but in New York.

"You would miss your family too much," he says, pulling me in for a kiss. "But I promise we'll come back."

"Between this little one being born and us taking over the shop, it's going to get crazy soon," I say with a sigh.

"Yeah," Brandon agrees, "it will, but in a good way. It's supposed to be a surprise, but your dad and uncles are turning a portion of the back office into a nursery while we're gone."

"What?" I gasp. "Really?"

I've been so nervous about having a baby and running Forbidden Ink, but I haven't mentioned it to my dad or uncles, not wanting to let them down. I agreed to run the shop before I found out I was pregnant, and it's always been a dream of mine. They've even agreed to make me a small partner, so I'll be earning a percentage of what the shop makes. My uncles are having the contract drawn up, and we'll be signing it when I get back.

Brandon and I have talked about opening our own shop one day, but until we're ready to do that, running my family's tattoo shop is the next best thing.

"Yeah, we've got this, babe." Brandon threads his fingers through mine and brings them up to his lips for a kiss. "You and me, with the support of your family."

"They're your family too," I point out. "You know my dad considers you another son."

"I know," he says with a shy smile. "And he's damn near the closest thing to a dad I've ever had." He heaves a sigh. "I never imagined being this happy, this content. Thank you."

The alarm goes off on my phone, the one I set to remind us when we need to head up to our room to get ready for dinner. Brandon made us reservations at an Italian restaurant I read is one of the best around. I love Italian, and I can't imagine anywhere being as good as the places in New York, but I'm excited to find out.

"It looks like rain," Brandon says as we gather our belongings.

"Yeah." I glance up at the darkening sky. "I hope it passes before our trip to the zoo tomorrow." I've been looking forward to going all week, and it will suck if it's ruined by rain.

Once we're ready, since the restaurant isn't on the strip, we call for the valet to bring around our rental car.

The restaurant is beautiful and authentic with the menu in English and Italian, and the waiters have lovely Italian accents. We learn that it's family-owned and -operated—from the cook to the hostess to the waiter.

I order shrimp Parmesan—my favorite—and Brandon orders chicken marsala since he hates seafood.

"So, what do you think?" he asks after I've taken my first bite.

"So good," I moan. "I think it just might give Antonio's a run for its money. Thank you for bringing me here."

Brandon takes a sip of the beer that he ordered and smiles. "Anything to see you happy."

After we're done eating, we step outside and find that it's pouring down rain and everyone is scrambling to quickly get in and out of their vehicles to avoid getting soaked.

"This weather is horrible," I say with a grimace.

I'm going to be so bummed if it's like this tomorrow. I've been looking forward to going to the zoo on our last day, and it will ruin it if it's raining the entire time.

"Look, a piano bar," Brandon says, giving me a pleading look.

"Let's go."

I hook my arm through his and walk toward the little hole-in-the-wall bar, making Brandon grin. He loves music, especially jazz, and drags me to various bars and clubs all over New York and Jersey to check them out.

The next few hours are spent with us listening to the live music, Brandon having a few drinks, and us dancing until my feet and back hurt, and he insists we go back to our hotel so I can get some rest.

"Shit, it's still raining," he says when we step outside. "And I've been drinking." He blanches. "I'm so used to New York that I didn't even think about having to drive."

"It's all good," I tell him. "We're on vacation. You should be enjoying yourself. But should we take an Uber?"

"Yeah." He nods. "We can come back tomorrow and get the car."

He pulls out his phone, types away, and then frowns. "It's saying it's going to be an hour."

"What? That's crazy."

"Welcome to Miami," the valet says. "This time of night, you could be waiting an hour or more, easily."

"I can drive," I tell Brandon.

"You sure?" he asks.

"Yeah, I do have my license," I say with a laugh. Because I've lived in the city my entire life, I don't drive often, but I do know how, and I haven't been drinking. "And the rain has slowed down a lot," I add.

I shift on my feet, regretting my decision to wear heels. "Besides, I don't think my feet can handle standing for an hour to wait for an Uber."

Because of how late it is, the bar and restaurant are closing, which leaves us with nowhere to wait.

"I'm sorry," Brandon says. "I shouldn't have drunk so much."

"Stop." I palm his cheek. "The point of this trip is to relax. I'm perfectly capable of driving us to the hotel."

The valet brings our rental car around and opens the door for me. Since my bump isn't small, I lift the steering wheel a bit higher so I can adjust my seat since I'm shorter than Brandon while he inputs the hotel address into the GPS.

"Did you have a good time?" Brandon asks while I drive us back to the hotel.

"The best. And I can't wait to go to the zoo tomorrow. I was thinking we could do Brenna's room with a zoo theme."

"Yeah, that would be cool. What if we—"

Brandon's words are cut off when the car hits something—a puddle? I'm not sure—and starts to hydroplane. I've driven in the snow many times, but as I try to hit my brakes to slow down, it feels like nothing I do works, and within seconds, the car is spinning out of control. Between the rain and the speed, everything becomes a blur.

And then we hit something hard.

There's a scream, followed by a cry, and then an immense amount of pain spreads throughout my body before everything goes black.

The Present

The beeping of the monitors and the smell of antiseptic shake me from my thoughts. I'm in a hospital, getting treated for OAS—oral allergy syndrome.

The last time I was in a hospital, I lost everything—my husband, my baby, and my entire purpose in life. But tonight, thanks to the paramedics who quickly got it under control, and the doctor and nurses who made sure I was stable once I arrived at the hospital, I'll be okay.

My throat hurts, and I'm a bit itchy, but I'll survive—unlike my baby girl and husband, who died that night because of me.

"Well, at least your face is less swollen," a gentleman says, leaning against the doorframe with his feet crossed at the ankles and his arms crossed over his chest.

I can make out the town fire department logo peeking out on his left pec, and when my eyes meet his, I recognize him as the paramedic who reassured me it would all be okay. The entire drive, while I begged him not to take me here, he worked on me while also calming my racing heart and saving me from adding a panic attack to my laundry list of issues.

"Thanks," I say with an awkward laugh. "I'm usually more careful about what I drink and eat. If the fruit is cooked, I'm good. It's the raw stuff I have to stay away from."

He nods, pushes off the doorframe with his shoulder, and steps inside. "I'm Shane Evans."

"I'd tell you my name, but I'm sure you already know it, thanks to the pile of paperwork I've probably caused you."

He chuckles, and if I wasn't immune to the opposite sex, the soft laugh, mixed with his warm smile, would affect me in a way that I haven't been affected in a long time. Not since my husband died.

"It's all good. I was just finishing up and wanted to come by and check on you."

"Do you check on all the patients you bring in?" I ask curiously.

The way his cheeks tinge a light shade of pink tells me my answer.

Shit, he's totally going to ask for my number.

"I appreciate you checking on me, but—"

"Oh my God! Thank God you're okay!" Natalia storms into the room like the hurricane she is, the door closing behind her. "I was so scared."

She throws her arms around me, and while she hugs me, my eyes meet Shane's. They're golden brown, reminding me of a warm brownie—delicious, but if eaten in large quantities, bad for your health. His arms are corded with muscle, and his shirt stretches across his chest in a way that's natural yet shows off the fact that he works out and keeps in shape.

I notice there's not a single tattoo in sight, and I briefly wonder if he has any ink. That thought has me averting my gaze because I shouldn't be thinking about him in any way, let alone considering what's underneath his clothes.

When Natalia pulls back, she notices Shane standing there, and even though she's not facing me, I can hear the smile in her voice when she says, "And who are you?"

"I'm Shane," he says. "I was the paramedic working on Kinsley."

"Ohh," she coos. "So, you're responsible for saving my cousin's life."

She saunters over to him, and I roll my eyes. I love my cousin, but she's such a flirt.

"She wasn't anywhere near her deathbed," Shane says with a chuckle, "but, yes, I helped alleviate her symptoms."

"Are you single?" she asks, getting straight to the point.

For some reason, even though Shane isn't mine, nor do I want him to be, the thought of her going out with him causes an emotion I haven't felt in a long time to stir within me—jealousy.

"Natalia, leave him alone," I chide, trying to keep my voice nonchalant.

"I am," Shane says, answering her question.

"Do you think my cousin is pretty?" she asks, making me gasp.

"Natalia!" I hiss, now wishing she were flirting with him instead of doing what I think she's doing.

"I do." Shane chuckles, his eyes, now filled with a mixture of mirth and lust, locking with mine.

"You should ask her out then." Natalia shrugs, then looks at me. "And you should say yes because you owe him for saving your life."

"Okay, Miss Matchmaker." I glare. "I'm betting my family is out in the waiting room."

"They are," she says. "I insisted on coming back since I felt responsible. It was my drink you consumed by mistake."

"It's not your fault. Things happen. Now, stop harassing that poor paramedic and go let my family know I'm okay."

"Fine." She sighs.

I think she's going to let it go, until she stops right next to Shane and says, "She works at Exposed Ink, in case you want to reach out," before making her dramatic exit.

"Ugh, sorry about her," I say once she's gone, dropping my face into my hands since I can feel the warmth that's crept up my neck and cheeks. With my semi-translucent skin, I'm positive my flesh is bright red.

"It's all good," Shane says, laughter in his voice. "I'm just glad you're okay."

I nod into my hands and then glance up, finding him smiling softly at me.

I open my mouth—to say what, I'm not sure—but before any words can come out, the door opens, and my entire family piles in.

"They couldn't wait," Natalia says with a huff. "I tried to tell them you were busy, but …"

She shrugs, and I glare. Then, I focus on my mom, who rushes to my side, ready to dote on me with her motherly love, and my dad follows, worry etched in his features.

My thoughts go back to the last time they showed up at the hospital, causing my insides to clench at the memory of having to tell them that Brandon and our baby were gone. They held me in their arms and told me everything would be okay even though we all knew it never would be.

Now, here they are again, visiting me in the hospital …

"I'm sorry," I tell them, hating to worry them. "I should've remembered my EpiPen."

"Stop it," Mom chides. "You have nothing to be sorry about. All that matters is that you're okay."

By the time they're done double- and triple-checking to make sure I am, in fact, okay, Shane has disappeared from the room, and I tell myself that it's for the best. I have nothing to offer him or anyone else.

But as I recall his warm brown eyes and boyish grin, I can't help but wonder what it would be like if I wasn't broken.

Would I have given him my number? Would he have taken it? Where would he have taken me to dinner? Would it have been the start of something fun and exciting, or would the date have been awkward and ended early?

My train of thought causes a lump of emotion to settle in my throat, making it hard to breathe. I'm broken because of my actions. I killed my unborn baby and husband, and if I hadn't, they'd be here. And instead of lying in a hospital bed, thinking about what it would be like for a man to ask me for my number and to take me out on a date, I'd be home with them, cuddled in bed.

I had my chance at a family.

At happiness.

At love.

And I single-handedly destroyed it.

Three

Kinsley

VALENTINE'S DAY.

A holiday I used to look forward to.

When I was younger, my mom would buy my siblings and me each a basket. She would fill it with chocolates and other goodies, always saying that regardless of who came into our lives, we'd always be her Valentines and that I was her first since I came along before my dad and siblings.

When I got older, it meant fun dances and the boy I liked asking me to be his Valentine. And when I started dating Brandon, it meant sharing the day with the person I loved.

Now that I'm a widow, it means spending the holiday alone and remembering all the good times Brandon and I had.

Today is the third Valentine's Day without him, and even though it gets easier, it still hurts to think about the fact that we'll never celebrate together again. We'll never kiss or hug or make love. We'll never conceive another baby together.

My hand goes to the area that carried our little girl. I was supposed to protect her, but instead, I killed her. She should be here, dressed in a pretty pink-and-red outfit. I should be following in my mom's tradition to buy her a basket of goodies.

Instead, her ashes sit next to my husband's in a glass cabinet that I can't even stand to look at because I did that. I killed them both, and because of my actions, I'll never celebrate another holiday with either of them.

A knock on the door brings me back to the present, and I climb out of bed, knowing it's my mom. Normally, she'd be here even earlier, but since we didn't get home from the hospital until late last night, she probably wanted to give me time to get some sleep.

"Happy Valentine's Day!" Mom says, holding up the white wicker basket and then enveloping me in a motherly hug. "I love you, my Valentine."

"I love you too," I choke out, hating that even after almost three years, I still get emotional.

"For you," she says, stepping into my place.

It was once a pool house that they turned into a mother-in-law suite my grandparents stayed in when they visited from Ireland. After the car crash, when I couldn't face going back to the townhouse, Mom and Dad insisted I move in here, so I'd be close and have my own space. Lately, I've been considering getting my own place, but I haven't taken the initiative yet.

"Thank you." I set the basket on the counter.

"How are you feeling?" Mom asks carefully.

"Fine." I shrug. "Tired but alive."

Mom nods, and then tears fill her eyes, and before I know it, she's got me wrapped up in another hug. "I was so scared," she cries. "When Natalia called …"

"I know, but I'm okay. The second I realized I forgot my EpiPen, she called for an ambulance."

"You're so calm and strong," she says, pulling back and wiping her tears.

"More like numb," I mutter, tears pricking my eyes.

"No," she says, shaking her head. "You're strong, Kins. What you went through, what you've lost. Only someone with a shit ton of strength could continue to wake up every morning and keep moving forward."

"It doesn't feel like I'm moving forward," I admit out loud. "It feels like I'm just existing."

"Oh, sweetheart." She pulls me into her arms. "It takes time. It took me six years, your dad tearing down my walls, and many years of therapy for me to truly move forward from my past," she says, referring to the time she was married to my sperm donor.

He cheated on her and then died during a carjacking while he was on a date with his mistress. My mom not only picked herself up and moved forward, but she did it while pregnant and then raised me for several years as a single mom.

"And it's even harder for you because Brandon was a good man and husband," she adds, making my heart clench behind my rib cage.

"He was the best," I whisper. "And I can't imagine finding anyone like him …" Nor do I want to.

Mom pulls back and looks into my eyes. "And you won't ever find someone like him. He was one of a kind, just like Lachlan is in my eyes. Nobody is asking or expecting you to replace Brandon, but that doesn't mean you don't deserve to find someone new to love."

"Who would want someone like me?" I mutter self-deprecatingly. "I'm broken, damaged …"

"And I felt the same way," she says, her eyes filled with emotion. "I was a widowed single mom with way too many rolls."

"You're beautiful and perfect just the way you are."

And that's the truth. Between her raven hair and matching eyes, her gorgeous tattoos, heart-shaped lips, and curvy body, my mom is a knockout. She might be twelve years older than my dad, but she doesn't look it.

"And so are you," Mom says, "on the inside and out. I couldn't imagine finding someone who would want broken, damaged me. But then I met your dad, and you know what?" She tucks several strands of hair behind my ear and then wipes away the tears sliding down my cheeks. "He showed me that I wasn't broken or damaged after all. And one day, you'll meet a man who—"

I start to shake my head in protest, but she keeps going. "I'm not saying you should go in search of a new husband, but you're young, Kinsley, and you have such a big heart. And even if you're not ready for anything serious, you still have needs, both emotionally and physically."

I groan, and she shrugs.

"What? You do. You've kept everyone at arm's length for years now. Maybe it would do you some good to go on a few dates and have some adult conversation with the opposite sex."

"I talk to men all the time," I murmur.

"I mean a man who doesn't work for Exposed Ink or isn't getting tattooed. A man who will remind you that you didn't die that night. That you're still alive, your heart is beating, and you deserve to be happy."

"It … it just fucking sucks," I cry out. "I found the one. I found the man I was supposed to spend my life with, and I fucked it all up."

"Stop it," Mom hisses. "Nobody blames you but yourself. If it were your fault, you'd be in jail. It was an accident. And you have got to stop blaming yourself. What if Brandon had been the one driving? What if he were the one alive and you and your daughter died? Would you want him to harbor that blame? To live the rest of his life alone and without love?"

She asks the same questions my therapist has asked me in the past. The questions I hate the most because I already know the answers. I know that my husband would've given anything for me to be happy, even if it meant without him. But the thought of being happy without him by my side is incomprehensible.

"No." I sigh, having had this conversation with my therapist more times than I can count.

The car crash was investigated, and no foul play was found. They deemed it a horrible, tragic accident, but it was just that—an accident. But even so, saying the word *accident* makes me feel like I'm being let off the hook, and I don't want to be … I don't deserve to be.

"I know today is hard on you, so it's okay to spend the day wallowing and reminiscing, but tomorrow is a new day, and I hope you'll wake up and choose to live instead of merely existing. I wasted too much time doing the same thing, and I don't want you to make the mistakes I made."

"I want to live," I admit. "I just don't know how."

"You'll figure it out," Mom says with a soft smile. "On another note, Celeste and Jase are hosting a barbecue next weekend for Melina and James. I hope you'll come."

"I'll be there. I'm happy for her, and I'm not going to break down over someone else finding love, I promise."

One reason why I've considered getting my own place is because of this. My mom is terrified of me breaking down, and I don't blame her. After almost losing her daughter in a car crash, she flew to Florida and witnessed me lose it. I had to be hospitalized and drugged, and she was scared I was going to end my life.

I'm not going to lie. At the time, I thought about it. But after seeing a therapist over the past three years, I've healed in many ways, and I'm happy for the most part.

I have a loving family, a great career, and I'm as content as a woman can be who lost her husband and baby. I enjoy visiting art museums, cooking, and baking. I've been going to the health club more often lately. I keep busy. I don't know why I didn't die that night, but I don't want to waste the second chance I was given living a life filled with negativity.

"Okay, good," Mom says. "I'm making breakfast if you want to join us."

"I'll get dressed and head over."

Once she's gone, I open my bag of goodies and groan when I find, right next to the adorable stuffed Baby Yoda, a black box that reads *Passion Kisses*—the online sex toy shop my mom buys her toys from. It should be weird that my mom bought me a vibrator of some sort—and it kind of is—but she's also my best friend, and she knows I haven't had sex since Brandon died, so it's also kind of sweet and thoughtful.

At some point, I'm going to have to figure out my sex life because I don't want to be abstinent forever, but it's hard when the last guy I was with was my husband and he was who I thought I would be with for the rest of my life.

Leaving the toy in its packaging, I open a Reese's Peanut Butter Cup, pop it into my mouth, and then get ready for the day. My dad wanted me to take off work, but I compromised by shifting my appointments to the afternoon. The last thing I want to do on Valentine's Day is stay home and wallow. I know Brandon wouldn't want this for me. He would want me to move forward and be happy. He loved me too much to want me to be unhappy. But it's easier said than done.

Four

Shane

"**D**AD! I NEED YOU!"

My seventeen-year-old daughter's panicked voice has me setting my coffee on the counter.

"What's wrong?" I ask, stepping out of the kitchen to meet her in the living room as our dog, Becky—a German shepherd Lab mix we rescued a few years ago—jumps up from the couch, wagging her tail and begging for attention.

Since Taylor only ran out the door a few minutes ago for school, I can't imagine what's happened to cause her hysteria in that short amount of time. But one thing I've learned from being a single dad to a teenage girl is that the things we wouldn't expect to cause stress seem to.

Wrong hair color, a pimple on her forehead, can't find the right shoes to match the dress—doesn't sound like any of that would be the end of the world, right? *Wrong.* Every one of those is serious enough to cause a breakdown—trust me, I've experienced it firsthand.

"My tire is flat, and I'm going to be late to school, and we have a pep rally today! If I miss it—"

"Breathe," I say with a laugh, thankful her outburst wasn't something serious.

"Dad!" She groans.

"Let's go." I nod toward the front door. "Today, you'll learn how to change a tire."

"But I'm—" she starts to complain as she follows.

"Late. I heard. What would you have done had I not been here?"

"Called you to come home."

I chuckle. "And what if I were on a call?"

"I would've asked Pop."

"They're out of town," I remind her.

My parents live next door, but since they officially retired a few years ago and my daughter is now old enough to stay alone overnight while I work my shifts at the station, they've started to travel more often.

"Fine, let's go," she says, knowing I'm not going to budge.

Since I work twenty-four-hour shifts as a firefighter paramedic, I always want to make sure my daughter is capable of handling things if I'm not available. I hate having to leave her, but thankfully, when she was younger, while I was saving for a place of our own, we lived with my parents, who helped tremendously. It also helps that we live in a small town and the station is walking distance from our house on Main Street.

"Look, it's right there," Taylor says, crouching in front of the tire and pointing out the silver screw wedged into the rubber.

"We'll put a spare on, and I'll bring it by Ron's garage later to get it plugged."

After getting the spare and jack out of her trunk and explaining how to raise her car properly so she can safely change the tire, I go about doing so, walking her through each step until the spare tire is on and her flat one has been thrown into the back of my truck.

"Thank you, Dad!" Taylor throws her arms around me and plants a kiss on my cheek. "Love you."

"Love you too, Tay. What time will you be home?"

"It's on the calendar," she mocks, repeating what I always tell her when she asks me the same question. "I have work after school, so not until late," she calls out as she hops into her white two-door Jeep Wrangler that she calls Snowball and then takes off.

Once she's gone, I let Becky out into the backyard and then heat up my coffee and make breakfast. While I sit at the table, eating and going through my calendar, I text my brother to see if he's up for any company today.

Eric and his wife, Katie, own a health club in town called Brookside Health Club. Before they opened it, the only fitness center was almost forty minutes away in the next town over. He saw the need and took a risk, and it paid off because the place is always busy.

Since I'm off five days a week, thanks to my two twenty-four-hour shifts, I go in a few days a week to teach various classes and help. It not only helps me stay in shape and gives me extra money in my pocket, but it also keeps me busy since my parents are gone a lot and my daughter is busy with school, friends, extracurriculars, and her job at the local bookstore and coffee shop.

> Eric: I was just about to text you. Katie has a doctor's appointment this afternoon, and I have a new member consultation. Wanna run through it for me?

Katie and Eric are expecting their first baby in May, and they're finding out soon whether it's a boy or a girl.

Me: Sure.

After I finish eating, I throw on my gym attire and head to the health club. I'm getting out of my truck when my eyes land on the business sign a few doors down—*Exposed Ink*—and my mind goes back to last week when we were called out to Neptune's for an allergic reaction.

Even though she had a swollen and splotchy face, I could tell the woman was beautiful. That normally wouldn't be enough to pique my interest. I've rescued plenty of pretty women during my fifteen years as a firefighter paramedic. But there was something about the way her blue eyes peered into mine as she begged me not to take her to the hospital that caught my attention.

After I finished the paperwork, I had every intention of leaving to go back to the station, but before I could question what I was doing, I was heading down the hall to the room I knew she was in to make sure she was okay—despite knowing she was since I'd left her completely stable. The only thing the doctor had to do was give her some fluids to be on the safe side and monitor her for a few hours before discharging her.

I could tell from my brief conversation with Kinsley that there was so much more to her than met the eye, and I wanted to dig deep and find it all out. I wanted to ask for her number, but then her friend showed up, and despite her making it clear I should reach out to Kinsley, when Kinsley got embarrassed—her pale skin turning a beautiful shade of pink—I second-guessed myself and left without her number.

Every day for the past week, I've been thinking about her. Every time I go to the health club and see the Exposed Ink sign, I consider walking in and asking to speak to her. But I keep chickening out.

My phone dings with an incoming text, so I pull it out and see it's from my brother.

Eric: Hope you haven't left yet. Newbie canceled due to an
emergency.

Me: No worries. Let me know if anything changes.

I pocket my phone and head inside, figuring since I'm already here, I might as well get a workout in. The entire time, I can't stop wondering if Kinsley is a few doors down. She obviously works at Exposed Ink, and based on the ink on her body, she's no stranger to being tattooed. But I'm not sure what she does there.

As I was leaving her hospital room, I saw what looked like her parents—judging by the number of tattoos they were both sporting and the matching Exposed Ink shirt the guy was wearing. Maybe she's a tattoo artist.

After I've gotten my workout in, I take a quick shower, get dressed in a change of clothes I keep in the locker room, and then head out.

I'm halfway to my truck when I change direction and end up standing in front of the tattoo shop. The open sign is illuminated, so I take that as my sign to go in.

A young guy with spiky black hair and several piercings in his face smiles at me as I walk up to the front desk.

"Welcome to Exposed Ink," he greets. "How can I help you?"

"I'm looking for Kinsley."

"Are you looking to get inked or pierced?" he asks.

"Um, neither. I was hoping to speak with her. Is she around?" I glance down the hallway, hoping to catch her, but it's empty.

The guy eyes me curiously for several seconds before he says, "What's your name?"

"Shane."

"And what do you want to speak to her about, Shane?"

Okay ... this guy is either protective or has a thing for Kinsley.

"I met her last week and wanted to talk to her about something personal."

After a long moment, he says, "Give me a minute," then disappears down the hall, going into the second door on the right.

While I wait, I check out the shop. I've never been in here before, but it's not how I imagined a tattoo shop would look. With an L-shaped black leather sectional, a sleek black coffee table with what looks like photo albums sitting on them, and a red felt pool table, the waiting area looks more like something you'd see in a wealthy person's house or an upscale club than a tattoo shop.

There's cool graffiti donning the walls, and I notice that several are sporting Kinsley's name underneath them. If the drawings on the wall are any indication, she's a seriously talented artist.

The front desk is sleek black, and to the right of it is a glass case with a bunch of jewelry inside it. Hanging above the case are several pictures in frames. I step closer to get a better look and immediately recognize Kinsley standing in between the two older people I saw at the hospital, the ones I assumed to be her parents. She doesn't really look like either one, but her soft smile is identical to the woman who has her arm wrapped around Kinsley's waist.

"Can I help you?" Kinsley says, steering my attention from the picture over to her.

She's wearing a similar outfit to the one she was wearing at Neptune's—a black Exposed Ink shirt and ripped jeans that mold to her shapely legs. Instead of the black Chucks she was sporting, she's in white today. And unlike the high ponytail her hair was in, it's down in two braids, making her look younger than her twenty-eight years.

"Hey, I don't know if you remember me …"

"I do," she says without so much as a smile, her expression giving absolutely nothing away. "You're the guy from the hospital."

"Yeah." I step closer to her, ignoring the guy who's now back to sitting behind the desk, watching our exchange. "How are you doing?"

"Wow." She laughs softly—a tiny smile curling up at the corners of her mouth—and tilts her head slightly to the side. "First, a hospital call, and now, you're at my work to check on me. They should give you a Paramedic of the Year award."

I chuckle. "I swear, I normally don't do this. It's just that I couldn't stop thinking about you, and I was wondering if you might want to hang out sometime." *Holy shit, I sound like a fucking teenage boy.* "I mean, I was hoping you might want to go out with me ... to eat." I push out a harsh breath and shake my head. "I'm sorry, I seriously suck at this. It's been a while since I asked a woman out and ..."

Kinsley snorts out a laugh, her blue eyes brightening with mirth, and I realize it's the first time I've seen her laugh and smile, and, holy shit, she was beautiful before, but when she smiles, she lights up the whole damn place.

"What I'm trying to say is, would you like to go on a date with me?"

Kinsley's smile drops, and before she speaks, I already know what her answer is going to be. "I'm sorry," she says, "but the only way we can spend any time together is if I'm inking you ... or you're treating me in an ambulance. And since I don't plan to consume any more raw fruit, the second option is out. I appreciate you saving me, and you seem like a nice guy, but I'm unavailable."

I'm confused by her words since her cousin said otherwise at the hospital, but before I can seek clarification, she dismisses me by quickly telling me to have a good day and then heading back down the hallway, disappearing into the room the front-desk guy went into.

"Sorry, man," front-desk guy says, shooting me a sympathetic look.

"Honestly, it doesn't surprise me that she's taken," I say as the guy from the hospital and picture steps out of the first room, his eyes focused intently on me.

"I'm Lachlan, Kinsley's dad," he says, pulling his glove off his hand and extending it.

"Shane." I shake his hand. "I'm the paramedic who brought her in last week."

"I know who you are. Thank you for saving my daughter's life. And FYI, she's not taken."

"But she said …" I begin, confused as hell.

First, her cousin suggested I ask her out, then Kinsley told me she's unavailable, and now, her dad is telling me she's single?

"That she's unavailable. Yeah, I heard," Lachlan says. "But it's not because she's in a relationship. She's single. Hasn't dated in years. But in her head, she's emotionally unavailable. Got a ten-foot wall erected around her big-ass heart."

"More like fifty-foot," front-desk guy mutters. "And the only way you're getting to her is by breaking down that wall, and in order to do that, you'd better be damn strong." He eyes me from head to toe with a smirk. "How strong are you, Shane?"

When my eyes go wide, unsure how to respond, Lachlan chuckles. "Ignore Scott's flirting. He's harmless. But he's not wrong." His features turn serious. "It would take someone extremely strong and determined to break down the wall my daughter has built."

I nod in understanding, her reluctance now making sense. "Gotcha."

I turn on my heel, ready to admit defeat, but as his words play on repeat, I stop at the door, unable to open it.

If I were smart, I would heed their warning and walk away. Kinsley made it clear she wasn't interested, and trying to break down the wall of a woman like her won't be easy. Hell, I've barely dated in the past seventeen years, focusing on being a single dad, so I'm no expert on women, and I'll probably fail miserably. But there's just something about her that I'm drawn to, making me want to try.

It's obvious from my two short encounters with her that she doesn't smile often, but when she does, it's worth the effort. Watching her laugh at my expense made me want to make her do it again. And when she frowned, I wanted to ask what had caused it.

I want to spend time with Kinsley, but instead of breaking down her walls, I want her to open the gate for me. I want her to let me in and show me every part of her. For the first time in a long time, I want to get to know a woman on a deeper level.

Why was she terrified of being brought to the hospital? What happened to make her emotionally unavailable? Why is it that even when she smiled at me for a brief moment a few minutes ago, she still looked like she was in pain?

"Is there something else you need?" Lachlan asks, shaking me from my thoughts and reminding me that I'm still standing in the doorway like a weirdo, thinking about his daughter.

"Actually, yeah," I say, turning around and walking back up to the desk. "I'd like to make an appointment to get a tattoo … with Kinsley."

Scott tries to hide his smile, but Lachlan doesn't even attempt to hide his smirk.

"You ever been inked before?" Lachlan asks, eyeing me skeptically.

"No," I admit. "Any tips?"

"Don't cry," Lachlan says, making Scott laugh.

"Kinsley's pretty booked up," Scott says.

"Let me see." Lachlan grabs the iPad and clicks around for a minute and then says, "I can get you in tomorrow at ten," making Scott throw his head back with a laugh.

Shit, that's soon. But fuck it. What's a little tattoo? I'll just get it somewhere hidden, and it will give me a chance to convince Kinsley to go out with me.

"Sounds good," I say. "I'll be here tomorrow at ten."

Five

Kinsley

"KINSLEY, IT'S BEEN A LONG TIME SINCE YOU REQUESTED an emergency appointment," Dr. Julia Benedict says with her warm smile that makes it easy to open up to her. "What brings you in?"

She sits across from me, dressed in a long, flowy floral skirt and a white blouse, with her legs curled under her and her latest knitting project in her lap.

After months of my mom begging me to see a therapist, I met with Julia. I had planned to see her, tell my mom I hated it, and continue to grieve the way I wanted.

But Julia shocked me when we bonded over our favorite romance novels, and then instead of her forcing me to talk, she handed me a piece of paper and coloring pencils and told me to draw whatever came to mind.

I spent the next year coloring more than speaking during our sessions, but eventually, they led to us talking, and now, I can't imagine not speaking to her.

Usually, our appointments are every two weeks, but after what happened this morning, I texted, asking if she had anything available.

"A guy asked me out today." I chuckle humorlessly. "God, that sounds so inconsequential when I say it out loud."

"Yet it was important enough to make you pick up the phone and text me. So, tell me what happened."

I take a deep breath and then tell her, "His name is Shane, and he's the paramedic who treated me for the food allergy." She already knows about that incident since I saw her a couple of days after. "He came into the shop to see how I was doing and then asked me out."

"And how did it make you feel when he showed up?" she asks with a soft smile.

"For a moment, when he was nervously trying to ask me out, my brain allowed me to pretend everything was simple. Like I was just a woman, standing in front of a man who was interested in her and wanted to take her out on a date.

"But then the question finally slid off his lips, and the memory of Brandon asking me out for the first time hit me like a ton of bricks," I choke out, tears filling my lids. "I hate this. I hate that I can't be normal."

"You know how I feel about that word," Julia chides playfully. "The expectation to be *normal* isn't one that is achievable since one can't accurately define it. What's considered normal to one person is different for another."

"I know," I mumble, having heard her say this on more than one occasion.

"You mentioned when he asked you out, he reminded you of Brandon," she says. "Are there similarities between the two?"

I think for a moment about Brandon. He was broody and

mysterious, the ultimate tatted-up bad boy with a rough exterior who didn't give a shit about what anyone thought of him besides me. He always had a soft spot for me. We had flirted for years, the chemistry between us sizzling, and when he asked me out, he was sure I would say yes. At that point, it was just a formality.

But Shane's nothing like Brandon—at least not from what I've seen. He's got this sweet sexiness to him, like he should be posing for a charity calendar in his uniform while holding a kitten he just saved. It's clear, based on the way his shirt stretched across his chest, he's in shape, and for a split second, I fantasized about him wearing that uniform in the bedroom as he reminded me what it felt like to be intimate with a man again.

As he stood in front of me and Scott, he was unsure of what I would say, yet he still took his shot. And when I turned him down and the look of defeat filled his features, I wanted to take back my answer and agree to go out with him just so that boyish grin would once again make an appearance.

But I couldn't do it.

"No," I tell her. "They're actually nothing alike from what I can tell. But it wasn't really about his looks or personality. It was the thought of getting to know another man—of possibly falling in love, having children, and creating a life with someone who wasn't Brandon—and the memory of my daughter, who'd never gotten a chance to live, that filled me with guilt and made me turn him down."

"Wow," Julia says with a smirk that tells me she's about to go all therapist on me. "You just created an entire fake future with a man before you even agreed to one date. For all you know, he was just looking to get laid."

I bark out a laugh and shake my head. "He seems too sweet for that."

"You don't know that because you don't know him. What if he

was only looking for something casual? Would you have said yes then?"

God, that's so hard because the truth is, I miss being intimate with someone, but the thought of being intimate with anyone but Brandon feels wrong.

"I don't know," I admit truthfully. "But it doesn't matter because I said no and he left."

"It still matters," Julia says, "because this is part of you moving forward. I want you to think about what you see your future looking like. I know I asked you to do this before, but that was over a year ago. And a year ago, had a man asked you out, you wouldn't have even considered it."

"I said no," I remind her.

"But you still considered it. We as therapists like to call that progress." She winks, and I groan. "Speaking of which, you should check out the book I'm reading. You might find it … enlightening."

She holds up the paperback, and my heart clenches at the couple on the cover. I used to love reading romance. It was my mom's and my thing. We could talk about the books we'd read for hours while checking out all the bookstores in our area. We attended book signings to meet our favorite authors, and my mom has an entire library of signed paperbacks we've collected over the years.

The day I lost Brandon and our daughter, I lost my desire to read romance. The first time I picked up a romance book to try to escape, I bawled my eyes out, unable to handle reading about someone else getting their happily ever after, knowing I would never get mine.

"It's so good," she says. "They're roommates but can't stand each other."

"Ugh," I groan. "You know I love a good enemies-to-lovers romance."

"Here," she says, handing it to me. "I have it on my Kindle."

I take it from her and eye it, wondering if maybe it's time for me to give romance books another shot. I won't be going out with Shane, but maybe I could live vicariously through a woman who isn't as fucked up as I am.

My thoughts go to the black box my mom left in my Valentine's Day basket. Maybe it's time I put it to use.

"Kinsley, your ten o'clock appointment is here," Scott says, poking his head into my room.

"I'll be out in a sec," I tell him as I finish prepping my station.

Yesterday, I didn't have an appointment for this morning, so I didn't plan to come in until noon, but last night, when Scott sent out our daily schedule reminders, one had popped up.

Which was fine with me since the last place I wanted to be was at home, staring at the romance book I couldn't bring myself to read.

After my appointment with Julia, I went for a run to the health club, and when I passed by the fire station, I couldn't help but wonder if Shane was in there and what he was doing.

So, when I got home, I grabbed the book, hoping to get him off my mind. But instead, three pages in, when I found out the hero was a firefighter—damn Julia for leaving out that crucial detail—I closed the book and refused to open it again, staring at it until I finally fell asleep. And then I ignored it on my nightstand as I got ready for work this morning.

Work is the best distraction, so while I'd usually be annoyed that Scott sprang a last-minute appointment on me, this morning, I'm looking forward to it.

Once my station is ready, I silence my phone and stow it away in my drawer and then head out to the waiting room to meet my client. Scott didn't leave any info about them, not even their name, which is very unlike him, so I have no idea what I'm working with.

Only when I step out of my room, my eyes lock with Shane, who's standing in the waiting room, dressed in a navy-blue shirt that reads *Station One* across his chest with a matching ball cap tucked low on his forehead.

What is it about a man sporting a ball cap that makes a woman swoon?

He's got on a pair of dark blue jeans that mold to his thighs perfectly, and on his feet are a pair of Nikes.

As if he can sense me checking him out, his head pops up from his phone, and his brown eyes lock with mine.

"What are you doing here?" I ask, my question coming out blunter than I intended.

"He's your ten o'clock," Scott says.

My gaze swings over to him, and from the smirk he's trying and failing to stifle, he knows exactly what he did.

"Have you ever been inked before?" I ask Shane, who shakes his head.

"And what are you planning to get today?"

"Umm …" He glances from Scott to me and then says, "I was thinking something small, like maybe …"

"Stop right there." I hold up my hand to emphasize my words and then look at Scott. "Did you make this appointment?"

"Yeah, but …"

"No buts," I hiss. "You know my rule. If it's not meaningful, I don't tattoo it. Did you even ask him what he was getting when you made the appointment?"

"He didn't make it," my dad says, stepping out from his station. "I did."

"Seriously?" I glare.

"It's not his fault," Shane says, stepping toward me. "You said you wouldn't talk to me unless I was getting inked or saving your life in an ambulance, so I made an appointment to get inked."

"You what?" I choke out, shocked by his admission. "A tattoo is permanent," I point out. "You were seriously going to let me put something permanent on your body just so you could talk to me for a few minutes?"

Shane shrugs, a small tilt of his lips quirking at the corners. "I figured it would be worth it, if I could use that time to convince you to go on a date with me."

Oh my God. This guy.

"I already said I'm unavailable."

"Which isn't the truth," my traitorous dad points out, raising a brow and daring me to argue.

"It's not happening," I say to Shane. "I appreciate the effort, but I'm not going out with you. And I'm definitely not tattooing something meaningless on your body. Come back when you have something worth tattooing … and don't even think about getting it off Google or Pinterest."

I glance at Scott. "Don't make appointments without asking them what they're getting!" I point to the wall where a sign hangs, saying, *If you'd like to book an appointment with Kinsley, please make sure your piece is meaningful. She has the right to refuse to ink anyone.* "You know my rule."

And then I look at my dad. "And you … find something better to do than play matchmaker. I'm. Not. Available."

Without waiting for any of them to respond, I stomp back down the hallway and straight to my room, where I slam the door and then lean against it, trying like hell to ignore the fact that Shane is getting under my skin. I can't stop thinking about him. And I'd be lying if I said that him concocting this plan with my dad and being willing to get a tattoo, just to spend time with me, isn't clenching the hell out of my broken and battered heart and reminding me that it still works.

I spend the rest of the day in my station, working on client after client, and once my last one leaves, I clean up quickly so I can try to leave without facing my dad. I feel bad that I yelled at him earlier, but he shouldn't have done what he did. And I'm not in the mood to discuss it.

But as I'm stepping out of my room, he steps out of his. Our eyes lock, and a small smile graces his features, and instead of being angry, tears fill my eyes.

"C'mere, Mini Q," he says, using the nickname he dubbed me with when I was little because I reminded him so much of my mom—Quinn.

He opens his arms, and I fall into them, burying my head into his chest as I cry while he holds me close. He moves us into his station and sits us on his couch that he has positioned in the corner.

"Shh, it's okay," he murmurs, rubbing my back. "I'm sorry. I shouldn't have done what I did. I just … *fuck*, I hate to see you like this."

"I know," I mutter through my cries. "It's just so hard." A choked sob pushes past the lump of emotion clogging my throat, and I cry harder. "I'm so sick of feeling like this, Dad. My heart hurts so much."

I cry in my dad's arms for several minutes, until the tears feel like they can't fall anymore, and then we sit in silence for a little while after that.

No words need to be spoken. There's nothing anyone can do or say that will bring my husband and baby back. Death is permanent, and the only thing I can do is try to move forward without them.

"I wanted to say yes," I whisper.

"What?" He pulls back slightly to meet my eyes.

"When he asked me out, I … I wanted to say yes."

But I couldn't.

I felt too much guilt.

I was too terrified.

My dad nods in understanding, then pulls me back into his arms. "You'll get there, Kins. Just keep doing what you've been doing. Take it one day at a time."

Six

Shane

"WHAT ARE YOU LOOKING AT?"

The sound of Taylor's voice has me jumping in my seat. When I got home from the station this morning, she was still asleep.

"Nothing," I murmur, closing my laptop.

"Don't lie." She laughs, lifting the screen back up so the Google page I was looking at is front and center.

"Are those"—she leans in closer—"tattoos?" She scrunches her nose up. "Dad, please tell me you aren't looking at Google for tattoo ideas."

I groan, remembering Kinsley's words. *Don't even think about getting it off Google or Pinterest.*

"How the hell else am I supposed to get inspiration?" I grumble, closing the laptop again and turning to face my daughter.

"Wait, you're really considering getting a tattoo?" Her brows hit her forehead as she looks at me like I've grown two heads.

"So what if I am?" I shrug, crossing my arms over my chest.

"Aren't you a little old to be rebelling?" Taylor smirks.

"It's not rebellion when you're of age."

"Right … so what is it then? A midlife crisis?" She cackles, and I huff out an annoyed sigh.

"Just drop it," I say. "You want to make breakfast or go out?"

Every Saturday or Sunday, depending on our schedules, Taylor and I spend some time together. It's our thing. We're both busy, especially her with her job and school and cheerleading and friends, so if our schedules align, we'll have breakfast together and then take Becky for a walk while we catch up on what we did during the week. Thankfully, my daughter likes me and goes along with it.

"I'm not dropping it," she says. "What's going on, Dad? I've known you my entire life, and you've never even mentioned getting a tattoo before. If you want one, that's cool, but searching for one online isn't it."

"That's what she said," I mutter.

"Who?" Taylor quirks a brow.

"The tattoo artist. She said she'd only ink something meaningful on me and told me not to even think about finding one on Google or Pinterest."

"She's not wrong." Taylor laughs. "Casey went to Exposed Ink to get a tattoo for her eighteenth birthday and dragged me along with her …"

My eyes lock with Taylor's. This is the first time I'm hearing about this. Casey is a year older than Taylor, but they're friends because they're both on the same cheer team.

If Casey went to get a tattoo and Taylor went with her, does that mean …

"No, Dad, I didn't get one," Taylor says, answering my silent question. "One, I'm not eighteen, and Exposed Ink won't tattoo or pierce anyone under eighteen without consent."

My thoughts go to Kinsley, and I wonder if she's met my daughter …

"The woman there refused to tattoo Casey because she wanted some stupid unicorn flower design." She rolls her eyes. "I told her not to do it, that it was cheesy as hell, but she told me it was cute, and she loved it." She cringes dramatically. "The woman at the shop … Kinsley, I think her name was … told Casey that a unicorn dies every time a woman gets one tattooed on them and that she couldn't contribute to the death of a unicorn."

She laughs, and I find myself grinning as I picture Kinsley saying this to Casey. The woman clearly cares, or she wouldn't refuse to ink people, but she's blunt, and she doesn't mince words, telling it like it is.

"What did Casey do?"

"There was nothing she could do. Apparently, what Kinsley says goes." She shrugs. "Casey left upset, saying she would go somewhere else, but she hasn't had the time. Which is for the best. You know I love her, but you wouldn't catch me getting a unicorn tattooed on me, and I'm glad she didn't get one either. I'm hoping she'll change her mind before she makes it to the city to get it done."

"What would you get?" I ask curiously.

"I don't know." She shrugs. "It would need to be something that I would want to look at every day, and when I'm older, it would make me feel something."

"Who raised you to be so wise?" I joke.

"Apparently not you, Mr. Google," she sasses back. "Now, let's go to breakfast. I'm starved."

As she runs back up the stairs to get ready, my eyes catch on the picture hanging on the wall, and an idea forms. The shop is closed today and tomorrow, but Tuesday, I'll call them first thing and make an appointment. Kinsley might have gotten me that round, but I'm in this to win it.

"You're back again?" Kinsley gasps, her eyes volleying from me to Scott, who's grinning from ear to ear. "I thought I told you—"

"I booked it under his name!" Scott says, lifting his hands placatingly.

"It said Evan!"

"No, Evans," I correct with a smirk. "That's my last name. Shane Evans."

Kinsley glares, and I stifle my laugh.

"I already told you that I won't ink—"

"Anything that's not meaningful. I know. I remember. And I have something meaningful." I pull out my phone and click on the picture I took of the painting this morning before I left to come here. "I want this inked on my arm."

"What is that?" Kinsley asks, furrowing her brows in confusion.

"It's a picture of me and my daughter," I admit. "She drew it for me on her first day of school. She had been home with me for years, but then she turned four, and everyone said I had to put her in school. She wasn't having it, said she only wanted to be with me, but I told her she'd have fun. She told me she hated me for making her go …"

I choke up, remembering the day like it was yesterday. Sending my little girl to school was the hardest day of my life. Trusting someone that wasn't family to care for my little girl sucked.

"I cried for a good hour," I admit, my voice filled with emotion as I recall that day. "I didn't have to work, so I was waiting at the door for her when she got out. I had already convinced myself that if she hated it, I would never send her back, education be damned."

I chuckle, but Kinsley doesn't smile. I can't read her expression, so I keep going. "She came barreling out of the school, her little pigtails flying behind her. She beelined straight for me and hugged my legs. And then she looked up at me and said she had so much fun and couldn't wait to go back."

I tap on my phone and show her the picture again. "When we got home, she pulled this picture out of her backpack and said it was for me. Her teacher told them to draw what they loved the most, and she drew me … well, us."

I point to the stick figures and then explain the rest of the picture. "That's the station. I was young when Taylor was born and only had my parents to help since her mom wasn't ready to be a mom."

She still really isn't, but I'm not about to open that can of worms. Kinsley just wants to know that my tattoo will be meaningful, not participate in a therapy session.

"The guys at the station are like family, so Taylor practically grew up there, considering them her uncles and aunts. When she showed me the picture, she said she loved me and I was her favorite person. And to be honest," I say with a shrug, "she's mine. She's seventeen now, and she has her moments, but in a lot of ways, since she was born when I was eighteen, we've grown up together, so I thought it would be cool to have a piece of her on me. Eventually, she'll go off to college and one day get married, but this picture will always remind me that from the beginning, it was just her and me against the world."

I glance up at Kinsley. Her eyes are glossy, but she quickly closes them, and when she opens them, she's back to her emotionless state.

"So, what do you say?" I ask. "Is it meaningful enough for you to tattoo on me?"

"Yeah," she whispers. "I'll tattoo it on you."

Seven

Kinsley

I DON'T KNOW WHAT I WAS EXPECTING SHANE TO SAY WHEN he pulled up the child's artwork on his phone, but it wasn't that. Honestly, it didn't click in my head at first. I was so frazzled by having him in my shop again that when he showed me the artwork, it didn't even compute that it was a child's artwork, let alone *his* child's artwork, until he started speaking.

As he spoke about his relationship with his daughter, I couldn't help but get emotional. In a lot of ways, it reminds me of the relationship I have with my parents, but it also reminds me of the relationship I'll never have with my daughter.

When I lost my husband and baby, I didn't just lose them. I lost all our future moments. I'll never get to hug or kiss them or tell them I love them. I'll never hear Brenna tell me I'm her favorite person. She'll never go to school or paint pictures to bring home. And looking at his picture reminds me how much I wanted all that.

"Where do you want the tattoo?" I ask once I set up my station and have somewhat gotten control of my emotions.

He mentioned his arm, but that can mean a lot of places.

"I was thinking we could do it here," Shane says, lifting the sleeve of his shirt and showing off his toned upper arm. "I saw on Google …"

I glare, and he laughs, lowering his sleeve back down.

"Calm down, Sour Patch. I didn't google this picture. It's mine. But I did google what it would look like on my arm to see if anyone else had done this sort of thing."

I love that he's put thought into this, which was my point when I turned him away, but my brain stops on …

"Sour Patch?"

"Yeah," he says with a grin, pulling a box out of his back pocket. "Sour Patch. They're my favorite candy. I'm kind of addicted."

He reaches into the box and pulls out a red one, his brown eyes sparkling as the sexual tension fills the room with his not-so-subtle inuendo. "They're sour on the outside, but once you get to the deeper layers, they're sweet." He places the candy on his tongue and then closes his mouth, moaning softly. "So good. Want one?"

He extends his hand but retracts it when I shake my head, unable to move, let alone take candy from this man who has crashed into my safe, carefully constructed world, threatening to tear down the walls I've built.

"You remind me of a Sour Patch," he says with a playful smirk. "Sour on the outside and—"

"I'm not sweet," I mutter, making Shane laugh.

"I beg to differ." He chuckles. "You met my daughter once," he says, shocking the hell out of me. "She came in here with her best friend, Casey."

It doesn't take me long to remember who he's talking about. "The unicorn girl?"

"Yep. You refusing to tattoo it on her was sweet," he says with a smile. "You can glare all you want, but underneath all that sour is a woman who cares."

"I just didn't want my name attached to that ugly tattoo."

"Sweet," he argues.

"Whatever," I mumble. "AirDrop me the picture so we can get this over with."

"Actually," he says, "this is only the first tattoo I want. When I searched arm sleeves, I saw a bunch of images where people got sleeves of their kids' artwork. I thought it would look cool.

"I have a few special pictures Taylor has made over the years, and I was thinking maybe you could design a few other images that are meaningful to me but make them cartoonish so they all have the same vibe—like my dog, Becky, and something to symbolize the fire station I work at."

"You want a sleeve," I say slowly.

I mean, I heard him, but I'm still trying to wrap my head around it.

"Yep," he replies, popping the *P*. "I was thinking I could come every week, and you could continue it."

Every. Fucking. Week. This guy can't be serious …

"You can only do every week a few times," I point out. "After a few sessions, your body will need more time to heal, and you'll need to wait at least two weeks in between appointments, if not longer."

"Okay." He shrugs. "So, every week until you say I need to switch to every two weeks. Got it."

I stare at him for several seconds, and when it's clear that he's being dead serious, I release an annoyed sigh. "Let's just see how this goes today before you make any future plans. For all we know, it'll hurt so badly that you'll pass out and throw up and never come back."

A girl can hope.

Shane barks out a laugh, not at all fazed by my words. "I already took pain reliever, and I'm a firefighter medic. I can handle a little pain."

He winks playfully, and I internally groan.

This man is going to be the death of me.

"Let's go," I say, pointing to the chair. "Sit down and lift your sleeve back up so I can look at what I'm working with."

"Would it be easier for me to just take off my shirt?" he asks with a flirtatious tone laced in his words.

I imagine his body on display, and based on his muscular arms, I'm sure his chest and abs are just as toned. Not only would that be distracting, but the last thing I need is to stare at this man shirtless. I'm having a hard enough time keeping him out of my thoughts.

"No," I say a bit too harshly as I open my drawer and grab a zip tie from the bag I keep on hand for this purpose. "Keep your damn shirt on."

Shane chuckles, unaffected by my rudeness. "So damn sour," he says, smiling at me. "I can't wait to get to all that sweet underneath."

I ignore him while I sit at my desk and, using the picture he sent to me, draw up the tattoo. It's a simple design, but it takes some time to make sure I get the lines and shading correct so it matches what his daughter originally drew.

"Okay," I say once I'm done, turning around in my seat. "Check this out and let me know if you want me to make any changes."

Usually, I'll have the client upload what they're looking to have done into our system so I can draw up a draft before they come in. Sometimes, it takes several times of going back and forth before the client is happy with what I've come up with. Some tattoo artists get annoyed by that, but it's permanent, and I want my clients to never regret what I inked onto their skin. So, if it means I draw up several drafts, then so be it.

He glances up from his phone and pockets it, then takes the iPad from me. He stares at it for several seconds, not saying a word, and I worry that he hates it. It doesn't matter how long I've been tattooing, I always question if my artistic capabilities are good enough. When I'm not tattooing, I spend hours drawing for fun, experimenting with different lines and shading.

"It's perfect," he chokes out, glancing up at me with glassy eyes. "Thank you. I'm glad you didn't let me get the first tattoo I was planning to get."

"What was it?" I ask curiously since I never gave him a chance to tell me—shutting him down the moment he said, "Maybe."

"A fire hydrant," he says with a chuckle. "This is way more meaningful."

"Well, that wouldn't have been horrible"—I roll my eyes—"and it's better than a unicorn."

Shane snorts out a laugh. "She has jokes. Look at that sweet coming out."

"I do not, and it is not," I grumble. "Now, focus. Is there anything you want me to change?"

"No. It looks perfect."

"Okay, cool." I point to the image. "I was thinking if you're serious about the sleeve … or half sleeve, we start small since you're a tattoo virgin …"

Shane chuckles like an immature teenage boy at the word *virgin*, but I ignore it.

"See this area here?" I run my finger along the grassy area of the picture. "We could shade it so that it will easily transition into another piece."

When Shane nods, I take the iPad from him and then go about prepping the area that will be inked. I print the design and then place it on him.

"Good?" I ask, showing it to him in the mirror.

"Yep."

"Let's do this."

I plug in my phone and click play on my playlist. Usually, I'll ask the client what kind of music they like, but the less I know about Shane, the better.

As Taylor Swift sings about having her heart broken, Shane glances at me with a smirk.

"What?" I huff, too curious for my own good.

"Just didn't take you for a Swiftie," he says. "Although I guess it makes sense since you got that whole broody-chick thing going for you."

Without responding, I grab his arm, turn the gun on, and get to work on his tattoo. At first, he tenses, but after a few minutes, his body relaxes.

"It doesn't hurt like I thought it would," he says, watching as I work.

"People who've never been tattooed think getting one hurts. But in reality, for most, it's more annoying than anything. For me, because I'm so used to it, it's therapeutic."

"What's the last tattoo you got?" he asks, his question forcing me to stop tattooing him.

The last time I was tattooed was …

Shit!

I turn the gun off and wipe his arm, then stand, peeling my gloves off and tossing them into the trash.

"I'm sorry. I need to use the bathroom," I rush out. "I'll be right back."

Before he can say anything, I storm out of the room, heading straight for the back office. Only before I get there, I run into my dad.

"Whoa," he says, looking at me with concern. "What's going on?"

"Nothing. I just need to go to—"

"Stop," Dad says, refusing to let me lie. "I thought you were in with a client. Did something happen?"

"No," I whisper. "Well …" I swallow thickly. "He asked what the last tattoo I got was."

Dad nods knowingly.

"I just need a minute."

"Do you need me to—" He nods toward my room.

"No, I'm just going to splash some water on my face. But thank you."

When I return to the room, Shane glances at me, his eyes zeroing in on my splotchy face. Thanks to my fair skin, I can't hide when I've been crying.

"Did I say something wrong?" he asks, his features etched with worry.

"No. I'm just a mess," I admit with a self-deprecating laugh. "Hence me not being emotionally available."

Shane nods in understanding, and then he says something that completely shocks the hell out of me. "As much as I would love to take you out on a date—and I still want to—it's clear you're not ready for that, so why don't we take a step back?"

"Okay," I say cautiously.

"My name is Shane Evans." He extends his hand. "And I would love it if we could be friends."

I stare at his hand for several seconds, and then, against my better judgment, I take it. It's warm to the touch and a bit rough. But for some reason, it's also comforting.

"I'm Kinsley Bryson," I tell him. "And you're going to find out that I'm a really shitty friend."

At my words, a sexy, boyish grin lights up his too-damn-handsome-for-his-own-good face. "Somehow, I doubt that," he says with a laugh.

And as he shakes my hand, his eyes boring into mine and his smile lighting up the damn room, I ignore the warmth that spreads through my body, particularly my lady parts, forcing my own smile on my face.

Friends, I tell myself.

Great.

We're friends.

That's perfect.

Then, why is it that I suddenly really freaking hate that word?

"Holy shit," Shane breathes, looking at his new tattoo in the mirror. "It looks so good." He snaps a photo of it in the mirror and then pockets his phone.

"I'm glad you like it. Did your daughter know you were getting it?"

"No. I figured I would show her after it was done. She was giving me shit about getting a tattoo at my age, saying I was going through a midlife crisis."

He laughs, and I join him. I don't know his daughter, but the one time I met her, she seemed cool. I could tell she wasn't at all on board with her friend's tattoo idea, and that makes me like her even more.

"They grow up too fast," he says, shaking me from my thoughts. "One minute, I was holding her in my arms and vowing to be the best dad I could be, scared to death that I'd somehow fuck it all up.

And the next, she's driving and working and giving me shit about my tattoo of choice."

Emotion fills my chest, and before I can think about what I'm saying, I blurt out, "My last tattoo was my daughter's heartbeat."

Shane's eyes widen in shock. "You have a daughter?"

"Had," I correct. "I mean, she's still my daughter, but she's not alive."

Tears fill my eyes as I lift my shirt to show him the tattoo that's inked along my left rib cage. And as he kneels in front of me to check it out, memories from the day I got it come back to me …

"I'm pretty sure it's somewhere in here." I open and close each drawer, trying to find the drawing I drew for my dad but somehow misplaced.

We hired a new cleaning company, and I think they're moving shit despite me telling them not to. When I reach all the way back in the bottom drawer, my hand latches on to a bunch of papers. I yank them out, and when my eyes land on a certain drawing, I drop it like it's on fire.

"Did you find it?" Dad asks.

"No," I whisper, staring at the paper I thought I had thrown out.

"Kins?" Dad says. "What's—"

His words come to a halt when his gaze lands on the picture.

"Oh shit," he whispers.

"I thought it was gone." Carefully, I take it from the pile. "I can't believe it's been two years since I lost her." I run my finger along the lines of her heartbeat.

Brandon was supposed to tattoo it on me after I gave birth to celebrate us welcoming our little girl into the world. Only there was no celebration or welcoming. Just the doctors taking my stillborn baby out via cesarean while my husband died on the surgical table in another part of the hospital.

I have nothing left of her but this picture I drew of her name and heartbeat. And for the longest time, I couldn't imagine getting it inked onto my body. But now, staring at it, knowing it's all I have of her …

"Hey, Dad," I say, glancing up at him. "Will you tattoo this on me?"

Dad's eyes widen. "Are you sure?"

"Yeah." I nod. "I want a part of her on me forever."

"Her name was Brenna," I say to Shane even though he can read it himself. "And I killed her before she even had a chance to live."

Eight

Shane

I STARE AT KINSLEY, UNSURE OF WHAT TO SAY, WONDERING how the hell we went from me reminiscing about my daughter to this …

Fuck, what is this?

She killed her daughter? That doesn't make any sense. If that were true, she wouldn't be standing here with me. She'd be in jail, right?

"Kinsley," I say, standing so we're back to being eye level.

Tears are streaming down her cheeks as she continues to hold her shirt up, exposing the tattoo she was showing me.

"I find it hard to believe you're a murderer, so can you explain what you mean?"

Kinsley sniffles back a sob and closes her eyes, forcing the liquid emotion to slide down her face. When she opens her eyes, I'm met with such devastation that my heart clenches in my chest for her.

"It doesn't matter," she mutters. "All you need to know is that being around me would be hazardous to your health."

"Your parents and cousin seem to be doing just fine," I point out.

"That's because I keep them at a distance," she admits, breaking my heart. "I learned the hard way that it's too easy to lose the people we love."

"And who else have you lost besides your daughter?" I ask, getting the feeling there's way more to this story than meets the eye.

"I don't want to talk about this," she says, lowering her shirt as she raises the wall that she temporarily lowered to let me in.

She applies ointment to my tattoo and then covers it up. "These are the aftercare instructions. If you have any questions, you can call the number on here."

Without giving me a chance to get a word in, she walks me to the front, lets Scott know I'm done, and then disappears back into her room, closing the door on the outside world.

"How'd it go?" Scott asks, obviously sensing the tension.

"It went well," I say, not giving anything away. "Kinsley is very talented and has convinced me to get a sleeve done, so I need to book another appointment for next week."

Scott's eyes widen, and then he barks out a laugh. "She convinced you, huh?" He nods to himself. "Yeah, okay."

After letting him know which days I work next week, we make an appointment, and then I take off, hating that I'll have to wait an entire week to see Kinsley again, but telling myself that I just need to be patient. Based on the way she reacted to her own admission, I'm guessing she doesn't open up to many people.

But she opened up to me.

"Hey, Dad!" Taylor yells from the kitchen when I walk through the door.

"Hey, kiddo. What are you doing home?"

"Half day. Came home to eat lunch, and then I've got cheer practice and then work." Her gaze zeroes in on the plastic wrap, and she gasps. "Oh my God! Did you actually go through with it? Did you get a tattoo?"

"I did."

"Well, let me see!"

She drops the sandwich she was making and walks over to me.

"It has to stay covered, but this is what it looks like." I pull out my phone and show her the picture I took of it when I was at the shop.

"Dad," she breathes, her hands going to her mouth. "That's … my picture that I drew for you."

"It was the day you told me I was your favorite person." I pocket my phone. "Figured I would take everyone's advice and get something meaningful, and this picture is as meaningful as it gets."

"I love it," she says, throwing her arms around me. "One day, I'm going to get one for you too."

I want to tell her not to do that, but I would be a hypocrite, considering the fresh ink on my arm, so instead, I hug her back and say, "Just make sure when you decide to do it, it's something you want on your body for the rest of your life."

"Speaking of which," she says, pulling back and giving me that look that says she's up to no good. "Since Casey didn't end up getting her tattoo, she mentioned wanting to get our noses pierced, and you know I've been wanting to get one forever. You said no before, but

I'm seventeen now, and it's not permanent." She side-eyes my tattoo, and I chuckle. "She's legal, but I'm not. So, what do you think?"

As I look at my beautiful, smart, mature daughter, I can't help but think about what Kinsley said today. I don't know what happened, but somehow, she lost her daughter. And as I recall the tears that spilled from her devastated eyes as she confided in me that her daughter had died, it makes me so damn thankful that my daughter is alive and here to ask for insignificant things, like a nose piercing.

"Sure," I say. "Let me know when you want to go, and I'll take you girls."

"Seriously?" Taylor gasps, obviously not expecting me to give in that easily.

"Seriously."

"Thank you, Dad! You're the best!"

Taylor hugs me and kisses my cheek. "Oh my God. I have to call Casey and let her know! Thank you."

With one last hug, she disappears upstairs to her room while I stand in the kitchen and thank God for the blessings in my life.

And then, once I've done that, I say a little prayer for Kinsley because even though I don't know exactly what happened, I know whatever it was, it must've been bad.

Nine

Kinsley

I WILL NOT THINK ABOUT SHANE.

I will not think about Shane.

I will not …

Dammit! I can't stop thinking about him.

It's been three days since he showed up at my shop and I tattooed him. Since I learned he had a daughter. Since I admitted out loud for the first time to someone other than my therapist and my family that I had a daughter and I was the reason she was gone.

"Her name was Brenna … and I killed her before she even had a chance to live."

I'm not gonna lie. When I told Shane I killed her, a part of me was hoping my word choice would push him away.

Boy, my therapist is going to have a field day with that one when we meet next week.

It's just that he was there, talking about his daughter, and I felt myself getting too close. So rather than stand by and risk getting burned, I put out the fire myself.

Only I didn't because even after what I said, he didn't look at me in horror, like someone would look at a murderer. Instead, his features were filled with sympathy and concern. And instead of running, he scheduled another damn appointment.

I tried to push him from my brain, telling myself he was just another client, but the way it felt when we shook hands after he proposed we start over and be friends told me that despite his possible good intentions, there was no being friends with that man.

My phone pings with a text from Natalia, asking if I'll see her tomorrow at her parents' house for the barbecue to introduce Melina's boyfriend, James, to the family.

> Me: Of course!

> Natalia: Good. We can talk about how you tattooed that firefighter hottie Shane and didn't tell me.

> Me: My dad?

> Natalia: You know our dads gossip like teenage girls when they play poker.

Ah, yes. Last night was their weekly poker date. All the guys get together in my uncle Jase's man cave and play poker for hours. They've been doing it for years.

> Me: It wasn't a big deal. He came in, I tattooed him, he left.

> Natalia: Nope! Not having this conversation in text. It's too easy for you to lie. We'll have it tomorrow so I can see if you're telling the truth.

Damn her and damn my face that shows every freaking emotion!
I throw my phone onto the nightstand in annoyance, and when

it lands, it knocks the book that's been mocking me since Julia loaned it to me and I found out it's about a firefighter.

I glare at it for several seconds and then lean over and swipe it off the table. It's Friday night, my parents are on a date, and I've pushed everyone far enough away that they've stopped inviting me out.

I open the book and, despite my hesitancy, get lost in the story. I don't even realize I've been reading for hours, until I glance out my window and see it's dark outside.

I'm about halfway through the book when the story begins to heat up. The heroine is a virgin who has practically zero experience, and the hero has no problem being her teacher …

"Have you ever given yourself an orgasm?"
Her cheeks tinge pink, giving me my answer.
"Oh, baby. Be prepared to have your mind blown."

As I read the scene, I can't help but imagine the characters are Shane and me, and while I'm not a virgin, because it's been years since I've been with a man, he's patiently walking me through it, taking his time and reminding me how good it feels to be intimate with someone.

I drop down between her legs and lick up her center, inhaling her sweet musk. While I slowly lick her clit, I reach up and tweak her nipple.

With one hand holding the book, my other hand skates underneath my pajama shorts and underwear and lands between my legs. I slide my fingers between my lips and find my clit. I'm turned on from the buildup of the scene, so it's easy to swipe through my wetness and use it as friction as I massage my swollen nub, quickly bringing myself to a climax.

"Chase," she breathes. "I'm … I think I'm going to—"

With a little bit of pressure, my orgasm hits me, and before I can think about what I'm doing, Shane's name spills from my lips as I come long and hard to the visual of him eating me out.

For several seconds, the release of dopamine and oxytocin helps me forget the world around me. In this moment, it's only me and Shane and …

Holy shit! I pull my hand out, drop my book, and sit up. I just came to the thought of another man … a man who isn't my husband.

With that realization, guilt rises, threatening to choke me. I climb out of bed, bringing my hands to my throat as I fight to breathe.

I can't believe I just did that. I'm married, and I got off to the thought of another man's touch, of his tongue. I cried out his name when I came.

"I'm a cheater," I choke out as tears prick my lids and spill over. "I'm a fucking cheater."

"No, Kinsley, you're a widow," I imagine Julia saying to me. *"Your husband is no longer alive. You can't cheat on the dead."*

I know she's right, but it still feels wrong … dirty.

I strip off my clothes and get into the shower without waiting for the water to warm, allowing the freezing cold drops to pelt my skin like a punishment.

Once it heats up, I wash my body, trying to rid myself of any thoughts of Shane, but it's no use because the more I try to forget about him, the more I think about him.

"There's only one way to get him out of my mind," I say out loud. "And that's to never see him again."

Once I towel off my body and get dressed, I grab my phone and pull up the online schedule. I find Shane's name and hover above it for several seconds before I click on it and then cancel his appointment.

Unprofessional? Definitely.

But it's the only way.

"You look so good," my aunt Celeste says for the third time, smiling at me.

I've only been at the barbecue for less than a half hour, and I'm already regretting showing up.

I love my family, but because of how close everyone is, that means they care even more. And everyone has spent the past three years worrying about me.

"Thank you," I say for the third time. "Are you excited about Milan?"

She shrugs and smiles. "Jase and I have spoken, and this is going to be our last Fashion Week. My girls have the company under control, so I've decided to officially retire. I miss my grandbabies when I'm gone, and now, with Melina …"

"Melina?" I ask, confused when Celeste clamps her mouth shut.

"Sorry," she whispers. "I'm not supposed to say anything."

Just as she finishes her sentence, James, Melina's boyfriend, clanks a knife against his glass to gather everyone's attention.

Once everyone is quiet, he begins to speak, thanking everyone for welcoming him into the fold. Then, he goes on to talk about how he and Melina met and how she's quickly come to mean the world to him.

And then, once Melina is standing in front of him, he pulls out a ring box and gets down on one knee. "Some might say what's happening between us is moving too fast, but I've always believed that when you know, you know. And I know that I want to spend my life with you ..."

As he continues to speak to her, my thoughts go back to the day Brandon proposed. We were in Forbidden Ink, having lunch. I laughed at something he'd said, and when he pulled his phone out of his pocket, the ring fell out. He had been carrying it around with him for weeks, waiting for the right time to propose. I told him I didn't need a perfect moment, and he got down on his knee and proposed. It was fitting since we had met and fallen in love in Forbidden Ink.

"Kins," someone says softly, shaking me from my thoughts.

When I glance over at my dad, I realize my vision is blurry because I've started to cry.

"I ... I need ..." I murmur, quickly standing.

"Go," he says with a sad smile gracing his lips. "It's okay. Go."

Without drawing attention to myself, I head out the side fence and don't stop until I'm safely on the sidewalk and away from everyone else.

My phone vibrates in my pocket, but I need a minute to myself, so I ignore it and walk down the sidewalk toward the development's main gate. Since it's a small town and I don't drive, I'm used to walking everywhere. Within minutes, I find myself sitting at Brookside Park. It's the town's main park, where most of the sports are played. There's a huge kids' play area, a trail for jogging, and even a dog park.

I sit on the bench and focus on the kids playing, trying to tamp down my emotions. Only the sight of a little girl squealing in delight has me spiraling further as I imagine being here with Brandon and our daughter.

I stand abruptly, ready to flee, when I run straight into a hard chest. When I step back, my apology on the tip of my tongue, I'm met with familiar bright brown eyes.

"Kinsley?" Shane says, gently holding on to my biceps to help steady me.

"Hey," I choke out. "Sorry, I was …"

"You're the tattoo artist from Exposed Ink, right?" a girl says, cutting me off.

I glance at her and recognize her as the friend of the girl I turned away. With her red hair and green eyes, she doesn't have the same features as Shane, but the second the corner of her lips curves into a smile, I know she has to be Shane's daughter.

"Yeah," I breathe out. "Taylor, right?"

"Yeah." She nods. "I was just talking about you with my dad."

My eyes land on him at the exact moment his tongue glides across the seam of his lips to wet them, and my thoughts go back to my fantasy in my room.

The second my neck begins to heat, I dart my eyes back to Taylor, praying my entire face didn't just turn red.

"My friend Casey and I are going to be coming in to get our noses pierced," she tells me.

"Oh, wow," I say, "Better than the unicorn tattoo."

Taylor snorts out a laugh. "And it's not permanent." She shrugs. "Unlike the tattoo my dad got."

"True," I agree. "But at least his is meaningful."

"Oh, you've seen it?" she asks, raising a brow. "Wait, do you two know each other?"

"I treated her for a food allergy," Shane says.

"And while you were doing that, you guys discussed my dad's tattoo?" Taylor quirks a brow, way too observant.

"Actually, I did the tattoo for him," I tell her.

Her eyes go wide, and then after several seconds, she bursts out laughing. "Oh my God. Now, it all makes sense!"

"What?" her dad asks, confusion laced in his tone.

"I couldn't figure out what made you get a tattoo after all these years of you saying you didn't want to mark your body permanently. But now, it all makes perfect sense."

"Taylor," Shane warns, but it only makes her grin wider.

"What?" I ask, clearly out of the loop. "What makes perfect sense?"

"It's like a scene from one of my romance books," she explains. "Guy saves girl, falls for her, and then gets a tattoo from her as an excuse to see her again."

It takes me a second to wrap my head around what she just said, but once I do, I can't help but laugh because she isn't wrong.

"I'm right, aren't I?" she says, her gaze flicking between her dad and me. "I should've put two and two together when he said the woman doing his tattoo said it needed to be meaningful. You're his tattoo artist." She glances at her dad. "You totally got a tattoo to impress her."

She smacks his arm playfully, and I snort out another laugh.

"Kinsley and I are just friends," he says with an eye roll.

"Oh no." Taylor's features turn serious. "Did she turn you down?"

She turns her attention on me. "Did you turn my dad down? He's a good guy. Doesn't sleep around or cheat. He's an amazing dad. He works hard. I mean, he's not a billionaire, but he owns his own home and can provide for his family, and since my mom is too busy traveling all over the world, he pretty much has zero other woman dram—"

Before she can finish, Shane reaches around and covers her mouth. "You'll have to excuse my daughter," he says. "She spends most of her free time reading romance and thinks every situation is straight out of a novel. We're not people. We're tropes."

I laugh again. "I get it," I tell her. "I actually love romance. But

I'm not looking to date. These days, I'm sticking to fictional men instead of the real thing."

I wink at Taylor playfully, and she laughs.

"Same," she agrees. "Romance books make it hard for real-life men to live up to the expectations book boyfriends set. I work at Books and Beans, so my life pretty much consists of romance books and caffeine."

"Oh, I love that bookstore! And their coffee is delicious."

"Right?" she agrees. "And I get a good discount on their books. I prefer to read on my Kindle, but you should see my library at our house. It's filled with so many trophies."

"Who's your favorite author?" I find myself asking.

What is it about these two that makes it so easy to talk to them?

Like father, like daughter, I guess.

Taylor wastes no time in telling me who her favorite authors are, and I find that despite our age difference, we love many of the same ones.

When she mentions having a special edition from one of my favorite authors, I can't help but blurt out, "I'd love to see it!" without thinking.

In my defense, it's extremely rare, and I really would love to see it.

I realize my mistake when Taylor responds by saying, "You should come over! We were just walking Becky." She points at the German shepherd I didn't notice until now. She's sitting pretty next to her owner and hasn't made a sound the entire time. "And then we're heading home to make dinner. Do you like ribs? Dad is a beast on the grill, and he's making them tonight."

"Oh, umm …" I glance at Shane, silently begging for help, but he only smiles softly, knowing I'm trapped and I'll be forced to spend time with him unless I want to turn down Taylor's invitation.

With a quick glare at him—which doesn't seem to faze him in

the slightest—I look back at Taylor, who's nibbling on the corner of her lip hopefully.

The word *no* is on the tip of my tongue, but at the last second, against my better judgment, I say, "Sure, I would love to have dinner with you and see your library."

Taylor squeals, Shane smiles, and my heart swells in my chest, once again reminding me that it's still there and working.

"Oh good, you're back." My mom envelops me in a hug. "I was starting to get worried."

"I'm okay," I assure her. "But I'm actually not staying."

My thoughts go back to Taylor and her dad. After agreeing to go over to their place for dinner, I remembered that the reason I was at the park was because I'd left the barbecue in a hurry. When I told them I would meet them at their place, Shane looked like he didn't believe a word I was saying, but Taylor, in all her innocence, shot off their address and said they'd see me soon.

I changed my mind a dozen times on the walk back to my aunt and uncle's house, but then I remembered I didn't have Taylor's or Shane's phone number, so bailing on them would be ghosting them, and I wasn't about to do that to that sweet girl.

"I ran into a friend," I say vaguely, "and she invited me over for dinner."

"Oh, that's good," Mom says, too happy that I'm actually willing to hang out with a friend to ask who it is. "Go have fun." She kisses my cheek. "I love you, Kins."

"I love you more."

After we separate, I find Melina so I can congratulate her on her engagement while avoiding Natalia so I don't have to tell her where

I'm going. My mom might give me some space, but there's no way I'll get past Natalia without her giving me the third degree. And the last thing I need is for her to know I'm going to Shane's house.

She'll make more out of it than it is, refusing to understand that I'm not going there to see Shane—he just so happens to be Taylor's dad. I'm going there to see Taylor and to check out her library and talk books. And Shane will just so happen to be there.

Now if only I can repeat that in my head enough times so that I'll believe it.

Ten

Shane

I F SOMEONE HAD TOLD ME THAT TAYLOR'S AND MY WEEKLY walk to the dog park would end with Kinsley in my house, chatting with my daughter about books while I cook dinner for the three of us, I would've laughed in their face and asked them what the hell they were smoking because there was no way Kinsley would go anywhere with me, let alone to my house.

Yet every time I walk from the back porch to the kitchen to grab something, I can hear Kinsley's and Taylor's laughter from the library that I built for Taylor.

Since it's only the two of us in a three-bedroom house with a living room and den and I don't need an office, I turned the den into a library as a surprise for her seventeenth birthday. The way she squealed and cried and hugged me, telling me I was the best dad ever, told me I'd picked the right gift for my book-obsessed daughter.

I set the plate of ribs on the table next to the grilled potatoes, veggies, and rolls, and then I head over to the library to let the girls know dinner's ready. But as I'm walking toward the back of the house where the library is, my phone pings with an email.

When I click on my mailbox, it's mostly spam, but my eye catches on an earlier email I must've missed from Exposed Ink. I click into it and read it twice, confused as to why my appointment has been canceled.

Since the only woman who can explain this is sitting in my house, I head straight back to ask her. I'm expecting to find her and my daughter, but only Kinsley is sitting in the middle of the room on the floor, looking through a paperback.

When she hears me enter, she looks up and smiles softly. "Taylor's in the bathroom. She has quite the collection." Her eyes track the shelves filled with hundreds of books. "I told her she'll have to come by my parents' place one day. My mom has a library that could rival this one."

"That would imply you're planning to see my daughter again," I say, stepping in front of Kinsley and then kneeling so I'm at her level.

"I …" She opens and closes her mouth. "If you don't want me to—"

"You're more than welcome to see Taylor anytime you want. I guess I'm just confused since you canceled our appointment."

I raise a brow, and she looks at me sheepishly.

"I'm sorry," she murmurs. "I know it was unprofessional, but …" Her cheeks turn a light shade of pink, and she sniffles. "I don't know what it is about you and your daughter, but you guys have this weird way of making me lower the wall I've worked so hard to build. I hadn't told anyone about my daughter, other than my family, who already knew, yet you confided in me about your daughter, and in turn, I was word-vomiting all over you."

I can't help but smile at her words, which makes her glare.

"I love how you're reveling in my misery," she mutters.

"I'm not reveling in anything," I say with a chuckle. "But you just admitted that even though you didn't want to let me in, you did, which means there just might be hope for you yet."

I'm only joking—sort of—but I know it's the wrong thing to say when Kinsley frowns.

"Shane." She sighs. "I canceled the appointment because, even though it's obvious that you're a good guy and you said you're okay with just being friends, you also made it clear you'd still like more from me, and the truth is, I don't have anything more to give you or anyone for that matter. I gave it all to my husband and unborn baby … and then they died."

A single tear slides down her cheek, and I reach out and swipe it away with my thumb, hating to see her cry.

"I'm so sorry," I say, palming the side of her face. "I hate that you went through something so devastating, and I won't even pretend to know how you must feel because I've never experienced any type of loss that comes close to what you went through."

"I did it," she whispers. "I was driving. I'm the reason they're dead."

Oh shit. Now, her comment about killing her daughter makes sense. And not only did her daughter die, but so did her husband.

"If I hadn't …" she chokes out, unable to finish her sentence.

Without thought, I drop to my knees and wrap my arms around her.

"It's okay," I tell her. "You don't have to say anything." I rub my hands up and down her back as she softly cries into my chest. "You went through something that no parent or spouse should ever have to go through, and the fact that you're still getting up every day and functioning proves how damn strong you are."

"I'm not—"

"What's going on?" Taylor says, cutting Kinsley off.

Reluctantly, I release Kinsley and stand. "Kinsley was just having a moment," I tell her. "Why don't we give her a second and you can help me get drinks? Dinner's ready."

Taylor glances at Kinsley with concern but says, "Okay, the bathroom is down the hall if you need to wash up."

"Thank you," Kinsley says, giving my daughter a watery smile. "I'll meet you guys out there."

"Is she okay?" Taylor whispers once we're in the kitchen.

"I don't want to tell her story, but she went through something horrific and is having a tough time getting through it."

Taylor nods in understanding, then tells me she'll be right back. When she returns, she has a stack of books in her arms.

"These are for you," she says when Kinsley walks out to join us. "They're my go-to reads when I need to forget about everything and escape."

Kinsley glances at me, then back at my daughter.

"Dad didn't tell me your business. He wouldn't do that, but he said you went through something horrible. I read these books last year when I caught my ex cheating on me because I wouldn't put out, and I swear they helped me forget all about his lying, cheating behind."

I already know what happened since my daughter and I talk about most things, but the amount of pride I feel from hearing her speak like that never gets old.

Kinsley cracks a smile and then hugs Taylor. "Thank you," she murmurs. "You have no idea how much that means to me."

"Of course! We're officially book friends, and that's what book friends do for each other." Taylor grins. "I'm going to grab a water. Do you want one?"

"That would be great," Kinsley tells her.

Once Taylor is gone, Kinsley says, "You have an amazing daughter."

"What can I say?" I smirk, hoping to lighten the mood. "She gets it from her dad."

"Welcome to—oh, it's you," Scott says with a laugh. "I wasn't aware you had an appointment today."

"He doesn't," Taylor says, practically bouncing into the shop. "My friend and I do."

"Oh, yeah?" Scott says. "Did you find something better than a unicorn to get tattooed?" he asks Casey, who rolls her eyes.

"They're getting piercings," Kinsley says, walking out and joining Scott at the front desk.

"Kinsley!" Taylor rushes over and hugs her. "Tell my dad that since I'm here, he should let me get my tongue pierced as well."

I shake my head, and Kinsley laughs. "How about we start with one piercing, and if it goes well, we can talk about doing another one?"

"Fine." Taylor sighs. "I'm going first," she says to Casey. "I can't watch it happen. I'll freak out. I need to just get it done."

After I sign the consent form, the girls head back with Kinsley. The room isn't big, and I figure they'll have more fun with it just being the girls.

While I'm waiting for them to get done, Lachlan appears from his room, his gaze locking on me. "Shane," he says, walking over and shaking my hand. "Good to see you back."

"I'm actually not here for me. My daughter and her friend are getting their noses pierced. My appointment is on Friday."

Lachlan smirks. "At this rate, you're going to end up inking your entire body in hopes of getting a single date with my daughter."

Scott laughs, and I shrug because what the hell do I say to that? He's not entirely wrong. I might be on board with getting the sleeve now, but it did start as a way to spend time with Kinsley.

"It'll be worth it," I tell him. "Besides, she's damn talented, so it's not exactly a hardship, having her ink me."

Lachlan nods. "I get it," he says, squeezing my shoulder. "I would've done anything for her mom to give me a chance. Hell, in the early stages, I pretty much did."

"And I'm assuming it worked out …"

"Yeah, it did," he says, smiling fondly. "We've been together for twenty-five years, we share three kids, and I couldn't imagine my life without her." He glances down the hall. "But if something happened to her, I don't even know how I'd move on."

Ah, so he's trying to feed me details without breaking Kinsley's trust.

"I know," I tell him. "And while I can't relate since I've never lost anyone, I get why she's so hesitant to put herself back out there."

"She told you?" Lachlan says, shock evident in his tone.

"I don't know all the details, but she told me the basics, and I hate that she blames herself. I barely know her, and even I know she would never purposely hurt anyone. Hell, the last place she wanted to go was to my house, but all it took was my daughter giving her, her signature puppy-dog eyes, and Kinsley caved."

"So, why do you keep coming back?" Lachlan asks. "If you know she doesn't want to be around you …"

"I wouldn't go that far," I say with a laugh. "I can see the attraction and curiosity when she looks at me. But she's been through something horrible. So, I took a step back and suggested we be friends."

"And what if she never gives you the chance to take her out on a date?" Lachlan asks. "Will you be okay with that?"

"At this point, I just want to get to know her," I tell him honestly. "The second I laid eyes on her, there was just something about her that pulled me in, and I wanted to know more about her. If all that comes out of it is a friendship, then I'm okay with that. But if she changes her mind and lets me take her out, I sure as hell won't say no."

Lachlan nods. "Well then, Shane, I wish you the best of luck." He pats me on the back. "May the odds be ever in your favor."

"What's your favorite food?"

Kinsley looks up at me through her lashes and raises a brow. She's been working on my tattoo for about a half hour, and every so often, I throw a question at her. The first few times, she answered without hesitation, but based on the look she's giving me, I'm assuming she's caught on to my sneaky way of getting to know her.

"Italian," she says, going back to inking me.

"I take it, you've been to Mario's?"

It's the only decent Italian restaurant in town, aside from the takeout pizza place.

"I have," she admits, her adorable nose scrunching up—an action I've learned she does when she's not keen on whatever is being said. "But it's got nothing on Antonio's in Hell's Kitchen."

"You're from the city?"

There's only one Hell's Kitchen that I know of, and it's in New York City.

"Yep. Born and raised. I didn't move here until …" She trails off and sighs, and I assume that's the end of the conversation, that she's once again slammed the proverbial gate closed to block me out, until she starts speaking again. "I moved here after Brandon and Brenna died."

She's never mentioned his name before, but I think it's safe to assume Brandon was her husband who died, along with their daughter.

"And then opened this tattoo shop?" I ask, shifting the conversation so she won't shut down. I've learned from our few conversations that if the topic isn't regarding her past, Kinsley is more likely to let me in.

"My dad did," she says. "He had enough of me moping around, and since there was no way that I was going back to work at Forbidden Ink …"

"That's where you used to work," I clarify, piecing her info together, "in the city?"

"Yeah, I practically grew up there. My uncles opened it and still own it. It's where my dad met my mom, and … it's where I met Brandon," she says with a sad smile. "He apprenticed with my dad and was eventually hired full-time."

"That's cool. You both were tattoo artists. Did you guys ever fight over who was the better artist?" I joke, trying to lighten the mood.

This makes Kinsley laugh, and the way her face lights up has me wanting to pull out every joke I know so she'll keep doing it. A sad Kinsley is tragically beautiful, but a happy Kinsley is downright breathtaking.

"No," she scoffs playfully. "It wasn't up for debate. I was the better artist."

I chuckle at her cockiness. "I can't even draw stick people. My daughter was a better drawer at four than I am as an adult," I say, pointing at the tattoo right above the one she's currently working on. "When we were forced to take art, I would have my friend do the assignments for me since he was artistically better than me."

Kinsley laughs again. "I've never heard of anyone cheating in art class. But the truth is, I couldn't really draw either when I was younger. I loved going to work with my dad, but I wasn't naturally good at drawing. My parents signed me up for art classes, and my love for it made me want to practice until I was great at it."

"I'd say it worked." I glance down at the tattoo she's currently doing. It's another image Taylor drew—of the fire station I've worked at since she was born with me in my fire suit and her standing next to the fire truck. She used to love riding in it when she was younger.

"You're extremely talented," I say, my gaze moving from my arm to her.

"Thank you," she mutters, a slight blush tingeing her cheeks.

"Taylor is creative," I tell her. "But she loves digital design. It's what she wants to go to school for."

"What grade is she in?"

"She's a junior. We're going to start looking at colleges soon, but she has her heart set on NYU."

"It's a good school," Kinsley says. "I went there."

"Really? What did you go for?"

She stops inking me and sits back, taking her gloves off to give me a small break, something she does every so often. So, I reach behind me and pull out my box of Sour Patch Kids. I pop one into my mouth and then offer her one.

She glances at the box the same way she does every time I offer her some, but this time, she reaches in and grabs one, and I take that as a win.

"Art and business. I wanted to learn all aspects of art, and I always wanted to open my own shop. I probably could've done both without going to school, but I wanted the best chance at being successful."

"Well, it looks like you did what you set out to do. This place is clearly a success."

"Yeah," she says with a soft smile, "it is."

She pops the red Sour Patch Kid into her mouth, and her lips pucker at the sourness.

"Ugh. I forgot how sour these are," she says, her face contorted in the cutest expression.

"Don't worry," I say with a laugh. "The sweetness that comes after is worth it."

Eleven

Kinsley

"WHAT THE HECK IS GOING ON?" I mutter.

I click out of the scheduling app and then back in, but it still doesn't work. Scott left early to go visit his parents for the weekend, so we're booking our own appointments until he gets back. Usually, I have no problem using the scheduling app, but for some reason, it's not working.

"I don't know what's going on with the app, so I can't schedule your appointment," I say to Shane, swiping out of the app. "And without getting into it, I can't see what I have available."

"That's okay," he says. "If you want, I can give you my number, and you can just text me …"

"Not happening." I shake my head. "Once it's working, I'll have Scott reach out to you."

Texting him—and in turn giving him my number—would be a bad idea. He's already finding ways to slip through the cracks of the wall I've put up. The last thing I need is to open the damn gate and let him walk right in.

Shane chuckles, but doesn't argue.

"How'd it go?" Dad asks when we get to the front desk so Shane can pay.

"Good," Shane says with a grin. "Kinsley is magic with a tattoo gun."

Dad chuckles as Shane pulls his card out from his wallet.

"Any plans tonight?" Shane asks me while my dad runs his card.

Before I can think of a lie, my dad throws me right under the bus. "This was your last appointment, Kins, so you can head out. I have a friend coming in to get some ink done, so I'll be here awhile, and I can close up."

I glare his way, but he either doesn't notice or pretends not to.

"In that case," Shane says, "want to go grab a drink?"

"I can't. I'm unavailable," I blurt out, flinching when I hear how stupid that sounded.

Shane laughs. "There's that word again," he says with a smirk. "Yet you're standing here, looking completely available."

My dad twists his mouth, obviously trying to hide his smile, but doesn't say a word.

"What about your daughter?" I ask, trying and failing to think of a reason to say no.

"She's working and then spending the night at Casey's." Shane steps toward me. "C'mon, Sour Patch," he murmurs, shooting me puppy-dog eyes that tell me exactly where his daughter gets them from. "Just one drink. It's Friday night, and neither of us has plans."

I know if I say no and really mean it, Shane won't argue. As insistent as he is about wanting to spend time with me and get to know me, he always respects my boundaries when I make it clear I don't want to go out with him—it just doesn't stop him from trying again next time—but for some reason, I find myself wanting to say yes tonight.

Maybe it's because I haven't been out since our girls' night at Neptune's or because I've spent the past three years isolating myself from everyone … or maybe it's because, despite Shane scaring the hell out of me with his charm and the way he seems to genuinely care, I enjoy talking to him.

"Okay." Shane's face lights up, but before he can get his hopes up, I add, "Just one drink, and it's not a date or anything like that. It's just two people who are kind of friends having a drink together."

His lips curl into a beautiful, boyish grin. "I'll take it."

"Have fun," Dad says with a knowing smile that I want to wipe off his face.

When we get outside, I follow Shane to his truck but then remember …

"If we're drinking, you can't drive."

I know it's stupid since I wasn't drinking the night I wrapped the vehicle around the pole, but Brandon's drinking led to him not being able to drive, which set off the horrible domino effect, and I never want to be in the position where I have to drive for someone who's been drinking again. Hell, I never want to drive again. So, if we're drinking, no one is driving.

Shane looks at me, confused for a moment, and then nods. "Okay, then let's walk."

He extends his hand for me to take, and without giving it thought, I do, letting him guide me onto the sidewalk.

"Do you work on the weekends?" Shane asks as we walk toward Main Street, where most of the restaurants and bars are located.

"We're open a half day on Saturdays and off Sundays and Mondays. What about you?" I ask, realizing that while he tends to hold most of the conversation, it's usually geared toward me.

"I work two shifts per week on different days. My next shift is on Monday."

"That's cool. So, you only have to work two days a week?"

"Yeah." He chuckles. "But I'm there for twenty-four hours, from eight to eight, for each shift."

"Have you been a firefighter paramedic for long?"

"My entire adult life," he says, glancing at me. "I found out Taylor's mom was pregnant a few months after I graduated from high school. I had already enrolled in college to become an EMT. Thankfully, my parents are amazing and helped out once she was born."

"She mentioned her mom the other day," I say carefully, knowing how hard it is to talk about heavy shit. "It sounded like she's not around much."

"She's not," he says with a sigh. "When Jamie found out she was pregnant, she wanted to have an abortion."

His words cause my body to stiffen and my steps to falter, and it's then I realize we're still holding hands. Glancing down at our threaded fingers, I can't help but notice how much bigger his are compared to mine. They're also rougher and stronger—probably because they're hands that are used to protect and save people—and I find myself being comforted by our hand-holding rather than being freaked out, like I'd expect to be.

"I'm sorry," he says quickly. "I didn't mean to …"

"No, it's okay. Sure, it's hard to think about women not wanting their baby when I wasn't given a choice when I lost mine, but I believe in women's rights and wouldn't judge anyone for making the choice they feel is best for them."

Shane nods in understanding, then continues, "We were young and not careful, and when she told me she was pregnant, I told her I'd go along with whatever she wanted. But then we went to her doctor's appointment and heard her heartbeat, and she had a moment of weakness, saying she wanted to keep the baby."

"Why do I sense a but?"

"Because isn't there always one?" he says with a humorless chuckle. "Everything was fine until a few months after Taylor was born. Jamie was offered an internship with a huge magazine overseas. She said it was too big of an opportunity to give up, that it would secure her entire future as a journalist, so she took it."

Shane stops in front of The Black Cat and releases his hold on my hand, and the coldness I feel at the loss of his touch doesn't go unnoticed.

"She said it would only be for one semester, like a study-abroad type of thing. So, I moved in with my parents so they could help me, and I prepared myself to be a single dad for a few months. Only she never came home."

"What?" I gasp. "But Taylor seems to know her."

"She does, as much as a child can know a parent who's been traveling their entire life. They text and FaceTime, and Jamie occasionally passes through town to visit. Less often since her parents passed away, so she doesn't have any ties to this town, aside from Taylor."

Aside from Taylor? That should be reason enough to never leave.

Shane sighs. "It's one of the reasons I haven't really dated since Taylor was born. I was so worried that I wouldn't be enough, that she would resent not having a mom around, that I tried to be twice the parent—for her mom and me."

Oh, this man. As if he couldn't get any more perfect.

"I've only been around you guys a couple of times, but even I can see that your daughter thinks you hung the moon. If you're worried about your relationship, don't be. It's evident you've done a damn good job making sure she's had a good life."

"Thanks," Shane says, hitting me with a warm smile as he opens the door so we can go inside.

It's busy since it's Friday night, but we're able to find a two-person high-top table near the bar. We've only just sat down when an older woman comes over and says hello, referring to Shane by his last name.

"This is Trudy," Shane says. "Her husband, Billy, works at the station with me on the same shift, and Trudy here owns this place."

"It's nice to meet you," I tell her. "I'm embarrassed to admit that I've never been in here."

Since it's a bar, there's no reason why I would've gone before I turned twenty-one, and when I moved here, I wasn't in any shape to try out different bars. I was too busy mourning from inside my room. And now, if I'm not at Exposed Ink, I'm either with my family or in the pool house.

Jeez, when I put it like that, maybe my therapist and Natalia— hell, my entire family—aren't far off when they gripe at me about not getting out and living my life.

"Well," Trudy says, "we have ourselves a Black Cat virgin." She smirks and glances toward the bartender. "Get this girl a Black Cat, stat." The bartender nods, and then Trudy looks back at me. "It's our house drink," she explains, "and it'll be the reason you keep coming back."

"Just make sure it doesn't contain any fruit," Shane says before I can. Then, he glances at me. "Anything else you're allergic to?"

"Carrots," I tell them both. "Raw fruit and carrots."

"Well, that's a damn shame," Trudy says. "So many good drinks are made with fruit. But you're good because the Black Cat doesn't contain any fruit." She looks at Shane. "Your usual?"

"Yes, please," he tells her.

"Oscar," she yells to the bartender, "one Berliner Weisse for this one." She nods toward Shane, and Oscar nods.

"Here's the menu," Trudy says. "I'll be back with your drinks and to take your food order. I recommend the sampler. It's a little bit of everything delicious." And with a wink, she saunters off to the next table.

"She's …"

"A lot," Shane says with a laugh. "But she and Billy are family."

"Oh, you're related?"

Shane shakes his head. "When you work twenty-four-hour shifts with the same people in the same station for years, they become like family. We've been through it all together. The ups and downs. I was there when they got into their first fight, when he proposed, when they got married, and when Trudy had the crazy idea to open this place. They've been to most of Taylor's birthday parties and watched her grow up. There are five guys on a shift, and aside from one guy who left last year to move to the city, we've all been working together for fifteen years."

"That's awesome." And completely relatable. "While I have my aunts and uncles, my parents have a few other friends that I grew up considering family. I didn't even know we weren't related until I got older."

Shane grins. "That's exactly how it is with us at the station. Even though I'm a single dad, between my parents and the guys I work with and their families, I've never felt like I was raising Taylor alone."

"That's how I imagined it would be when I got pregnant," I admit. "I mean, I had Brandon, but from the moment I found out I was pregnant, my little girl was loved by so many people."

Shane smiles sadly, and I expect him to ask what happened—sure, he knows the basics, but I didn't go into specifics—but he doesn't. I've noticed that while he asks questions, they're never too deep, and he always lets me tell him how much—or little—I want. He might guide the conversation, but he lets me control it.

"I can believe that," Shane says. "I've only met your cousins and dad, but it's clear you're loved."

I can't help but smile at that. "I am."

We go over the menu, and when Trudy returns with our drinks, we order the sampler, as she suggested. Once she leaves, I take a sip of my drink, and the perfect mix of sweet and bitter hits my senses.

"What do you think?" Shane asks, taking a sip of his beer.

"It's really good," I say, taking another sip.

"Trudy is obsessed with making new drinks. At every party and several nights a week here, she's testing out new drinks and forcing everyone to try them."

"I love cooking and baking, but making drinks isn't my area of expertise," I admit with a laugh that has Shane grinning. "I swear, no matter what I do, they're never as good as the ones at the coffee shop."

"You should ask Taylor to show you," he says. "She's been working at the coffee shop for several months now, and she makes all types of frappe mocha latte shit."

I throw my head back with a laugh at his words, and it hits me how long it's been since I've enjoyed myself with anyone, let alone a man.

Fuck … a man.

Who isn't Brandon.

My husband.

No, not my husband. My late husband.

Because he's gone.

And I'm here.

Just as the guilt starts to seep through the cracks that Shane has created, my favorite song comes on. Memories of dancing to it with my mom in our living room while we sang at the top of our lungs hit me, and before I know what I'm doing, I'm standing and extending my hand to Shane.

"I love this song! Dance with me?" I ask, wanting to push the guilt away and just be in the moment with him.

Without argument, Shane gets off the stool, takes my hand, and guides me onto the dance floor.

It's a fast-paced pop song, and as we dance to the beat, both of us lip-sync the lyrics, making us crack up in laughter and reminding me how good it feels to let loose and have fun.

But then the song morphs into a slower, more sensual tune, and for a second, I'm unsure of what to do.

Then, Shane twirls me around, until my back is flush against his front. The hand that's linked to mine rests on the curve of my hip, and his other hand slides around to my front, causing butter-flies to swarm my belly.

With his body wrapped around mine, I catch a whiff of his mas-culine scent, the spicy essence sliding through me like a shot of whis-key, filling me with warmth I haven't felt in too long. Not since …

I swallow thickly and close my eyes, pretending for a moment that Shane is Brandon. I know it's wrong on so many levels, but I miss this. Being held by a man, feeling safe and wanted and cher-ished. And if I let myself admit that this is Shane and not Brandon, the guilt is going to take over, and I'm going to be forced to push him away.

And I don't want to push him away. For just a little while, I want to stay like this, in Shane's arms, enveloped by his scent and comforted by his touch.

My head, of its own accord, tilts back against his muscular chest, and his chin rests on my shoulder as we sway to the music. And even though I want to pretend it's Brandon, I can't because Shane is taller, more rugged. His body fits around mine differently. When I glance down, his hands are ink-free. His skin is smooth, tanned. His scent is intoxicating and addictive in a different way than Brandon's was.

The song morphs into another and then another, and it isn't until my stomach rumbles that I realize we've been dancing just like this for a while, and I've been enjoying it.

When I twist around to face him, with our bodies so close, our mouths are only inches apart. His brown eyes, filled with desire, meet mine, and I wonder what he sees in mine.

Fear?

Guilt?

Sadness?

Then, Shane's gaze slides down to my mouth, and for a split second, I wish for him to kiss me so I can feel his lips on mine because above any emotion I'm feeling, lust is the strongest.

Without thinking about anything other than right now, I reach up and press my lips to his. They're hard yet soft, and I can smell the beer he was drinking on his breath.

At first, he doesn't make any move to kiss me back, and I'm about to retreat, cursing myself for getting lost in the moment, for letting myself feel, when Shane's arm snakes around my waist and he pulls me into him so our bodies are flush against one another.

His lips curve around mine, and the hand not holding me comes up and cups the side of my face. We stay like this for several seconds—our bodies and lips connected—and then I sigh into his mouth, silently pleading for more.

Shane takes that as his cue to deepen the kiss, and his tongue slides past my parted lips and into my mouth. As our tongues move frantically against one another, I find myself trying to get closer to him, craving more of him. It's like the dam that was holding back my need for stimulation has burst, and I'm craving to be touched, to be kissed.

As if Shane can hear my inner thoughts, he effortlessly reaches around and lifts me off my feet. Instinctually, my legs wrap around his torso, and my fingers delve into his soft hair.

With his mouth never leaving mine, he walks us over to a darkened area and gently pushes me against the wall. Our kiss heats up, both of our mouths ravenous for the other.

But then his arousal pushes against my center, and I gasp into his mouth as what we're doing hits me.

"Stop," I breathe out, reaching between us and shoving my hand against Shane's chest.

His eyes snap open, and he immediately releases me, setting me on my feet and taking a step back.

"I'm sorry," I choke out. "I didn't mean to …"

"Hey," he says, reaching out to touch me. "It's—"

I flinch, moving back slightly, and his brows furrow in confusion.

"I shouldn't have done that," I whisper, bringing my fingers to my swollen lips.

Shane's features morph into understanding, mixed with sadness, and I hate myself for leading him on.

"I meant it when I said I couldn't give you anything more," I murmur. "I shouldn't have kissed you and—"

"It's okay," he says softly. "I know. We just got caught up in the moment."

"I need to go," I tell him, only my words are muffled by the embarrassing sound of my stomach growling.

"Stay and eat. The food should be at our table by now."

I stare at him, at his pleading eyes, his lips, puffy from our kiss, and I war with myself. I want to stay, but I also want to go because as much as I enjoy Shane's company, he scares the hell out of me. He has me talking and laughing and feeling things I never thought I'd feel again.

"Don't run, please," he adds, as if he can hear my thoughts. "I promise I won't do that again."

"You didn't do anything," I point out. "I did this. I asked you to dance. I kissed you. I got lost in the moment."

"Yeah, and it was a damn good moment," he says with a soft smile that causes those pesky butterflies to reappear, this time in my chest. "But it's okay if that's all it was … a moment," he adds. "Come back to the table with me and eat. We can pretend it never happened."

I want to tell him that I don't want to pretend it never happened. If anything, I want to do it again and again. Now that I've been reminded of what it's like to feel, I don't want to stop. But that can't happen. Because as I look into Shane's compassionate, patient eyes, I know he deserves better than anything I'm capable of giving him.

I'm broken. Damaged. I had my chance at a family, but I ruined it, and the last thing Shane needs is to be weighed down by my guilt.

"Okay," I choke out. "Let's go eat."

And pretend it never happened.

Twelve

Kinsley

"**M**OM, YOU'RE HOME!" I RUSH INTO MY MOM'S ARMS, having missed her like crazy even though it's only been a few days since she left and we've talked every day that she's been gone. "How was your trip?"

"Busy," she says. "It's good to be back home in our quiet little town." She laughs. "I actually got in last night, but when I came by to see you, you weren't home."

She raises a curious brow, and my thoughts go back to last night. The rest of the evening with Shane was spent with delicious food and drinks, conversation, and laughter. I thought it would be awkward, but true to his word, he pretended like the kiss never happened.

I wish I could say the same thing, but the truth is, when I got home, I couldn't stop thinking about it. And those thoughts turned into fantasies, and before I knew it, I was pleasuring myself to the thoughts of Shane doing more than kissing me.

"I went out for a drink and food with a friend," I say vaguely.

When she smirks, I roll my eyes, remembering my dad was there last night and he tells my mom everything.

"He's just a *friend*," I insist, making it a point to emphasize the word *friend*—for her sake and mine.

"Uh-huh," she says. "I was thinking we could go get coffee and pedicures. Make it a mother-daughter afternoon. What do you say?"

"I say that sounds perfect. Let me change, and then we can go."

Since I had a couple of appointments this morning, I'm wearing my Exposed Ink shirt, so I change out of it, leaving my jeans on, and throw on a soft beige sweater since it's cool out.

When I step out of my room, I find my mom looking through the stack of books from Taylor.

"You're reading again?" she asks, hopefulness laced in her words.

"Yeah."

After devouring the firefighter romance Julia lent me and returning it to her at our last session, I couldn't stop and ended up reading all the books Taylor lent me.

Speaking of which …

"We should go have coffee at Books and Beans. Taylor, Shane's daughter, lent me these books, and she works there. If she's there, I'd like to return them to her."

It will mean not having to see Shane outside of the tattoo shop, and I enjoy her company. Win-win.

"Sounds good."

When we walk into Books and Beans, I immediately spot Taylor, standing behind the counter, talking with someone. She looks up at the sound of the doorbell chiming, and a smile spreads across her face.

"Kinsley!" She rushes around the counter and envelops me in a hug. "I was just asking my dad this morning when we were going to see you again. I saw the addition to his sleeve you did, and it looks so good."

"Thanks. I'm glad I can ink your work onto him so he can have them as memories."

"Are you here for coffee or books or both?" she asks.

My mom laughs at her upbeat personality, and Taylor turns her attention to her.

"You must be Kinsley's mom. You have the same smile."

Mom's grin widens. "I am. I'm Quinn."

She extends her hand, but Taylor ignores it, wrapping her arms around her. "It's so nice to meet you. Kinsley told me you love reading. I can't wait to see your library one day!"

"You're welcome over anytime," Mom tells her.

"Here are your books," I say, handing Taylor the tote bag of books.

Taylor eyes the bag and frowns. "Did you not want to read them? I don't mind how long you borrow them for."

"Quite the opposite," I admit with a laugh. "I devoured them all."

Taylor's eyes widen. "Dang, you are a hard-core reader. I like it." Then, her eyes light up. "Oh! I have a BookTok account. You should go live with me so we can discuss the books. It would be so much fun, and I can totally name-drop your shop." She winks dramatically, making my mom laugh. "Not to brag, but I have, like, fifty million followers."

"What?" I gasp because I'm pretty sure I have, like, twenty— and not with the word *million* following it. Like, literally just twenty. And half of them are probably my family.

"My dad helped me make it a couple of years ago because I wanted to post about the books I'd read and loved, and it totally blew up. He used to monitor it, but now that I'm seventeen, he trusts me to handle it. He won't let me touch any of the money it brings in, but it's going into my savings account."

She waggles her brows, and my mom and I laugh. The girl has such a big personality.

"So, what do you say? Want to go live with me to talk books?"

"I'd love to," I tell her.

"Cool!" She beams. "So, books or coffee or both?"

"Both," Mom and I say in unison.

After ordering our lattes and pastries, we sit on one of the comfy couches.

"She's fun," Mom says, nodding toward Taylor, who's helping another customer. "I'm glad you're getting out again … even if it's just simply making friends."

"They haven't really given me much of a choice," I grumble, taking a sip of my coffee. "Shane keeps showing up, and his daughter makes it hard to say no to her."

Mom chuckles. "Oh, if you didn't want them around, you'd make it clear."

She quirks a brow, daring me to argue, and I roll my eyes.

"So, what are you reading?" I ask, hoping she'll drop the subject of Shane.

"A curvy single mom romance," she says with a grin. "She meets a sexy younger tattoo artist, and he won't stop until she agrees to go on a date with him."

"Sounds a lot like yours and dad's love story."

"Right?" she agrees and then proceeds to tell me all about the book, leaving the topic of Shane behind.

"Ugh, I'm exhausted," Taylor says a little while later as she dramatically plops onto the couch next to us. "This whole working life isn't for me." She brings her hand to her forehead and sighs, making Mom and me laugh.

"You'll get used to it," I say, patting her knee. "Are you on break?"

"Nope." Her green eyes pop open. "I'm off. Came in at six a.m. for the early shift."

"We're going to get pedicures," I find myself saying. "Want to join us?"

Taylor's eyes light up. "Yes! I'm totally in need of a good pedi. We're going to be heading to Florida for cheer camp soon, which will mean plenty of pool and beach time. Gotta make sure my toes look cute."

Mom snorts out a laugh while I shake my head.

"Okay, let's go."

Since the nail salon is in walking distance, we leave Taylor's and Mom's cars in the parking lot and head over.

The salon isn't super busy, so they're able to sit us next to each other, and the entire time, Taylor chats away about everything and anything. I learn she was in a relationship for a while, but the guy cheated on her with her now ex-friend. Casey is talking to a guy on the football team, and since Taylor is single, she feels left out, but she's trying to be supportive since Casey was always supportive of her relationship with her ex.

She's heavily involved in cheer, and she has a competition coming up. She gets good grades and plans to go to NYU for graphic design. A lot of this I already know from Shane, but I enjoy listening and getting to know her, so I don't mention that, simply letting her talk.

"Kinsley went to NYU," my mom says with a proud smile. "Maybe she can take you on a private tour. Show you behind the scenes."

Taylor gasps. "Oh my God, that would be awesome!"

Taylor's phone goes off, but when she checks it, her smile morphs into a frown.

"Everything okay?" I ask.

"Yeah, I was supposed to have dinner with Casey, but she bailed on me to hang out with the guy she's talking to." She rolls her eyes like it doesn't bother her, but I can tell it does.

"Why don't we go to dinner?" I offer. "I don't have any plans, and I've been wanting to check out that new hibachi restaurant that opened, but it seems weird to go alone. Do you like hibachi?"

"Oh, yes!" Taylor squeals, clapping her hands. "I've been wanting to go to that place."

"Mom?" I ask, turning toward my mom.

"Oh, no, you girls go and have a good time. I have a date tonight with my husband."

She waggles her brows, and Taylor giggles while I mock gag.

Twenty-five years later, and I'm still not used to the amount of PDA I've had to witness between my parents over the years. I can't even tell you how many times my siblings and I have walked in on them or heard them when they thought no one was home.

On the other hand, I love that my parents love each other so fiercely. It's what I wanted for myself, and the thought that I'll never have it again makes me sad. Yet I can't bring myself to move on because the fact is, I already had it, and I destroyed it.

The rest of our pedicure is spent talking about various books we've read and loved and the hundreds we have on our TBR list. Once our feet are clean and pretty, we walk back to the cars, and Mom takes off.

Since Taylor drove, I hop into her Jeep with her, and she puts the top down, swearing it's the only way to ride in a Jeep. I love her free spirit, and as she drives us down Main Street, I can't help but feel like maybe Shane and Taylor were meant to come into my life.

Before them, I was barely living, but since I met them, I've gone out, dancing and drinking, started reading romance again, and I'm currently singing pop songs at the top of my lungs with Taylor as we cruise through town.

But when Taylor pulls into a parking spot in front of the restaurant, my eyes lock with Shane's, who's leaning against the side of the building, and my stomach drops. Because as much as I enjoy their company, hanging out with him is also hard, especially knowing how attracted I am to him while trying like hell not to act on it. Because when I do, the guilt eats me up inside—something I spoke about with Julia during our last session.

I whip my head around to look at Taylor and she at least has the decency to look a little sheepish when she says, "He texted, asking what I was doing for dinner, so I figured he could meet us. You guys are friends, right?"

She bats her lashes at me, telling me she knows exactly what she's done, and I groan.

"Taylor, if you knew I'd be okay with him going, you would've mentioned it, but you didn't, which tells me you thought there was a small chance I wouldn't be."

Taylor sighs. "You're right. It's just that my dad really likes you. He talks about you all the time, and I don't know why, but you don't want to give him a chance, so I thought maybe if I gave you a shove in the right direction, you'd see how awesome he is." She shrugs. "I'm sorry. I shouldn't have done that, and if you want to cancel, I'll tell him it's all my fault. He honestly thought you were on board."

"I'm not going to cancel, but in the future, I need you to be honest. I consider you a friend, and friends don't go behind each other's back."

Taylor nods in understanding. "Can I ask why you don't like my dad?"

Oh boy … I wasn't prepared to have this conversation with Shane's daughter—and not while he's standing fifteen feet away and we're sitting in her Jeep.

"It's not your dad," I tell her honestly. "Three years ago, I was married and pregnant, and I lost my husband and baby girl in a car crash that I'd caused while I was driving."

Taylor gasps, her hands going to her mouth. "Kinsley, I'm so sorry."

"It's okay," I choke out, blinking back the tears that are filling my eyelids. "You couldn't have known. Your dad seems like a wonderful man, but I'm just not in a place to love someone the way they deserve."

"But what about you?" she asks. "Don't you deserve to be loved? Finding love after loss is a popular trope for a reason. Because everyone deserves to find love. What if my dad is the man you're meant to fall in love with? He's such a good guy.

"He takes care of me and loves me enough for my mom and him since she hates staying in one place for too long, and I know he would love you so much if you let him."

Her words cause the threatening tears to fall.

"I'm sure he could," I say, forcing a watery smile on my lips. "But he deserves better than a heartbroken woman who can't love him the way he deserves to be loved."

"Everything okay?" Shane asks, making me jump.

I was so focused on Taylor that I forgot he was here.

"Yeah." I clear my throat. "Everything's good."

Shane doesn't look convinced, but he nods.

"I didn't tell Kinsley you were meeting us for dinner," Taylor admits, throwing herself under the bus.

While I'm not thrilled about what she did, I can respect her taking responsibility. It also speaks volumes of their relationship that she knows she can tell her dad anything.

Shane sighs. "I'm sorry. I don't have your number, so I didn't even think to ask if you knew and were okay with it."

"It's all good," I say, hopping out of the Jeep. "Taylor and I spoke. Now, let's go eat."

When I look back and see Shane hasn't moved, I grab his hand and pull him along. "Come on, you two! A hungry Kinsley is a cranky Kinsley."

Thirteen

Kinsley

"DID YOU SEE THE FINAL MOVIE JUST RELEASED?" TAYLOR asks as she takes a sip of her drink while we wait for the waitress to run Shane's credit card since he insisted on paying for dinner.

I wasn't sure how dinner would go, but every time I'm around these two, they have a way of making me feel comfortable, like I've known them for years rather than weeks.

"Yeah, my mom hated the series." I roll my eyes. "But I loved it, so I'm planning to binge them all."

"I've already seen the first two, but I would totally be down for watching them all again. We should watch them tonight," Taylor suggests. "Casey won't watch them either, which is fine since she's never read the books and she won't appreciate the movies properly."

"I think Kinsley has given you enough of her time," Shane cuts in, using a tone I haven't heard him use with Taylor before. It's deep and serious, and, holy shit, it's kind of hot.

"Okay, sorry," she says without argument, looking completely deflated.

"Actually, I'd love to watch the movies tonight," I say to Taylor, then glance at Shane, who's looking at me in shock. "If it's okay with you."

"You don't have to do that," he murmurs. "I love my daughter, but I know how difficult it can be to say no to her."

"I know, but I want to. But if you're not up for company, I could have her come to my place."

"Of course you're welcome to come over," he scoffs. "I just don't want you to feel obligated."

"Well, I don't. I happen to like hanging out with Taylor."

The waitress drops off the receipt and Shane quickly fills it out, then pockets his card.

"Just Taylor?" he asks, as we stand to leave.

"Your dog is cool."

Shane shakes his head, and his eyes light up with mirth.

"Plus, now, you're going to be stuck watching them with us." I playfully stick my tongue out at him and take off toward the restaurant's exit.

I've barely made it out the door when Shane grabs my hand and tugs me toward him, so my back is flush against his front. In this position, I can smell his masculine scent and feel his hard body against mine, both of which do crazy things to my lady parts.

"Watching a movie with you, on my couch, in my home, is the opposite of *stuck*," Shane murmurs into my ear, sending a shiver through my body.

It doesn't matter how much I try to resist the feelings I'm developing for Shane. They're there and increasing with every look and touch and minute we spend together. The chemistry between us is sizzling, and if I'm not careful, that heat is going to become a fire and burn him. And the last thing I want is for another person to be hurt from caring about me.

The thought of Shane getting hurt—or worse, dying—because of me has me opening my mouth to tell them I can't go over to their house to watch the movies after all.

But before I can think of a believable lie to use, Taylor says, "Dad, can we go by the store and get snacks? We can't have a movie night without all the goods."

And the words evaporate on my tongue because there's no way I'm witnessing her disappointment by bailing on her.

"The goods?" I ask, stepping away from Shane so our bodies are no longer touching.

"Yeah," Taylor says. "Popcorn, soda, Sour Patch Kids, which are Dad's favorite …"

I can't help the blush that creeps up when she says Sour Patch, and even though she doesn't notice, too busy naming all the junk food she plans to get, Shane notices and grins that sexy, boyish grin that's going to be the death of me.

"Stop it," I mutter.

"What?" He shrugs.

"What?" Taylor asks, confused.

"Kinsley doesn't understand or *appreciate* my fixation with Sour Patch Kids," Shane explains, his eyes never leaving mine.

He might not be touching me anymore, but with the way he looks at me, it feels like he's reaching inside of me and caressing my soul.

"But like I told her," he says to Taylor, his eyes still locked on mine, "there's just something about getting through the sour to get to the sweet that makes it worth it."

"I would rather just buy something sweet instead of dealing

with the sour," I volley, even though I already know nothing I say will sway Shane from the way he feels.

The man is nothing if not determined.

"I was always told hard work makes you appreciate what you have that much more." He smirks. "Besides, who said I didn't like the sour?" He raises a brow. "I enjoy *every … single … part* of my Sour Patch."

And just like that, I'm left speechless … and turned on.

Fuck.

"Okay, we've got the popcorn and drinks and candy." Taylor points to each item, checking it off her list. "I think we're good to go."

She drops onto the couch and pats the seat next to her. "Come on, Kinsley. Sit next to me."

Without thought, I sit next to her on the middle cushion, but the second I do, I realize what she's done because the only spot left is the one next to me—unless Shane were to sit on the love seat, but that doesn't have a good view of the TV, which means …

Shane steps into the room, takes in the situation, chuckles, knowing exactly what his daughter has done, and then sits next to me, so damn close that his scent envelops me while his thigh rubs up against my own.

"Oh! I forgot the chips and salsa!" Taylor exclaims, jumping up from her seat and making a beeline for the kitchen.

"Sorry about her," Shane says, not at all sounding sorry. "She's clearly read too many romance books."

"I get it," I tell him. "Before my husband died, I believed in happily ever afters. She wants her dad to find love. She's just picked the wrong person for her dad."

"Or the right one," he argues, tilting his head slightly to the side so his eyes meet mine.

This close, I can make out the flecks of gold in his brown eyes and the stubble on his face and the cut jawline that slightly takes away from the baby face he has. Everything about this man is beautiful, and if things were different, I have no doubt I could let myself fall for him.

"Okay, here we go," Taylor says, rushing back in.

She sets the tray of food on the coffee table, turns off the lights, and sits back down, clicking play on the movie. Since it's a romance—and a spicy one at that—it doesn't take long before the couple is getting hot and heavy. Taylor is enraptured by the movie, but I can't help glancing at Shane, who I've caught looking my way several times.

The couple is at a club, dancing just like Shane and I were, and as the guy's mouth connects with the woman's, my mind goes to the night I kissed Shane at The Black Cat. The way his mouth devoured mine while his hands roamed my body.

Things between the couple heat up as the guy pushes her against the wall and then lifts her into his arms, similar to the way Shane picked me up like I weighed nothing and brought us to the darkened corner and then deepened the kiss.

The guy on the screen finds an empty room and drops her onto the desk, and without my consent, my thoughts go to Shane and me at the bar.

Me not stopping the kiss.

Him carrying me to the back office.

The two of us ripping each other's clothes off.

Our mouths consuming one another.

Him spreading my legs and filling me.

My lady parts tingle, and I clench my thighs in an attempt to tamp down how turned on I am. But it's too late. The fantasy feels too real, and when I shift slightly, I can feel the wetness between my legs.

"I need to use the bathroom," I say, quickly jumping up without waiting for Taylor to pause the movie.

I take my time going pee and washing my hands, willing my body to calm the fuck down. But of course, when I step into the hallway, I find Shane leaning against the wall with a knowing smirk on his face.

"What?" I snap, my body filled with pent-up sexual tension and no way to release it.

"I saw the way your legs were clenching," he says, stepping into my space. "The way your eyes went glossy at the couple on-screen."

"It was an intimate scene." I shrug, trying and failing to appear unfazed. "It would turn anyone on."

"Maybe," he says, "but when I was watching it, I couldn't help but think about that night at The Black Cat."

"It was a mistake."

"You really feel that way?" he asks, lifting my chin when I drop my gaze. "Because it was the best kiss of my life, and I refuse to believe that anything that good could be considered a mistake."

My eyes snap up to his, and I open my mouth, wanting to argue. But I can't because he's not wrong. The kiss was damn good. And as much as I want to regret it, I can't find it in me to do so. So, instead, I say the only thing I can think of that's not a lie.

"It can't happen again."

Without waiting for him to argue, I skirt around him and quickly go back to the living room. Shane sits next to me, and Taylor presses play. And even though I should be focusing on the movie, I can't get the visual of Shane and me having sex on the desk out of my head.

When the first movie ends, Taylor starts the second one.

It's getting late, but I tell myself that I can make it through this one and then tell her we'll need to watch the last one another day.

As if Shane can sense me slowly losing the battle, he grabs the blanket from behind the couch and drapes it across our laps. With the warmth of the blanket, the fight to stay awake gets harder, and before I know what's happening, my eyes are closing, and my head is landing on something firm yet soft. And even though I should question it, the masculine, comforting scent lulls me to sleep.

Warm.

Masculine.

Comforting.

I nuzzle my face further into the scent, wanting to keep this feeling wrapped around me. And then it hits me—Brandon is dead, which means …

My eyes pop open, and I'm met with a hard chest that's thankfully covered with a shirt.

Oh shit. I fell asleep and somehow ended up spending the night with Shane on his couch. Without moving, I take in my surroundings. Shane is passed out, and his head is at a weird angle that looks like it might hurt. His arm is wrapped around me, and my face is pressed against his chest. We're in the same positions we were in last night while watching the movie, only closer.

I glance around and find a clock hanging on the wall—ten in the morning. Holy shit, I can't remember the last time I slept in this late and without waking up once in the middle of the night.

Usually, I suffer from nightmares, my mind replaying what happened the night I killed Brandon and Brenna, and I'll wake up several times throughout the night, or my brain will kick into overdrive, and

I'll wake up far too early, starting my day before the sun comes up. But last night, I not only slept all night, but I also had zero nightmares and slept in.

And of course, it happened while I was sleeping in Shane's arms.

"I know you're awake," Shane's raspy voice says, making me tense up. "But feel free to continue to pretend you're asleep. I happen to like you snuggled up against me like this. Hell, if you want, I can carry you to my room, and we can continue to sleep …"

"No, you can't," Taylor says, making me jump out of Shane's arms. "We have to get ready to leave soon."

I sit up and glare at Shane, and he chuckles.

"What?" he asks, sounding all innocent, like he didn't just worm his way into my … okay, not bed. Couch? Cushion? Whatever it was, he wormed his way into it last night.

Okay, maybe he didn't so much as worm since I fell asleep first, but …

"You know what?" I hiss. "You should've woken me up."

"Why?" He shrugs, then sits up and stretches, and his shirt rises, exposing the smatter of hair that makes up his happy trail.

Jesus, why does this man have to be so damn good-looking?

"Maybe because it's highly inappropriate for me to be spending the night with your daughter here."

"His daughter doesn't care," Taylor says with a laugh, reminding me she can hear every word I'm saying. "I'm seventeen, and I know how the birds and the bees work. Besides, you two falling asleep during a movie and sleeping on the couch with your clothes on is hardly bad parenting."

"See, Sour Patch?" Shane grins. "All good."

I sigh and roll my eyes, and he grins wider.

"What?" I glare.

"Nothing." He shakes his head. "You just look cute in the

morning with your hair all over the place and a red mark from where your face was smooshed against my chest."

He runs the back of his finger along my cheekbone, and a shiver racks my body.

"I need to go," I grumble, scampering off the couch and away from him.

"Oh, don't go," Taylor says. "I'm actually about to make breakfast." She lifts the mixing bowl up for me to see. "Dad, come help."

"On it," Shane says, getting up and walking past me.

Since I know where their bathroom is and I suddenly have to go, I excuse myself. After going pee, I wash my hands and then attempt to clean up my face and fix my hair into a messy bun. Since I can't do anything about my morning breath, I call it good and tell myself after we eat breakfast, I'll make an excuse to leave before Taylor can convince me to stay.

But then I walk out to the kitchen, and Taylor stops what she's doing to look at me.

"Guess who we're going to see today," she says in a singsong voice.

Before I can even attempt to guess, she reaches across the counter and grabs a book, holding it up. The look on my face must be filled with awe and shock because she smirks and nods slowly.

"Yep. She's doing a signing in the city today, and I got two tickets to go."

"What?" I gasp. "I'm so jealous."

Because I haven't been reading, I haven't been keeping track of who's signing and where. But the book she's holding up is from my favorite author.

"You don't have to be," Taylor says with a laugh. "One of the tickets is for you."

"What?" I say again. "How? You didn't even know I'd be here."

"I know, but it's only one ticket per signed copy, so I got two so

I could get you one. You mentioned it was your favorite book when you came over for dinner, so I planned to surprise you with a signed copy. Dad was going to wait in line with me."

Oh, my heart.

Why do these two have to be so damn sweet? They're seriously making it hard to keep them at arm's length.

"But now, you're here," Taylor says happily. "So, you can come with us and meet her yourself."

Damn it! Looks like I won't be leaving after all … except …

"I'm going to need to shower and change," I point out.

"We can swing by your place after we eat," Shane chimes in. "Now, do you want one pancake or two?"

And just like that, I'll be spending my day with Shane and his daughter. I was supposed to be working on pushing them away, yet somehow, they just keep on reeling me in closer.

Fourteen

"I seriously can't believe I met Anna Peterson today," Kinsley gushes. "And not only that, but I got a signed special edition and a picture with her." She holds her book to her chest and leans against the bookshelf, her eyes filled with happiness.

I've learned from spending time with her the past few weeks that it's hard for her to be genuinely happy. I can see it in glimpses here and there, but it's rare that she lets the guilt completely melt away and simply enjoys the moment.

But every time I see her smile like this, it makes me want to do everything in my power to make her understand that it's okay to be happy. That just because she's smiling and laughing and enjoying her life doesn't mean she no longer cares about what happened to her late husband and baby.

"And to think, when I woke up this morning, I was trying to plot how to escape you." She winks playfully, and I chuckle.

"Speaking of which …" I glance at my daughter, who's busy

piling books into her basket, to make sure she's out of hearing distance. "I know Taylor has quickly adopted you as her book bestie or whatever she calls it, but I promise, it's okay to tell her no sometimes. She'll live."

The second the words are out of my mouth, I instantly regret them. "Fuck, I meant …"

I'm racking my brain, trying to think of a better way to word what I was trying to say, when Kinsley gives me a sad smile and says, "It's okay. I know what you meant … and didn't mean. People do it all the time, and I promise that despite being a bit messed up, I'm not that fragile."

"I'm sorry," I say anyway. "I can't even imagine how hard it is for you. If I lost Taylor …" The mere thought of losing my daughter causes my heart to clench in my chest.

I don't even know how the hell Kinsley gets up every morning and functions after losing not only her daughter, but her husband too. She might not realize it, but she's so damn strong.

"It's hard," she says, "but the truth is, your daughter has helped me more than she knows. She got me reading again, something I hadn't done since my entire life had changed, and hanging out with you two is the most I've gotten out since they died, aside from going to work and the occasional night out forced on me by my family.

"And I'm not saying this like I'm trying to use your daughter … I know I lost my daughter, and she isn't coming back, and I would never try to replace her. But," she chokes out, tears filling her eyes, "sometimes, when I'm with Taylor, I imagine what it would have been like if my daughter had survived.

"She'd only be three years old, but …"

She sniffles back a sob, and I pull her down the aisle and into an isolated corner of the store where nobody can see us, not wanting to have this conversation in the open. I'd rather have it in private, but when Kinsley is willing to talk, I'm not going to look a gift horse in the mouth.

"I get it," I murmur once we're alone. "And trust me when I tell you, when she looks at you, she wonders what it would be like if her mom was capable of being a mom."

"I don't want to judge her mom," she says, "but I don't know how she can go weeks or even months without seeing that precious girl."

"I don't know," I agree. "I guess for her, it's out of sight, out of mind." I shrug. "She's not a bad person. And in her own way, she loves Taylor. She calls and texts, and they video-chat. When she has time, she visits and brings her stuff from the places she's been to. But she just wasn't meant for the full-time mom life."

Kinsley nods in understanding, then shocks me when she says, "After I lost Brenna and Brandon, I told myself that I would never get married and have any more kids. After all, I had my chance at a family, at being a mom, and I destroyed it. But sometimes, when I'm around Taylor, I think about what it would be like … to carry a baby to term and give birth to her the right way, like I was supposed to with Brenna. Only instead of her being stillborn, she would come out warm and crying. The doctor would lay her on my chest, and I would promise her that I'd do everything I could to be a good mom."

Kinsley releases a strangled sob, and I reach out to wipe her tears.

"You already are a mom," I tell her.

She shakes her head, more tears sliding down her face. "No, I'm not."

I reach up and palm her cheek, and surprisingly, she nuzzles into my hand, accepting the comfort.

"Yes, you are," I say. "You carried her for months, then gave birth to her. She's just in heaven now. But I have no doubt that if given the chance, you'd be an amazing mom again. I see it in the way you are with Taylor. One day, you'll be given a second chance, and you'll get to hold your baby and tell them all about their sister who's looking down on all of you."

"No." She shakes her head harder. "That's not going to happen because I'm not having any more babies. The doctor said that due to the placental abruption that occurred when I hit the pole, I might have a harder time conceiving."

"Might doesn't mean you can't," I point out.

"No, but I don't want to," she murmurs. "I was given the most beautiful gift, and I couldn't keep her safe, and it makes sense that my punishment would be that I not only lose her and my husband, but that my body also has a lower chance of conceiving. It's like it's the universe's way of telling me that I had my chance and I ruined it."

"Stop," I say, swiping my thumb under her eye to wipe her falling tears. "It was an accident. Do you think I'm a good dad?"

"You already know you are." She rolls her eyes.

"Well, what if we got in the car right now and I got into an accident and Taylor died? I hadn't been drinking or doing drugs. It was raining, and I hit the road the wrong way and—"

She gasps, covering my mouth with her hand. "How did you … how did you know?"

"What?"

"That's what happened," she says. "We were in Miami for our babymoon, and it was raining, and I hit a patch of water and hydroplaned, losing control and hitting a pole."

"Oh, Kins." I frame her face with both hands. "I didn't know. I was just using that as an example. But you didn't answer me. What if it was me driving? Or hell, Brandon? Would you think I'm a bad dad? Would you be looking down on him from heaven, thinking he was a horrible husband and father?"

"No," she chokes out. "I know you're a good dad, and I can't imagine blaming Brandon, but it's just so hard. Every time I'm enjoying myself, I feel like I shouldn't be because they don't get to. I know it's absurd because he loved me and would've wanted me to be happy, but I was supposed to be happy with him … with our daughter.

"The night at The Black Cat was the first time I let myself go. Drinking and dancing with you … kissing you. But then I got home, and the guilt consumed me."

"I can't tell you how to feel," I say. "But I know that if I were lucky enough to be with you and something happened to me, I would want you to move forward and find happiness. Maybe it's because as a paramedic, I'm exposed to death more often than most, but it's made me see how precious life is, and it shouldn't be wasted. Every day, I wake up and try to live my life as if it's my last because the fact is, it very well could be."

Kinsley nods in understanding as she sniffles back her cries.

"I want to do that," she admits. "I want to live my life. I just don't know how."

"Let me help," I tell her, sliding my hand around to the back of her head and gently pulling her face toward mine. "Let me help you live again."

"How?" she whispers, her mouth only inches from mine.

If I wanted to, I could lean in and kiss her, but I don't want to do that. I want it to be her choice.

"Kiss me."

"What?" she breathes, her beautiful blue eyes widening in shock.

"Kiss me, Sour Patch. Kiss me and let me help breathe life into you again."

She stares at me for several seconds, and just when I think she's going to tell me no, she leans in the rest of the way and presses her soft lips against mine.

We stay like this for a few beats, and as much as I want to take over, I stand still, letting her lead the way, needing for it to be on her terms.

And then her lips curve around mine, and her tongue slides between my lips, and I take that as my cue to take control.

Tightening my hold on her hair, I tug her toward me so our bodies are flush, and then I deepen the kiss. Our tongues tangle around one another, and when mine catches hers, sucking on it and getting a taste of her sweetness, she moans into my mouth.

The loud noise in the otherwise quiet bookstore has her opening her eyes and realizing where we are.

"Oh my God," she breathes, her cheeks tinged that adorable shade of pink. "What is it about you that has me losing my mind and letting you kiss me in public places?"

She scrunches her nose up, and without thinking, I lean in and kiss the tip of it.

My hand lands on the wall, and my body presses up against hers.

"Actually," I say, running my lips across her cheek and over to her ear, "you kissed me both times."

I'm considering kissing her again because, fuck, I can't get enough of this woman, but before I can, I see Taylor rounding the corner.

"There you guys are!" She huffs. "I've been looking everywhere for …"

She stops in her tracks, her perceptive eyes taking in the

situation. With Kinsley leaning against the wall and me caging her in with my body pressed up against hers, it's obvious what we were just doing.

"Oh, actually, I'm just going to go," Taylor says with a knowing grin. "Continue on."

"Not happening," Kinsley mutters, ducking under my arm. "Let's go." She links arms with Taylor and glares back at me. "Your dad is trying to get us kicked out for PDA."

Taylor barks out a laugh. "Who knew my dad had game?"

"Technically, we have one and a half movies left," Taylor says on our way home, "since you totally passed out within the first half of the second movie. Plus, I took off today to go to the book signing, so I don't have to be anywhere the rest of the day. I'm just saying, today would be the perfect day to finish the movies."

I'm about to tell Taylor that it's not happening and we're dropping Kinsley off at home, that she's given us enough of her time and she probably has things to do, when Kinsley says, "You're right. And it's probably best if we watch them during the day because I'm the worst at staying up late. But we're only watching them on one condition. Your dad needs to make us ribs again because they were so good, and I've been craving them ever since he made them the last time."

Taylor glances my way with a look that says I'd better say yes. So, of course, I have to give her a hard time.

"Sorry, kid. I was planning to order Chinese."

Taylor glares, and Kinsley laughs.

"I'm kidding." I glance over at Kinsley, who's sitting next to me in the front seat. "You want my famous ribs? All you have to do is ask."

"Oh my God, I'm so full." Kinsley leans back and rubs her flat stomach. "Those are the best ribs ever. You should consider opening your own restaurant."

I chuckle and reach over to wipe the corner of her mouth that has some sauce on it. "If I had known food was the key to your heart, I would've offered to cook for you sooner."

She rolls her eyes, but since she doesn't attempt to flee at the mention of her heart or me touching her, I take that as a double win.

Once we've done the dishes, the girls grab snacks and drinks, and we pile on the couch to watch the movies. This time, instead of Kinsley shying away from me when I sit next to her, she snuggles into my side, laying her head on my shoulder.

I don't know what that means, but it feels like there's been some kind of shift between us after our conversation at the bookstore. One that I'm not even sure Kinsley is aware of.

Reaching into my pocket, I pull out my box of Sour Patch Kids and pop one into my mouth. Kinsley glances up at me, and I think she's going to give me shit for eating my favorite snack, but instead, she opens her mouth, silently asking for one.

I reach in and grab a red one and set it on her tongue. Within seconds, her face puckers, making me laugh.

We watch the movie for a few minutes before she reaches into my box and pops another one into her mouth.

"Ugh, why are these so damn good?" she mutters, looking up at me.

"It's the sweet and sour," I tell her as my eyes lock on her plump lips, wishing I could kiss her. "I'm telling you, it's the perfect combination."

Her cheeks tinge a beautiful shade of pink, telling me she knows I'm referring to her and not the candy, and then she rests her head back on my shoulder, but not before taking another one and eating it.

"Be careful," I warn, my voice low so Taylor can't hear. "They're addictive."

"I think I'll take my chances," she murmurs, grabbing one more.

Not even thirty minutes later, soft snores fill the room, making Taylor and me lock eyes and quietly laugh.

"She's not a very good movie watcher," Taylor says, pausing the movie. "At this rate, it's going to take us a month before we finish them."

"I think she's emotionally drained," I tell her, thinking back to our earlier conversation at the bookstore. "All of this is a lot for her. She's spent the past few years isolating herself from everyone."

"When she told me she lost her husband and baby, my heart hurt for her," my daughter says softly. "She's so nice, and I hate when bad things happen to good people. Sometimes, life can be so unfair."

"Yeah, it can be," I agree.

"So, are you going to wake her up or let her sleep?"

I glance down at Kinsley, sleeping peacefully. "I think I'm going to let her sleep."

Taylor shakes her head but grins. "Okay, then I'm heading to bed. Casey has texted me a million times, wanting to tell me about her and her new boyfriend."

Taylor heads up to her room, and I switch from the movie to a game that's on, letting Kinsley continue to sleep.

At some point, I must've fallen asleep as well because when I wake up, I'm met with sleepy blue eyes staring up at me.

"Morning," I rasp.

"Morning," she says lazily, making no move to get up. "I don't think we finished the movie."

I chuckle. "No, and Taylor joked that it's going to take a month to finish them."

Kinsley groans and sits up. "I can usually stay awake." She pouts, her brows bunching together. "There's just something about … *this house* that has me passing out."

"You mean there's something about me," I say, refusing to mince words. "You're comfortable, Sour Patch. In my home, in my arms. And it allows you to fall asleep."

I expect her to deny it, so I'm taken aback when she says, "Yeah, it's you. But, Shane …" She sighs. "I feel like I'm leading you on because I know you want more from me than I'm capable of giving you."

"I just want you," I find myself saying. "However I can get you."

"You say that now, but eventually, you're going to want to get married and have more babies. Look at how close you are with Taylor."

"How about we just take it one day at a time? No labels or promises. Just enjoy each other's company." I tip her chin so she'll look at me. "Okay?"

"Okay," she breathes. "I can do that."

"Good. Now, as much as I love cooking, I have to get to work this morning, so how about we grab some breakfast, and then I'll drop you off on my way to work?"

"Where's Taylor?" she asks, glancing around.

"Right here," Taylor says as she descends the stairs with her bag draped over her shoulder. "And I'm about to be late to school." She rushes over and gives me a kiss on my cheek and then gives Kinsley one as well. "Have a good day! I have cheer practice and work, so I'll be home late. Love you!"

"Wow, she's chipper in the morning," Kinsley notes.

"It's the cheerleader in her."

While I get ready for work, Kinsley insists on taking Becky for a quick walk. Usually, in the morning, I just let her out into the backyard to do her business, but if Kinsley wants to walk her, I won't stop her.

When we arrive at Thea's Breakfast Nook, everyone stares at us curiously. It's a small town, and with me being a local firefighter and having lived here my entire life, I know just about everyone.

"Shane," Thea says with a smile. "How are you doing this morning?"

"Good," I tell her. "Just grabbing some breakfast before work."

"And who is this beautiful woman?" Thea asks, smiling at Kinsley.

"This is Kinsley. She owns Exposed Ink, the tattoo shop downtown."

"Oh." Thea's eyes light up. "How fun! I've always wanted to get a tattoo," she says to Kinsley. "A little butterfly or unicorn." She waggles her brows, and Kinsley stifles a laugh. "Maybe one day, I'll get brave enough or drunk enough and actually go through with it." She winks. "Your mom and dad come in often, so it's nice to finally meet you."

"Nice to meet you too," Kinsley says, her eyes filled with mirth. "And anytime you want to come in, just ask for me."

"Will do," Thea says, showing us to our table and setting the menus down. "Take a look, and someone will be with you shortly to take your order."

"What happened to refusing to kill all the unicorns?" I murmur once Thea is out of earshot.

"To see that woman, who is probably in her eighties and has never been inked, get a tattoo would be worth killing a unicorn." She smirks, grabbing the menu. "Now, tell me what's good. I'm starved."

"Everything," I say honestly because I've yet to eat anything here that wasn't delicious.

While we eat, Kinsley gushes about how she still can't believe she got to meet one of her favorite authors, which leads to who she'd love to meet in the future, and while she talks, I can't help but think about how much she's changed in the month since I met her. She's laughing and smiling and talking animatedly. She might not want to admit it, but I'm totally growing on her.

After paying the bill, I swing by her place to drop her off.

"Thank you for this weekend," she says, sounding almost shy. "I had a good time. Even if it started against my will."

I bark out a laugh. "Does that mean I've earned your number?"

Kinsley shakes her head and grins. "Not a chance. I had a good weekend, but not *that* good."

Fifteen

Kinsley

"There she is." Mom glances back at me from where she's cooking at the stove and smirks. "Have a good weekend?"

When I don't respond, she raises a knowing brow and adds, "What? You didn't believe anyone bought your vague *I'm hanging out with a friend* text after I invited you to breakfast yesterday morning, did you? And when I dropped by this morning, I noticed you still weren't home. I assume you spent the weekend at Shane's?"

"Sorry," I mutter, sitting on the barstool at the island. "I should've called. But in my defense, I didn't plan on—"

"Stop." She waves me off. "I was only giving you a hard time. You're a grown adult."

"Yeah, a grown adult who lives in her parents' pool house."

Mom stops stirring whatever's in the pan and turns around. "Are you thinking about moving out? You know you're welcome to stay as long as you want, but if you're ready …"

"I know, and I appreciate it. A few months ago, I wouldn't have even considered it, but lately …" I shrug. "I don't know. I feel like I'm finally starting to heal, and I've been thinking about what my future looks like."

"And it's not in our pool house?" Mom says with a wink.

"As nice as it is, no." I laugh. "With the money I've saved from living with you guys, I can afford a place, so …"

"So, you should start looking. And if you need a second opinion, your dad and I are always around."

"Second opinion for what?" Dad asks, strolling into the kitchen. "And what are we around for?"

He makes a beeline straight for my mom and wraps her in his arms, giving her a kiss on her cheek. Rather than it hurting my heart like it used to because I would think about how Brandon would never hug or kiss me again, it makes me think about the way Shane kissed the tip of my nose yesterday. It was such a simple gesture, yet it felt big. Like things between us are shifting, and I'm not sure how I feel about that.

It's one thing to kiss him out of lust, but it's another for him to be cute. Making out can be chalked up to hormones and chemistry, but kissing my nose felt intimate. Like something couples do.

And when he told me he wanted to help me live again and asked me to kiss him, to let him breathe life into me, instead of saying no, I kissed him, and for the second time since I'd met him, I really did feel like I was living again. And instead of feeling guilty, it felt good.

"Kinsley is thinking about moving out," Mom says, shaking me from my thoughts.

Dad turns around to look at me. "Really?" he says with a smile.

"Try not to sound too excited," I drawl.

"I'm not excited," he says gently. "But the fact that you're considering it and with the anniversary coming up … I love you, and I'm glad to see you finally starting to climb out of the darkness. Moving out is a big deal …"

He continues to speak, but his words are drowned out by the pounding in my heart at his mention of the anniversary. How did I forget about it? I've been so busy with Taylor and Shane that it completely slipped my mind.

I glance at the date on my phone—March 11th. The anniversary of their deaths is in four days. And I completely forgot.

"I need to go shower," I mutter, taking off out their back door before they can stop me.

When I get to my place, I peel my clothes off and turn the water to hot, needing to wash Shane off my body. I can smell his scent from sleeping on the couch with him. We kissed yesterday.

After my shower, I try to get lost in my book, but my brain is too busy thinking about this week.

"Kins," my mom says, stepping through the front door. "You okay?"

"Hey. Yeah." I set my book down.

"I knocked a few times, but when you didn't answer, I got worried."

Of course she got worried because this week is the anniversary of their deaths.

"I forgot," I admit, blinking back my tears. "I was so busy with Shane and Taylor that I forgot until Dad reminded me. What kind of shitty person does that make me?"

"That doesn't make you shitty," Mom says, having a seat next to me. "That just means you're moving forward."

"While they're dead."

"And nothing you do will bring them back," she says. "But for the first time since their deaths, it feels like you didn't die with them."

"I … think I need to call Julia."

Mom nods. "Okay, if you need anything, I'm here."

"Thank you." I reach over and hug her. "I love you."

Once she's gone, I text Julia and ask for an emergency session. Since we were due to speak tomorrow anyway, she moves it to today.

"Kinsley," she says when I walk into her office a few hours later. "How are you?" She has her legs crossed with her most recent knitting project in her lap.

"Not good," I admit, having a seat. "I forgot that this week was the anniversary of Brandon's and Brenna's deaths."

She nods. "And why do you think that is?"

"Because I was distracted by Shane and his daughter."

"Distracted how?" she asks, not letting me get away with my vague answer.

"I spent the weekend with them."

Julia raises a brow and sets her knitting project down. "Well, now, we're getting somewhere."

"Shane asked me to let him in," I admit, remembering the way he looked into my eyes and asked me to kiss him.

"And what did you say?"

"I said yes?"

She quirks a brow. "Was that a question?"

I laugh. "Well, I tried to push him away by telling him that I'm leading him on because I don't want any more kids or to get married, and eventually, he'll want those things, but instead of him running, he said he just wants to take it one day at a time. No promises or labels."

Julia nods. "Getting back to the babies and marriage. Is that a sure thing?"

I take a moment to think about her question, trying to imagine moving forward and getting married again, making promises for forever … growing another baby, one who isn't Brandon's, but instead Shane's.

"A month ago, I would've said there was no way in hell that would happen, but now … I'm not so sure. Shane just makes it so damn easy to be myself around him. He doesn't judge the way I'm grieving. He simply wants to spend time with me, and when I'm with him, I feel less sad. I feel like the old me, before the accident."

"Did you just hear what you said?"

I shake my head, unsure of what she's referring to.

"You said *before the accident*. You've never done that before. You always make a point to say you caused it, but you just admitted it was an accident."

She's right. I've always avoided that word because using it would mean taking the blame off me and I didn't want to be let off the hook.

"Shane and I spoke about it the other day. He asked me if he got into a car accident with his daughter, would that mean he was a horrible dad, and it made me realize that even though I hold myself responsible, I hadn't done it on purpose. I loved my husband and baby, and if I had known that by us getting into the car that night, they would lose their lives, I never would've done so.

"I wasn't drinking or doing drugs. I wasn't on my phone or distracted. I was going the speed limit. But still, we crashed, and they died. I didn't kill them," I breathe out. "It was a horrible accident, and hanging out with Shane has reminded me how short life is. I've spent the past three years acting like I died with them, and I don't want to do that anymore."

I release a sigh of relief, feeling both nervous and exhilarated after admitting that.

"And what do you want?" Julia asks.

"I want to live again."

"Are you sure you want to do this?" Mom asks the next morning.

"Yes, I'm sure. I don't want to sink back into that dark hole, and getting out and staying busy will hopefully help prevent that."

Speaking with Julia confirmed what I'd already known and not wanted to admit—I've developed feelings for Shane, but more than that, I'm ready to move forward. And I plan to focus more on that … after this week is over.

"Okay." Mom smiles. "Then, let's go."

When we arrive at the health club, we rush straight back to the studio where the yoga class is being held since it's about to begin and grab a mat. I haven't done any classes yet since I started coming here, but my mom loves the yoga class and mentioned it's a good stress reliever, so I figured since I don't have any clients until this afternoon, I'd check one out. At this point, I'll do anything to get through this shitty week.

I'm getting situated when the instructor announces the class will start shortly, and I whip my head around to find where the voice is coming from because I would recognize that voice from anywhere.

"Isn't that …" my mom begins.

"Holy shit."

I glance at my mom, then back at Shane just as his eyes meet mine. They quickly widen in shock, but when they drag down my body and back up, meeting mine for a second time, they're filled with lust. It's then I remember I'm dressed in leggings and a tiny sports bra that leaves little to the imagination. And if looks could give orgasms, I have a feeling I'd be screaming out Shane's name.

"Jesus," Mom whispers. "I knew the man had a crush on you, but holy hell." She dramatically fans herself. "I had no idea the chemistry between you two was so hot that it could set this place on fire."

"Mom!" I hiss. "What are we, in high school? He doesn't have a crush."

Mom shrugs, Shane smiles at me, and I wave awkwardly, which makes Mom laugh, and in return, I glare at her.

"Sorry." She laughs again. "It's just so cute."

"It's not cute," I grumble even though it is in fact kind of cute.

Shane goes about introducing himself to those who haven't met him before. Apparently, his brother and his brother's wife—Eric and Katie—own the health club, and while he usually teaches other classes like boxing and cardio, he is fully trained to teach yoga.

"Is Katie okay?" one of the women in the front asks.

"Yes," Shane says. "But she woke up this morning feeling a bit sore and asked if I could take over her class. She's hoping to come back later this week, but with her due soon, she's taking it day by day."

"Katie's so sweet," Mom says. "I'll have to send her a little pick-me-up. She's having a little girl."

I wait for the pain to come, and it does because I wouldn't be human if I didn't ache for my baby girl, but another emotion also makes an appearance—hopefulness. Because for the first time, I can see it—getting pregnant again, carrying a baby, feeling him or her growing in me. I loved being pregnant, and I couldn't wait to be a mom.

I glance at Shane, and he smiles softly, and images of him doting on me hit me. We're obviously nowhere near the creating-a-family stage in our relationship—hell, are we even in a relationship? But the fact that I can visualize a future with Shane and a baby has my heart swelling.

"All right, ladies," Shane says, snapping me from my thoughts. "Let's do this."

The yoga class is only an hour long, yet it feels so much longer than that. Between Shane eye-fucking me, my mom noting the way

Shane is eye-fucking me, and me trying and failing not to eye-fuck Shane right back, when the class is over, I'm hot and sweaty and turned on.

Mom says she's going to shower at home, but since the shop is right next door, I brought my clothes with me so I could shower and get dressed here.

But before I get to the women's locker room, a hand wraps around my wrist and pulls me through a door marked *Private*. When I spin around to see what's going on, I'm met with Shane's body pressed against mine.

"Do you have any idea how hard it was to instruct a class to do the downward fucking dog with your ass wiggling in the air?"

My thighs clench at his admission, and I thank the bra gods that my sports bra is thick enough that my nipples won't poke through the material.

"I'm pretty sure rule number one for teaching at a health club is not to eye-fuck your students," I sass.

Shane growls—legit growls—into my ear. "Oh, Sour Patch, I wanted to do way more than eye-fuck my student." He runs his nose along the side of my neck and plants an open-mouthed kiss to the sensitive area just under my ear. "Tell me I wasn't the only one imagining fucking you in that position."

"You weren't," I admit, my hormones winning out over all common sense. "I'm pretty sure I imagined you fucking me in every position."

I shift my hips forward, and my pelvis rubs against his front. He's taller than me, so his hard length hits my belly, making us both moan in anticipation.

"Fuck," Shane murmurs. "I can practically smell your arousal."

He lifts my leg and hooks it around his waist, and in this

position, when he grinds himself against me, it hits my center, eliciting a moan from me.

"You like that?" he murmurs into my ear.

"Yes, don't stop."

He grinds harder, hitting my center over and over again.

"Oh God. Yes, just like that," I groan. "I'm so—"

My orgasm hits at the same time Shane's skillful mouth devours mine, swallowing down my moans as I come completely undone.

High off oxytocin, I crave more of Shane, so I reach down and wrap my fingers around his hard, thick length, silently telling him what I want.

But instead of giving it to me, he shakes his head.

"Fuck, I have another class to teach," he murmurs against my lips. "Come over for dinner tonight. We can continue this in private."

His brown eyes plead with mine, and I almost agree, but then I remember I have inventory tonight. I've been putting it off, and I need to get it done. My dad sent me a list of things we're almost out of that need to be reordered.

"I can't. I'm working late."

"With a client?"

"No, inventory."

Shane nods and then leans in, brushing his lips against mine. Then, taking my hand in his, he leads us back down the hall and stops in front of the women's locker room. He sweeps a few errant hairs from my face and then presses a chaste kiss on my forehead. "I'll see you later."

And for the first time, his words feel like more of a promise than a threat—one I'm looking forward to.

Sixteen

Shane

"**D**AD, MOM'S ON THE PHONE FOR YOU." TAYLOR STOMPS down the stairs and thrusts her phone at me. "And try to make it quick because I need to get to work."

"Why didn't she just call me?" I ask, taking the phone from her.

"Maybe because you never answer your phone unless it's me."

Taylor laughs, and I don't bother to argue because she's not wrong. I'm not big on the phone, I can't stand social media, and I prefer to make a phone call rather than text. So, unless it's Taylor's ringtone, I tend to ignore it. The truth is, I couldn't even tell you where my phone is right now. The thing is old as hell, and I'm shocked it still works.

"Hey, Jamie. What's up?"

"Shane, how are you?"

"Good. And yourself?"

It's been several months since I've spoken to her, so my guess is, she's coming into town, and she'd like to spend time with Taylor.

"I'm good. I'm finishing up a documentary in Brazil and then planning to make a trip back to the States. I was wondering if it would be okay if Taylor and I went on a little girls' trip."

"You mean a work trip?"

She's done this before. Tries to turn a work trip into a mother-daughter trip, but it ends with her working around the clock and Taylor being bored, asking to come home.

"No, Shane, an actual vacation with just our daughter and me. Though if you wanted to go, I wouldn't be opposed."

I can hear her smirk over the phone, and I mentally roll my eyes. When we were younger, she'd stroll into town, and because I was young and dumb, I'd give in and hook up with her, hoping to put my family back together. I grew up with two loving parents and wanted the same for Taylor.

But then I grew up, saw that Jamie had no intention of settling down and was only looking to scratch an itch, and I put a stop to it, not wanting to complicate shit between us. With Jamie, the lines need to be clear. Otherwise, she'll try to blur them.

"Where?" I ask, ignoring the not-so-subtle invitation to join them.

While I'll miss my daughter—if Jamie follows through—a few days of having Kinsley all to myself would be nice. Maybe I'll even take some days off work so we can do something, just the two of us.

You're getting ahead of yourself.

She's barely agreed to see where things go. Planning trips is probably moving too fast for her.

"She mentioned wanting to go to the city. Something about wanting to see a college. I was thinking she could take a few days off school so we could make it a little longer than the weekend."

"Jamie," I sigh. "You know how important school is, hence her wanting to visit NYU. That's where she wants to go to college."

I know she's in her own world ninety-nine percent of the time, but would it kill her to pay the smallest bit of attention to the shit our daughter says?

"I'm well aware of where our daughter wants to go to school," she snaps defensively. "And it's only a few days. I don't get to spend a lot of time with her and—"

"By choice," I point out, refusing to let her get away with acting like her daughter is being kept from her.

She could spend time with Taylor whenever she wants. She chooses not to come around more than once a year.

"Well, not all of us were destined for the small-town life," she volleys.

And not all of us were destined for parenthood, I think, but don't say out loud since Taylor is standing in front of me, begging me with her eyes to say yes.

"I don't know."

"Dad," Taylor groans. "Please."

She doesn't see her mom often, and we both know if I say no, it'll probably be several months before she's back in the area again.

"I'll think about it," I tell them. Then, to Jamie, I say, "Once you know the dates, text them to me, and I'll look to make sure they don't interfere with any exams or school functions."

"Thank you, Dad!" Taylor exclaims, grabbing the phone. "Love you!"

She takes off up the stairs to continue her conversation with her mom while I finish preparing dinner for Kinsley and me. She didn't invite me to the shop, but she did mention she'd be there, doing inventory, so I figured since she couldn't come over for dinner, I'd bring dinner to her.

I called Scott, who let me know Kinsley's last appointment of the day should be done by six o'clock, so at a quarter till, I head over to Exposed Ink.

"Sorry, we're—" Kinsley looks up from the desk, but when she sees it's me, she changes directions. "What are you doing here? Is our appointment tonight?" she asks in confusion.

"Nope." I lift the cooler I packed. "I brought dinner."

Her eyes light up in shock and curiosity. "What did you bring?"

I lock the door behind me, switch the Open sign to Closed, and have a seat on the couch. "Come see for yourself."

Kinsley gets up and joins me while I place the containers of food on the table.

"Whatcha got there?"

She leans over my shoulder, but when I turn to answer her, our faces almost collide. Her eyes meet mine as she drags her tongue along the seam of her lips to wet them.

"Chicken Alfredo," I say, my eyes not leaving hers. "But right now, I'm thinking the only thing I'm hungry for is you."

Kinsley's cheeks heat up a beautiful shade of pink. "Too bad because I forgot to eat lunch, so I'm actually starved for real food."

"You got it." I lean in and kiss the tip of her nose and then back away. "Here you go." I hand her the container and silverware and then pull out the drinks and cups I brought.

"Is that sweet tea?" Her eyes go wide.

"Yep, and it's homemade."

"Shane Evans." She sighs. "You really do know the way to my heart."

She opens the lid, pours some sweet tea into a cup, and takes a sip.

"Oh my God." She moans, taking another sip.

"Damn, Kins," I say with a laugh. "Keep making noises like that, and I'm going to toss you on that pool table and eat *you* for dinner."

"Maybe if you're a good boy and eat all your dinner, you can have me for dessert." She leans in and brushes her lips against mine. "But I can't promise how sweet I'll be."

She smirks playfully, and stick a fork in me because I'm done.

Sour Kinsley was already a force to be reckoned with.

Sweet Kinsley captured my heart.

But sexy Kinsley … she just might be the death of me.

"My goodness, that Alfredo was delicious." Kinsley sets her container down and leans back to rub her food belly.

"I'm glad you liked it. I know Italian is your favorite, so I figured you might."

Kinsley smiles softly at me. "You're like the perfect book boyfriend, only you're real. You're a good dad and a great cook. You have a noble profession and a cute dog, and you own your own house."

"But …" I prompt because with Kinsley, there usually is one.

"No buts." She shakes her head. "I just want you to know how amazing you are."

"Amazing enough to get your number?" I joke, making her laugh.

"Not that amazing." She stands and bends over to clean up, but before she can, I reach out and turn her around, pulling her into my lap.

She comes willingly, her thighs resting on either side of me.

"What will it take?" I ask, gripping the curves of her hips and scooting her toward me. "What will it take for you to give me your number?"

"I don't know," she breathes. "A number just feels so personal."

"I got you off in the office of the health club. You can't get more personal than that."

"Giving you my number will lead to texting and phone calls, which will lead to talking and making plans and getting to know each other, which will lead to getting serious, and that will end in heartbreak."

"I won't hurt you," I promise, curling my fingers around her nape.

"I know you won't," she says softly. "I'm more afraid of hurting you."

"Don't be. I'm a big boy, and I can handle whatever you throw at me. I want this, Kins. I want you. I want us."

I know I agreed to taking it one day at a time with no strings, but I need her to know where I stand.

"I do too," she admits, shocking the hell out of me.

"Really?"

"Yeah," she says, wrapping her arms around my neck. "I know we said no promises or labels, but I want them. I'm just scared. I'm damaged, only a shell of myself, and you deserve to be with someone whole."

"Let me decide what I deserve. I want you, Sour Patch, however I can have you."

Kinsley looks at me for several seconds and then nods. "Okay, you can have me."

Before I can ask what she means, her delicate hands cup my jaw, and her lips gently press against mine. The kiss starts off slow but quickly deepens when she exhales a soft moan and I slide my tongue into her mouth.

And suddenly, we're ravenous.

Our tongues unite.

Our mouths fuse.

"Tell me I can have you," I murmur against her lips.

She said the words earlier, but I need to hear them again to make sure she's completely on board with taking this next step.

"I want you," she says, sliding her hands around to my nape until her fingers are entangled in my hair. "Please, Shane. Tell me that I can have *you*."

I lift her into my arms, and her legs wrap around my waist, and I walk her over to the pool table, setting her on the edge with her thighs spread so I can stand between them.

"Do you know how many times I imagined fucking you on this table?" I tell her as I lift her shirt over her head, exposing her simple black bra.

I plant an open-mouthed kiss on the swell of her breast while I reach around and flick the clasp open. The material falls down her arms, and I'm left with the gorgeous view of her perky tits.

Her nipples are pebbled and begging for attention, so I take one breast into my palm and lean in, wrapping my lips around the hardened tip, sucking and licking it.

"Oh shit," Kinsley moans, thrusting her chest toward me.

Unless I'm completely off base, it's been three years since she's been with a man, so she's got to be overstimulated and desperate to be taken care of properly. She might've gotten herself off over the years, but I know firsthand that using my fist isn't the same as sinking into a warm, wet pussy.

After giving her other nipple some attention, I gently push her down so she's lying on the table, looking like a meal that's only meant for me to enjoy.

I trail kisses down her flat torso until I get to the top of her jeans. I unbutton and unzip them, and then after pulling her Chucks and socks off her feet, I pull her jeans down her legs, leaving her in only a tiny black thong. Then, I take a step back so I can take in the woman in front of me.

"Shane," she groans. "What are you doing?"

"Admiring you," I admit. "I've been fantasizing about this since the moment I met you, and here you are, giving yourself over to me."

I take a step closer so I'm between her legs once again, and then I lean down, fisting the back of her head gently and bringing her face up to mine so I can kiss her, taste her. There's so much I want to do to this woman that I have no idea where to start. What if this is my only time with her? She said she wants promises and labels, but she could change her mind.

"Shane," she murmurs against my mouth. "Please."

The desperation in her voice shakes me from my thoughts. If this is the only time I get to be with Kinsley, I'm going to make damn sure it's a night she never forgets.

While trailing kisses down her neck and along her collarbone, I reach between us and cup her material-clad pussy. I haven't even touched her down there yet, but I can already feel the wetness.

When my mouth hits the waistband of her underwear, I hook my fingers around the sides, and she lifts so I can slide them down her legs.

I bend so I'm eye level with her neatly trimmed pussy and give it a kiss before I move a little lower and stick my nose between her lips, inhaling her scent.

"Fuck, you smell so good."

She reaches out and drags her fingers through my hair. "Please, Shane," she begs.

Separating her lips, I lick up the center, stopping at her clit and giving it some attention.

Kinsley moans in pleasure, telling me she likes what I'm doing, so I do it again and again, until her pussy is dripping onto the edge of the table and she's practically shaking.

"More," she commands, fisting my hair and pushing my face toward her when I stop for a second to get a good look at her pink pussy.

"You got it, Sour Patch," I murmur before I dive back in.

I lick and suck on her swollen clit, and I could easily make her come like this, but I want to give her the more she asked for. So, with my tongue massaging her clit, I thrust one finger, then two into her pussy. It takes a few times before I find the right spot, but once I do, between my tongue on her clit and my fingers in her cunt, she finally lets go, coming long and hard, soaking my mouth and hand as I lap up her juices, trying to memorize the taste of her.

"I feel like this is all very one-sided," Kinsley mutters as I stand, mentally wondering how I should make her come for a second time.

"As it should be," I tell her, reaching over and tweaking her nipple. "Tonight is about you."

"No," she disagrees. "Tonight is about *us.*"

She grips the bottom of my shirt and pulls it over my head, then leans in and presses a soft kiss to the area right over my heart. "It's about the start of something new."

She unbuttons my jeans and pushes them down my legs, then wraps her hands around my neck and pulls me down to her. "It's about me accepting that the past happened, that it can't be changed, but wanting a future with you."

Her mouth captures mine as her hand slides between us and wraps around my shaft. I could fuck her on the edge of this table, but it won't be comfortable for her. So, instead, I climb onto it, making her giggle into my mouth.

Our kissing intensifies as I grip her thighs and guide myself inside of her. She's drenched from her orgasm and so goddamn warm.

When I bottom out inside of her, we both moan into each other's mouth. And then I start to fuck her slowly, not wanting the connection between us to end. Wanting to stay like this, inside of her, for as long as possible.

"Shane," Kinsley murmurs, breaking the kiss and meeting my gaze with hers. "I promise I won't break. Please, fuck me harder."

"Your wish is my command," I tell her as I drop my hands onto the table on either side of her head.

With the felt of the pool table helping with the traction, I start to fuck her harder, deeper. Her walls clench around my cock like a vise, and too soon, she's screaming my name as her climax hits, taking me straight over the edge with her.

"God, that was so good," she breathes as we stay just like this, both of us attempting to catch our breath. "How soon can we do that again?"

I glance up at her and shake my head. "Are you even real?" I ask, wondering how the fuck I got so lucky to have her in my life, in my arms.

While her grief is a part of who she is, she's so much more than that. She's sweet and selfless and so goddamn sexy and strong and talented. She has a huge heart that she wears on her sleeve, and it's the reason why she took the accident so hard. She cares deeply and passionately.

"I am," she says, palming the sides of my face, "and thanks to you, I finally feel like I'm living my life again."

Seventeen

Kinsley

"Y
OU'RE REALLY NOT GOING TO GIVE ME YOUR NUMBER?" Shane looks at me incredulously from the driver's seat of his truck. "I gave you not one, but two orgasms, and I still haven't earned your number?"

"I mean, the orgasms were good," I say with a smirk. "But I'm just not ready for that level of commitment yet."

I shrug, and he chuckles.

Shane ended up staying while I did the inventory. We listened to music, argued over whose playlist was better, and talked about nothing of importance. We laughed and flirted, and it felt nice … comfortable. The way it always does with Shane.

"Whatever," he grumbles before he gets out and rounds the front of the vehicle, coming over to my side.

I'm not sure what he's doing, until he opens my door, and for a second, I sit there, staring at him, wondering how the hell this man is real and what flaws he's hiding because nobody can be this perfect.

He extends his hand, and I take it, hopping out of his raised-up truck. I'm not short, but in his truck, I feel like I am.

"Are you, um … coming in?" I ask when he walks with me around the back of my parents' house and past the pool, stopping in front of my door.

"No, Taylor will be home soon, and while she's left to her own devices when I have to work my shifts, I like to be home on the nights I can be." He reaches out and tucks a few wayward strands behind my ear. "I just wanted to walk you to your door, so I could do this."

He leans down and captures my mouth with his, his tongue sliding past my parted lips and uniting with mine. It's only meant to be a kiss good night, but once his mouth is on mine, I can't help but crave more. It's like Shane has opened the door to my hormones that I kept locked away for too long, and now, my body is desperate for his touch, for the connection I feel when I'm with him.

As if we're both on the same page, Shane reaches down and lifts me into his arms. My legs wrap around his waist at the same time my arms wrap around his neck as he walks us inside.

It's dark, and he bumps into the couch and then the table, making us laugh.

"I need you now," I murmur against his lips.

He nods in agreement and then sets me on my kitchen island, where we proceed to rip each other's clothes off. Once we're both naked, he thrusts two fingers into me while I trail kisses along his neck, sucking and licking along his flesh.

It only takes less than a minute before I'm coming all over his skilled hand, and then he's replacing his fingers with his hard length.

"Fuck, Sour Patch," Shane moans as he fills me inch by

delicious inch, until we're connected in the most intimate way. "I was addicted to you before, but now …" He shakes his head. "I don't think I'll ever get enough."

Before I can say anything in response, he pulls out and then thrusts back in, damn near taking my breath away. The counter is smooth, and my ass slides back and forth along the surface as Shane fucks me fast and hard.

With him holding on to my hips, I pull his face back down to mine, kissing him like I need his air to breathe. And in many ways, I do.

In such a short amount of time, he's come to mean so much to me. He saw me drowning in the darkness, and instead of walking away, he refused to leave me there. I tried like hell to push him away, but still, he stayed, and every day, he coaxed me toward the light, one foot at a time, until I was on the other side of the door with him, the sun shining down on us.

"Shane," I choke out, breaking our kiss so I can look at him.

I don't know what I want to say. My feelings are all over the place. The brightness nearly blinding me. But of course, Shane understands without me having to say anything. Because he gets me.

"I know," he murmurs, leaning in and nipping my bottom lip before looking at me. "I know."

With our eyes locked on each other, we both find our release, and maybe it's because I've finally accepted that I have strong feelings for him, but it feels like this time is even more intimate, like I've bared not only my body, but also my soul to him. And he's done the same to me.

Once we've both come down from our high, he carries me through my bedroom and into the bathroom. With me still in his arms, he manages to turn on the water and then steps into the shower. Only then does he set me down and proceed to wash my hair and body.

When it's my turn to wash him, I take my time, exploring every inch of him. Both times we've been together were in the heat of the moment, so I didn't get a chance to appreciate his body.

"Keep touching me like that, and I'll be fucking you against the wall in here," he says, his eyes filled with a mixture of mirth and lust.

"You have to get home to Taylor," I remind him.

Once we're out of the shower, he gets dressed in the clothes he was wearing, and I throw on an old shirt and sweats.

I'm walking him to the front door when my phone rings. I glance at it and see Taylor's name on the screen, along with a picture of us at the book signing.

Shane glances at it, then does a double take. "Seriously? My daughter has your fucking number, and I don't?" He pouts, grabbing my phone and hitting Accept. "How did you get—"

"Hey!" I say through my laughter. "Give that back. We are definitely nowhere near the stage where you get to answer my phone."

Taylor barks out a laugh as I snatch my phone from Shane and put her on speaker.

"Is that my dad with you?" she asks even though she already knows the answer.

"Yes, and he's butthurt that you have my number and he doesn't."

Taylor giggles over the phone. "What can I say? Hos over bros."

Her dad scoffs, "There is so much wrong with all of this that I don't even know where to start. Are you at home?"

"Yeah, I just got home. I was calling to see if Kinsley has read the new Anna Peterson book that came out this morning. I devoured it during school today, and I need to vent."

"Glad to know you're getting such a wonderful education," Shane deadpans.

"I haven't," I admit. "Between yoga with my mom this morning, working all afternoon, and …" I glance at Shane, my cheeks heating up at the thought of how we spent this evening, and he smirks. "I've been busy," I say after clearing my throat. "I'm hoping to read it tonight if your dad will ever leave."

He rolls his eyes. "Give me your number, and I'll go."

"Nope," I say, popping the *P* for dramatic effect.

At this point, I'm just having fun, messing with him.

"I'll text you once I start it and let you know what I think," I say to Taylor.

"Okay, sounds good. See you when you get home, Dad. Bye!"

Taylor hangs up, and Shane grips the curve of my hip, pulling me toward him until our bodies are flush.

"I think it would only be right that your boyfriend has your number," he murmurs, his eyes twinkling with mirth.

"Who said anything about you being my boyfriend?" I scoff.

"You," he says, bending slightly and licking the seam of my lips. "You said you wanted labels and promises."

"And I do," I admit, my heart thumping in my chest at the thought of moving forward. Only instead of being consumed by guilt, I'm filled with excitement. "It's been years since I've been in a relationship, but I'm pretty sure the guy is supposed to actually ask the woman to be his girlfriend, not demand it like a Neanderthal."

I quirk a brow, and Shane barks out a laugh.

"All right, Sour Patch." He gives me a chaste kiss, and I expect him to follow it up with asking me to be his girlfriend, so I'm shocked and confused when he steps back. "I'd say I'll call or text when I get home, but I don't have your number, so … I guess I'll see you when I see you."

With a panty-dropping wink, he opens the door and walks out, leaving me wondering what the hell just happened.

One second, I thought Shane and I were going to make things official, and I was ready to, and the next, he's walking away while leaving whatever is going on between us in limbo.

Men. They can be so damn frustrating.

Eighteen

Shane

"Ask her to be my girlfriend? Seriously? What are we, teenagers?" I grumble as I mix the pancake batter for breakfast.

It's been thirty-six hours since I left Kinsley's house after she told me the only way that we're making shit official is by me asking her.

Since I had to work my shift yesterday and the station was slow, I had a lot of time to overthink this, and the only thing I've come up with is that it needs to be romantic because she's a romance reader, and if my daughter has shown me anything, it's that romance readers have high expectations when it comes to shit like this.

I let out a sigh of annoyance, at a loss as to how to go about this, and nearly drop the bowl when Taylor appears out of nowhere.

"What's got you all huffy?" she asks, reaching around and grabbing a few blueberries and popping them into her mouth.

"Kinsley wants to date me."

"Really?" she squeals. "That's amazing!" She jumps up and down, but when I don't show my own enthusiasm, she stops and looks at me. "Why does it sound like you're unhappy about it? I thought this is what you wanted."

"Oh, I am happy," I tell her, pouring the batter onto the skillet. "But apparently, mentioning that I'm her boyfriend without actually asking her to be my girlfriend is unacceptable."

Taylor gasps, her hands dramatically going to her chest. "You didn't ask her out?"

"I haven't asked anyone out since your mom, and I was seventeen. I wasn't aware that I needed to do that at thirty-five."

"You know, for a smart guy, you really can be dumb sometimes," she chides. "Your future girlfriend reads romance. Of course she would expect her potential boyfriend to properly ask her out."

"Okay," I say, flipping the pancakes. "I get it."

I don't …

The second Kinsley told me she wanted more, that she wanted the promises and labels, I immediately considered her mine. But if she wants me to ask, I can do that. The problem is, I have a feeling that simply saying, *Hey, will you be my girlfriend?* won't suffice.

"Do you?" Taylor questions, as if she can read my thoughts.

"Yeah, I need to ask her to be my girlfriend in a romantic way."

I slide the pancakes onto our plates and hand her one.

"And how are you going to do that?" she asks, pouring syrup over her pancakes and then having a seat at the island.

"No damn clue," I admit, having a seat next to her. "Any ideas?"

She thinks for a few minutes while we both eat our breakfast, and then her face lights up. "I got it! What if you bought her a pizza and wrote her a note that reads, *This might be cheesy, but will you be my girlfriend?*"

"Seriously? That's the best you got, kid?"

"I saw it in *The Princess Diaries*." She shrugs.

"All those romance books, and you can't think of a single way to ask her out?"

"Well, in most of my books, the guy is either in high school or college and hates her until, like, the last chapter, where he finally admits he's loved her forever … or he's a billionaire, and he takes her somewhere super fancy on a helicopter and makes a grand gesture. And since you're far from a billionaire …"

"Screw this." I shove the last of my pancakes into my mouth and swallow it down with a sip of my coffee. "Kinsley doesn't need a grand gesture. She just wants me to ask, not assume. So, I'll go by her work and ask."

Taylor looks at me like I've lost my mind. "Wow … well, I hope you like being single because with that attitude, that's how you're going to die. Alone and single."

"Dramatic much?"

I drop my plate into the dishwasher and rinse out my glass.

"I'm out of here," Taylor says. "Don't forget I leave tomorrow morning for state."

"Am I driving you to the bus, or do you want to drive yourself?"

Before she started driving, every time she had a cheer competition, I'd drive her to the bus to see her off, but now that she has her own vehicle, she's more independent.

"Nah, you can say goodbye to me tonight or tomorrow morning. I have to pick up Casey, and I'm leaving Snowball at the school."

"All right, have a good day at school."

"Will do! Love you."

"Love you too."

After she takes off, I jump in the shower and contemplate how to go about asking Kinsley to be my girlfriend. I'm still thinking about it while I walk Becky, and by the time I'm in my truck, heading over to Exposed Ink, I've decided that we're adults, and she isn't looking for a grand gesture—just for me to ask—and while my daughter's advice is sweet, we're not in high school anymore like she is.

But before I make it to the shop's front door, I eye the pizza shop two doors down and groan because what if she is looking for a grand gesture?

"Fuck it."

I walk over to the pizza shop, order a large pie so the other people she works with can have a slice, and then ask for a piece of paper I can write on … because apparently, I've become *that guy*.

Nineteen

Kinsley

I'm standing by the desk when Shane walks inside, holding a pizza box in his hand. I wasn't expecting him today—and I know he's not on my client list since I went over it this morning—but I can't help but smile at him surprising me here since he can't call or text me. Well, he can … he just doesn't *know* that he can.

"Pizza?" I ask, stating the obvious.

"Hopefully you haven't had lunch yet," he says, setting the pie down. "I would've called or texted but …"

Scott chuckles, knowing all about Shane wanting my number. "I'm starved."

He reaches over to open the box, but Shane grabs the box first and sets it out of Scott's reach. "Not yet." He glares at Scott, then looks at me, his features softening. "I've tried to think of how to ask you to be my girlfriend since I left your house the other night, and the only thing I've come up with is that I suck at coming up with romantic shit, so I'm just going to throw it out there."

Scott snorts, and I stifle my laugh at the same time my dad walks out to join the party.

"What's going on?" Dad asks, leaning against the wall and crossing his arms over his chest.

"I'm about to ask Kinsley if she'll be my girlfriend," Shane says.

In the corner of my eye, I see my dad's brows hit his forehead because he thinks I'm going to say no.

"Kinsley," Shane begins, "since the moment I saw you all puffy and struggling to breathe, I knew I wanted to make you mine."

The guys laugh, and I shake my head because this just might be the worst speech I've ever heard, but it's also, in a weird way, very sweet.

"You've got this way about you that draws me in, like a bag of Sour Patch Kids. I crave the sour and look forward to the sweet." He steps toward me, and suddenly, it feels like we're the only people in the room.

"Even when you were trying to fight the inevitable and push me away, you still welcomed my daughter into your fold with open arms."

He places a hand on my hip, and hot tears sting my eyes because I wasn't prepared for this. I thought he'd just ask, not give an entire speech.

"I love how creative you are, how passionate you are about your work, and the way you can't stay awake during a movie to save your life."

Dad chuckles, and I quickly glare at him before looking back at Shane.

"But there's so much more I want to know about you. I want to spend every day with you, getting to know you, learning about what you love and hate. I love spending time with you, and when I'm not around you, I wish I were. I meant what I said before—I want to help breathe life into you again because when I get to see you living your life, laughing and smiling and being carefree, it breathes life into me as well."

Shane reaches out and palms my face, and his thumb wipes away a tear I didn't realize had fallen. "Kinsley Bryson, will you be my girlfriend?"

I don't even have to think about it when I choke out a, "Yes," and then jump into Shane's arms and kiss him like we're the only two people in the room.

"Great. Now, can we have pizza?" Scott asks, reaching for the box.

"Sure," Shane says, carrying me over to the desk and setting me down on it.

"What the hell is this?" Scott asks, holding up a paper. "*This might be cheesy, but will you be my girlfriend?*" He glances between Shane and me. "Was this your doing?" he asks Shane.

"Yep," he says with a shrug. "In my defense, Taylor suggested it, and I vetoed it, but then I second-guessed myself and grabbed it in case I needed a grand gesture. That"—he points to the pizza—"was my backup plan."

I bark out a laugh, totally imagining him and his daughter discussing how he could ask me to be his girlfriend.

"It was either that or I rent a helicopter." Shane leans in and kisses me. "Thankfully, this worked because I'm not going to lie. I looked up helicopters, and they're expensive as hell. I'm going to need you to stick with the firefighter trope and stay away from the billionaire ones. I can't have you getting any ideas."

He shoots me a playful wink, and butterflies swarm my belly because—holy shit!—I'm Shane's girlfriend.

"What's going through that beautiful head of yours?" Shane asks, handing me a slice of pizza.

"I never imagined being anyone's girlfriend again," I admit. "I really hope I don't suck at it."

"Hey," he says, "I haven't had a girlfriend since high school, so if we suck at it, at least we can suck at it together."

After we have lunch, my next client arrives, so Shane leaves, but not before inviting me to dinner with him and Taylor tonight. Apparently, she's leaving for a cheer competition so they're having dinner tonight together, and he'd like to introduce me to her formally as his girlfriend.

I tell him he's a goofball, but since my last client is a small tattoo and I should be done by five o'clock, I agree to meet him at his house. But since he doesn't want me walking, he insists on picking me up from work.

"Kinsley!" Taylor rushes over and envelops me in a hug. "I can't believe you're actually dating my dad. This is so awesome. I thought for sure he was going to blow it, but look at him, handling it like a good book boyfriend."

I laugh at her, and Shane rolls his eyes.

"He handled it very well," I tell her, remembering his speech. "You would've been proud." I glance at Shane, who smiles warmly at me.

"Great," he says. "Now that we got that out of the way, let's eat."

He cooked a delicious meatloaf, and while we eat, Taylor tells us all about her upcoming competition and what it will mean if they place.

When we're done with dinner, Taylor helps with the dishes and then takes off to her room—because she and Casey need to go over their weekend outfits—leaving Shane and me to spend some time alone.

He pours me a glass of wine and grabs himself a beer, and we head out back. I haven't been out here yet, and I immediately notice the big yard and beautiful porch, complete with a wooden swing. While Becky runs around the yard, we sit on the swing, me tucked into Shane's side and his arm wrapped around my waist.

Neither of us is speaking, simply enjoying the cool night while sipping our drinks and watching the dog, but it feels nice. Relaxing … for the first time in a long time, I feel content.

"What are you thinking about?" Shane asks after a while, as if he can hear my thoughts.

"I didn't realize how alone I felt," I admit. "I pushed everyone away, and I didn't grasp how badly I'd isolated myself until you came along and pushed back."

"You did what you had to do," he says, leaning in and placing a chaste kiss on my temple. "I looked it up, and they say everyone handles grief differently."

"You looked it up?" I ask, shocked by his admission.

"I needed to know what I was working with," he says, glancing down at me when I look up at him. "I've never been where you are, and I wanted to make sure I didn't cross the line or say something stupid."

Oh, my heart.

Without thought, I set my wineglass on the table and climb into his lap, needing to be closer to him. He immediately catches on and sets his beer down so he can hold me with both hands. With my legs straddling him, I wrap my arms around his neck.

"Thank you," I murmur, my eyes locked on his. "I couldn't see beyond my grief until you came into my life, and for the first time since I lost my family, I can see a future for myself, and it's with you and Taylor. The way you both welcomed me into your life means so much to me. I'm so grateful for your patience and persistence … I just … I feel like I'm living a completely different life."

Shane smiles and then captures my mouth with his, giving me a quick but emotionally filled kiss before he pulls back. "That's all I want, Sour Patch. To live my life with you. To enjoy each other's company. There will be good days and bad, happy and sad, but I want to have them with you."

"I want that too," I tell him, moving my arms down so they're wrapped around his waist and I'm able to rest my head on his chest and inhale his masculine, comforting scent.

Shane tightens his hold on me, and we sit like this for a long time, content with just simply being together.

When my eyes start to drift closed, Shane chuckles, his chest vibrating and making me look up at him.

"As much as I love that I'm comfortable enough for you to sleep on, I should take you home, unless you want to spend the night." He waggles his brows playfully.

"I'd like that, but I don't want to set a bad example for Taylor. We only just started dating, and I think it would be best if we take things slow. For me too."

"I love that about you," he says, tilting my chin and giving me a quick kiss. "I always told myself that whoever I dated would have to accept the fact that I was a single dad. I dated a few women, but we never made it past a few dates before they would make comments about not wanting to deal with another woman's child or saying that it must be rough, raising a teenage girl. One asked if I expected her to fill in the role of Taylor's mother." He shakes his head. "But with you, it's different. Hell, I think you accepted Taylor before you accepted me." He smirks.

"You're not wrong," I say with a laugh. "And those women were stupid because they had no idea what they were missing out on. Taylor is such a breath of fresh air. Anyone would be lucky to have her in their life in any capacity, and the fact that you two come as a package only makes it that much sweeter."

I think about something and then sit up, needing to get this off my chest. "I really like Taylor," I tell Shane. "And I know we don't know what the future holds, but if things don't work out with us, I need you to promise that I can stay friends with her. I mean, if she still wants to."

"Of course," Shane says, his brows furrowed in confusion. "Your relationship with Taylor is between you two, and I would never interfere with that. No matter what happens with us, your friendship won't be affected. But, Sour Patch …"

He slides his hands down to my butt and pulls me closer to him so our bodies are almost flush and our mouths are only inches apart. "Unless you do something crazy, like cheat on me, nothing will make me walk away from you." He traps my bottom lip between his teeth and tugs on it playfully. "I'm in this for the long haul."

Beep. Beep. Beep.

I wake up and reach for my phone, ready to start my day. Last night ended with Shane kissing me goodbye with the reminder that he would see me today.

Only, when I turn off my alarm, I notice today's date … and just like that, everything goes to shit.

Twenty

Shane

Your appointment for Friday, March 15, at 11:00 has been canceled. Please call the office to reschedule.

STARE AT THE EMAIL IN CONFUSION. IT'S BEEN LESS THAN twelve hours since I said good night to Kinsley on her doorstep with the promise of seeing her today. She didn't mention not being at the shop, so either a mistake has been made or something happened between last night and this morning. And of course, I don't have her damn number, so I can't call her directly.

I click the number to the shop, and Scott answers on the second ring.

"Hey, man. It's Shane. My appointment was canceled. Was there a glitch or something?"

"Hey," he says. "It automatically sent that when I canceled it. I was just about to call you to reschedule."

"Did something happen? Is Kinsley okay?"

Scott's quiet for several seconds, telling me something is wrong, before he says, "Sorry, man, I can't give out personal information. Let's just say, today is a bad day."

A bad day? What the hell does that mean?

"Okay, then can I have her number? I'd like to check on her."

"You know I can't do that. If she wanted you to have it, she would've given it to you herself."

"Fine, can you at least tell me where she might be?" From the sound of his voice and his vagueness, something is wrong, and I want—*no, I need* to make sure Kinsley is okay.

"No clue, but her dad mentioned she prefers to be alone on days like today."

More vagueness … great.

"Hold on." There's muffled speaking, and then he says, "You didn't hear this from me, but she likes going to the park to think."

The park …

We only have one main park in town, and it's where I ran into her before when Taylor and I were walking Becky.

"Thanks."

The drive to the park doesn't take long, but when I get there, Kinsley is nowhere to be found. Next, I stop by her place, but she doesn't answer, so I knock on her parents' front door, but nobody's home.

I drive around, looking for her for a while, but when it's clear I'm not going to find her, I head back home, frustrated and worried.

Until I step out of my truck and find Kinsley sitting on my front porch. Her eyes are rimmed red, and her cheeks are splotchy, telling me she's been crying.

I walk over and sit next to her. "I've been looking for you. When you canceled our appointment, I got worried. Drove all over in search of you, but I didn't consider you'd be here."

"I'm sorry," she says. "I didn't realize you had an appointment today. I mean, I probably did, but my brain wasn't all there when I canceled the appointments this morning. I planned to go to the park, but when I was on my way there, I realized I didn't want to be alone." She looks up at me with tears in her eyes. "It's been three years."

I don't need to ask what she's talking about because I already know. Three years since her late husband and daughter died.

"Three years," she says again. "And it still hurts so damn much. But for the first time, I didn't want to be alone. I wanted to be with you."

I hate that she's hurting, but my heart soars at the thought that while I was looking for her all over, assuming she wanted to be alone and was pushing me away, she was sitting right here, wanting me the entire time.

"Tell me what you need, Kins."

"You," she says softly. "I just need you."

"Done."

I lift her into my arms and carry her into my house and go straight for my en suite bathroom. Taylor's gone for the weekend, so I don't bother shutting the bedroom door since I know we won't be interrupted.

I set her on the counter while I run the hot water in the tub, then go to Taylor's bathroom to grab some necessities since she's got tons of girlie shit, like bubble bath stuff and candles.

After getting everything set up, I turn the music on my phone on soft and then go about stripping Kinsley out of her clothes. She's quiet and withdrawn the entire time, but she goes into the tub willingly.

"Join me," she murmurs, her glassy eyes pleading.

I wasn't planning to, wanting to keep it about her and not us, but when she looks at me like that, there's nothing I wouldn't give her.

"Of course," I say, quickly getting undressed and then sliding in behind Kinsley so she's able to lean against me.

I had my bathroom renovated when I bought the house, so the tub is a decent size and fits us both easily. With the music playing, we sit in silence for a few minutes. I use the silkiness of the water to rub my hands up and down her arms, hoping I'm comforting her, and when she sighs further into me, I know it's working.

"Tell me about him," I say, continuing to wash her.

She momentarily tenses up, and I wonder if I said the wrong thing. Another guy might be jealous or resentful that his girlfriend loves another man, regardless that he's no longer here, but I accept that Kinsley's heart will always be filled with love for other people. Luckily, she has a huge heart that can hold love for several people at once.

"He was rough around the edges," she begins. "Came from a shitty home and was lost when he showed up at Forbidden Ink, the tattoo shop that my family owns in the city …"

She goes on to tell me about their friendship and how it eventually turned into something more. Their wedding, moving in together, deciding to have a baby, and the night her life changed for the worse. While she talks, I listen and wash her so she knows I'm paying attention. Nothing I say will change what happened, and really, Kinsley doesn't need me to say anything. She just needs me to listen, to understand, to know that she's safe, talking to me about an important part of her life that will always be a part of who she is.

"I told my therapist about you," she says, shocking me. "I told her that for the first time, because of you, I feel things I didn't think I would ever feel again. Feelings I wasn't sure I ever wanted to feel again."

She glances back at me sheepishly. "I wish I could snap my fingers and move forward, leaving the past where it belongs. I feel like you deserve so much more than a woman who's still hung up on her dead husband three years later."

She goes to turn away, but I grasp her chin, holding her gaze.

"That's not how I see it at all. I'm proud of you, Kins." I lean in and press my lips to hers and then pull back. "Every year, you've spent today alone, and had you chosen to spend today alone, I would've understood because I'm not trying to compete with your past. It's part of what makes you who you are, and I love you exactly the way you are. But the fact that you showed up on my doorstep on your own, trusting me with your broken heart, means the world to me."

Her eyes widen at my use of the L-word, and truth be told, I didn't mean for it to come out like that, but I don't regret it because it's the truth. I love Kinsley Bryson, and I'm going to do everything in my power to show her that.

"Shane." She turns around so she's facing me, and the water in the tub sloshes around, but neither of us pays attention to it, too focused on one another. "I need you to help me forget." She frames the sides of my face. "To remind me that even though *they're* gone, I'm still here, and I deserve to be."

"Kinsley ..." I brush my lips against hers. They're soft and plump, and they taste salty from the tears sliding down her face. "You deserve to be here, and if I have to remind you of that every day for the rest of our lives, I will."

Twenty-One

Kinsley

"YOU DESERVE TO BE HERE ..."

Shane's words permeate deep within me as he cups my jaw, and his mouth gently presses against mine. The kiss starts out slow and tender, until he pushes my lips apart and deepens the kiss, giving me what I need.

"... if I have to remind you of that every day for the rest of our lives, I will."

Craving more of Shane, I slide my palms down his chiseled torso, my fingers exploring every ridge of his six-pack, until I get to the hard length that's bobbing between us.

"Kins," he groans into my mouth when I wrap my fingers around his shaft and pump it up and down, relishing in the velvety-smooth skin. "Fuck, baby, I need to be inside you now."

He grips the curves of my hips and, without preamble, lifts and lowers me onto his cock, causing us both to moan in unison as he stretches and fills me completely.

"You feel that?" he murmurs, locking eyes with me.

"What?" I breathe out, half dazed from the way his cock is filling me.

"This." He presses his hand to my chest, right above my heart. "Your heart is beating wildly." He pushes up from the bottom, and his cock hits a spot deep within me, making me moan. "Your body is on fire." He slides one hand around and reaches between us, his thumb grazing my clit and making me squirm in want.

"You're alive," he says, rubbing my sensitive nub in a way that has my insides clenching. "And every fucking day, I'm going to remind you of that."

"Shane," I choke out, fresh tears welling up in my eyes.

"You're alive," he repeats, continuing to circle my clit with the pad of his thumb. "Now, the question is, are you ready to start living?"

When I don't answer him right away, he brings me to the brink of my orgasm, only to take it away, making me cry out in frustration.

"You want to come?" he says, leaning in and nipping at my bottom lip. "Then, answer me."

He adds a bit of pressure to my clit, enough for me to feel the stirrings of my orgasm. He does it again and again, bringing me to the edge and then pulling me back.

"Shane, please," I beg, knowing what he wants, but unsure if I can give it to him. "You said you'd help me forget."

"But that's not what you really need," he says as he continues to wind me up so tightly that it feels like I'm going to implode if I don't get some relief soon.

"Don't you see, Kins?" He applies more pressure to my clit. "You can't push what happened to the side and pretend it didn't happen. It happened. Two people you loved died, and you survived." His brown eyes lock with mine, and it's as if he reached into my body and tugged on my soul. "And now, it's time for you to live."

My heart pounds against my rib cage as his words penetrate deep, filling the fissures in my heart like a soothing balm. Butterflies swarm my chest, and my head feels fuzzy. It's all too much, yet not enough, and even though I'm scared shitless, as I look into Shane's eyes, there's nothing I want more than to live with this man. So, I give him the only answer I can …

"Yes," I choke out. "I'm ready to live."

His lips curve into a beautiful smile, and then his mouth is back on mine, nipping, licking, sucking, as he breathes life back into me one thrust at a time. His thumb presses against my sensitive clit, and with a couple more skillful strokes, I detonate around him, screaming his name as he takes me straight over the edge with him.

"I want to take you out on a date."

I glance up at Shane from beside him on the bed, wondering if I heard him right because after everything that's happened between us, he wants to take me out on a date?

"Huh?"

I know I'm a bit dazed from all the sex we've had—after we got out of the bath, we rinsed off in the shower, and then after drying off, he carried me to his bed, where he worshipped my body until I couldn't take it anymore and I collapsed against his chest, curled into his side, where we both passed out—but did I hear him right?

Shane chuckles and kisses my forehead. "I said, I want to take you out on a date."

"We are dating," I say with a laugh.

"Exactly." He reaches around and strokes the side of my bare breast, making me squirm. "Yet we haven't gone on a single date."

He rolls us over so he's hovering above me and cages me in with his arms. "What do you say, Kins? Will you go on a date with me … in public?"

Ah, so that's where he's going with this. We live in a small town, and the second we're seen together, people are going to talk. And before we can even order dinner, everyone will know that Brookside's very own hero and single dad is dating the town's recluse.

"I don't know," I say in a serious tone that has his face falling. "If I'm seen out with you in public, people will assume that I'm off the market, and now that I'm ready to move forward, I'm not sure I want to tie myself down to one man."

His eyes narrow in confusion, and as much as I'm having fun messing with him, I can't keep my straight face going. He's just too damn sweet.

"I'm just kidding," I say with a laugh, reaching up and poking his hard stomach with my fingertip. "Yes, Shane, I would love to go on a date with you in public."

"You brat." With one hand holding himself up, his other reaches between us and tickles my side, making me bark out a laugh. "Keep that shit up, and I'm going to lock you up in here and never let you go."

"Mmmm," I moan, pulling his face down to mine. "Is that a threat or a promise?"

I wrap my legs around his torso, and because we're both naked, he slides right in, both of us groaning in unison.

"A promise," he says against my lips as he slides in and out of me. "Definitely a promise."

"Is that your stomach grumbling?"

Shane rolls me onto my back and glances down at me with a frown while I blink several times, attempting to wake up.

"Well …" Before I can finish, my stomach grumbles again, and I giggle. "We never ate last night," I point out.

"Jesus." He frowns. "I've only been a boyfriend for like a day, and I'm already sucking at this."

"Oh my God, stop," I say with a laugh, pulling his face down to mine for a chaste kiss. "You do not suck. Besides, the amazing orgasms you gave me last night more than made up for you not feeding me."

"It was good sex," he agrees, peppering kisses along my jawline.

When my stomach growls loudly, we both laugh.

"That's it," he says. "Jump in the shower, and I'll make us breakfast before you wither away."

I roll onto my stomach, torn between wanting to remain in his comfy bed and getting out of it so I can eat.

"Now," he demands, playfully smacking my ass.

"Fine." I groan, crawling to the edge and rolling off. "But how about instead of cooking, you shower with me, and then we can go out?"

I waggle my brows, and Shane smirks. "I like the way you think."

After our shower and the two orgasms he gave me while in there, we get dressed—me in my jeans from yesterday and a shirt of Shane's he lent me since I hadn't planned on spending the night and have no clothes—and then head out.

Since we're both starved, we head to Sunny Side Up Café to get something to eat, agreeing to stop at my place afterward so I can change.

I usually work on Saturdays, but Scott canceled all my appointments until Tuesday when he realized he scheduled me on the anniversary of Brandon's and Brenna's deaths.

"I was thinking," Shane begins, but before he can finish his thought, he's caught off guard by the sound of my mom's voice.

When we look over, we find her and my dad sitting at a booth.

"Kinsley," Mom coos, standing and hugging me. "I'm so happy to see you. You look … radiant."

In other words, she's shocked and thrilled to see that I'm not drowning in the darkness. When she texted me yesterday, asking if I was okay, I told her I was at Shane's so she wouldn't worry. All I got back was a blushing emoji.

"I look like I haven't changed my clothes since yesterday," I mutter, making her laugh.

"Shane," Dad says, sliding out of the booth and giving him a handshake. "It's good to see you."

"You too," Shane says.

"What are you two up to today?" Mom asks.

"First, I need to feed this one," Shane tells her with a laugh as he pulls me into his side and kisses my temple. "Apparently, we forgot to eat last night and …" At the insinuation of us being too busy to eat, Shane's eyes go wide, and his face—what's not hidden under his facial hair—heats up in an adorable shade of pink, making my mom giggle and my dad snort out a laugh.

"What I mean is …" he stammers.

"We're hungry," I finish.

"Why don't you join us?" Mom suggests. "We only just sat down."

I glance at Shane, unsure if he's okay with that, but without looking at me, he slides into the booth across from my parents and pulls me down next to him.

"Where's Taylor?" Mom asks after the waitress takes our drink order.

"At a cheer competition," I tell her. "Look how pretty she looks!"

I pull out my phone and click on the picture she sent me this morning, then turn it around to show my mom.

"Aww, I love it," Mom says.

"She sent you that?" Shane asks, glancing at the picture. "What the heck? She hasn't even texted me this morning," he grumbles. "What am I, chopped liver?"

"I'm sure she's going to text you," I tell him.

Just as he pulls his phone out, it dings with an incoming text.

I look over and see a text from her, letting him know she'll be cheering all day and to wish her luck and she'll FaceTime him later.

"See?" I say with a laugh. "She just likes me more."

I stick out my tongue playfully, and he mock glares.

"You have such a sweet girl," Mom tells Shane. "She reminds me a lot of Kinsley when she was younger."

"Thank you," he tells her. "I definitely got lucky."

"It's not luck," Dad says. "It's good parenting. Give yourself some credit."

Shane nods. "Yeah, but she makes it easy. I was worried that she would rebel, especially since her mom isn't around much, but she's a damn good kid."

"Well, I think all kids rebel at some point or another," Mom says.

"I didn't," I note.

"Really?" Dad says. "I can recall a few times you rebelled."

"Do tell," Shane says with a glint in his eye.

"Remember when you were sixteen and you snuck into the tattoo shop and tattooed your boyfriend?" Dad says with a smirk.

"Oh my God, am I ever going to live that down?" I groan. "In my defense, he was a football player and a senior, and I was young and dumb and trying to impress him."

"His parents nearly flipped a gasket when he came home with a tattoo of the school's mascot," Mom says with a laugh.

"Thankfully, he was eighteen, and Kinsley made him sign a waiver," Dad adds with a chuckle.

"Oh yeah!" Mom laughs. "What about the time she drew all over Natalia and the other models right before a fashion show?"

Dad laughs. "Her aunt Celeste was so pissed that her models had *Free the Tatas* written on them with lifelike breasts underneath, but it was too late to try to cover it up, so they all had to walk the runway with it."

"Hey!" I exclaim. "That was for a good cause."

Mom laughs. "Remember the time she body-painted—"

"Okay, enough about me," I say, leaning over and covering my mom's mouth. "Where the heck is the waitress? I'm starved."

I glance around, and Shane laughs.

"I like learning about you," he says, tucking me into his side and kissing my cheek.

One of the things I love about Shane is how touchy-feely he is. It doesn't matter where we are or who we're with, he always shows me how much he cares, whether it's holding my hand or kissing me. I always feel cherished.

"Well, in the future, anything you want to know, ask me, not them." I glare at my parents, who don't even have the decency to look ashamed.

"Are you two doing anything fun today?" Mom asks.

"After I get her fed," Shane says, "I'm going to convince her to go away for the night with me."

I whip my head around to look at him. We discussed going on a date, but going away wasn't mentioned.

"Where?" I ask.

"I don't know." He shrugs. "Maybe we can find a last-minute hotel on the beach."

"You guys should go to the cottage in the Hamptons," Mom says. "When was the last time you were there, Kins? It's probably been …" She trails off, her eyes widening as she connects the dots at the same time I do.

The last time I was there was with …

"Actually …" She clears her throat, shooting me an apologetic look.

"Am I missing something?" Shane asks.

"The last time I was at the cottage in the Hamptons was with Brandon," I tell him. "We went there for a short vacation while I was pregnant."

I can see my parents gaping at me, shocked that I'm speaking so candidly with Shane, but I meant what I said last night. I'm ready to live my life with him, and that means accepting the past instead of running from it.

If I avoid everywhere Brandon and I went, we'd have a lot of places I would have to avoid, and that's not what I want for Shane or me.

"We should go," I tell him. "It's free, and I haven't been there in years." And then I consider what I just said and pedal back. "Unless that would be really awkward and …"

"Hey, stop," Shane says gently, smiling softly at me. "A trip to the Hamptons sounds good, as long as you're up for it."

He reaches down and squeezes my hand, and my heart swells in my chest.

"I think that would be nice," I admit.

I can't avoid the cottage forever, and going there and making new memories with Shane sounds kind of perfect.

"Then, we'll go," Shane says, glancing at my parents. "Thank you for the invite. I'm ashamed to admit that even after living in Brookside all these years, I've never made the trip to the Hamptons despite it being only a couple of hours away."

"I know it well," I tell him, snuggling into his side. "I can be your tour guide."

I glance up at him, and he smiles down at me for a second before he leans in and gives me a quick kiss that has me craving more.

"I can't wait," he murmurs against my lips.

When we break apart and look at my parents, my dad is smiling, and my mom legit has tears in her eyes, and for the first time, it really hits me how down I've been these past few years and how worried they've been about me.

"Do you guys want to go?" I offer.

"No, we're good," Mom says. "You two go and have a good time. Once it's warmer out, we'll have to do a long weekend and invite everyone. I'm sure I can convince your brother and sister to join us."

"Looks like it's just you and me," I tell Shane, kissing the corner of his jaw.

"I can't wait."

Twenty-Two

Shane

AN INSECURE MAN WOULD PROBABLY BE WORRIED THAT he's about to spend the night in a place where his girlfriend and her late husband spent time together while she was pregnant with their baby. Where they no doubt had sex and created fond memories. And, yeah, there's a small part of me that hopes what Kinsley and I are doing is enough that she doesn't wish Brandon were here instead of me, but mostly, I'm just so damn proud of the strides she's made since I met her. She's come a long way in a short time, and I'm happy that I get to witness it.

"This is it," Kinsley says, stepping into the cottage that she told me has been in her family since her parents got married and her dad bought it for her mom as a wedding present.

"It's beautiful," I tell her, wrapping my arms around her from behind.

"Do you want a tour?" she asks, glancing up at me.

"Maybe later." I lean down and kiss her exposed shoulder and then the curve of her neck. "Right now, I just want you to show me to a bed so I can get lost in you."

"That sounds perfect."

Taking my hand, she guides me down the hall, but before I can toss her onto the bed, her phone rings.

"Oh, it's Taylor!" she says, jumping onto the bed and answering the call. "Hey, you! How's it going?"

"We did so good!" Taylor exclaims, her face covered in stage makeup and her hair up in a tight ponytail. They must've just finished performing. "We won't know the results until later, but I'm almost positive we're going to place."

"That's awesome, Tay!" I move into the picture so my daughter can see me.

"Hey, Dad!" Taylor grins before her brows furrow. "Where are you guys? That doesn't look like our house."

"We're at Kinsley's family's cottage in the Hamptons," I tell her. "We'll be back before you."

"Ohh, look at you, taking things to the next level." She waggles her brows, and I shake my head. "At this rate, I'll be calling Kinsley my stepmom by the end of the year."

She cackles at her joke, but I notice the way Kinsley stiffens. She forces out a laugh, but something about what Taylor said doesn't sit right with her.

"So, what happens if you place?" Kinsley asks, changing the subject.

"We go to Nationals, which is in Daytona Beach, Florida, and then Worlds, which is in Orlando. If we make it to Worlds, I plan to beg my dad to take me to Disney."

I chuckle. "You don't have to beg. We can go even if you don't make it. Gotta get a few trips in before you leave me for college anyway."

Taylor grins. "Kinsley, you'll go, right? To Nationals and Worlds if we make it?"

"Umm," she chokes out, thrown off by Taylor's request, "I should be able to."

"Awesome." Somebody says something to Taylor, momentarily distracting her. "I gotta go, guys. But I'll call you tonight once the results are in. Love you. Bye."

Without waiting for us to respond, Taylor ends the call.

"That girl has so much energy," Kinsley says with a light laugh.

"Since the day she was born." I pluck her phone out of her hand and toss it onto the nightstand. "Now, where were we?"

She leans back and bites her bottom lip, her eyes looking at me with lust. "I think we were about to make new memories here."

"Ah, yes." I pull her shorts down her thighs and spread her legs. "Starting with an orgasm so good that every time you think of this place, your only thought will be how hard I made you scream my name."

I drop her shorts onto the floor and lie on my stomach, spreading her legs so her perfect pussy is at eye level. Then, with the determination of a starved man, I go to town on her pussy. She's already wet, and it doesn't take long until she's coming all over my tongue and fingers.

"Shane, I need you," she says, dragging her fingers through my hair.

Quickly discarding my clothes, I climb on top of her, and she pulls my face to hers, kissing me like she's desperate for the connection. When she tastes herself on my lips, she moans and clenches her thighs, clearly turned on.

"Fuck me, please," she demands, licking the seam of my lips as her ankles dig into my ass and she pushes me toward her.

I slide in without any resistance, fucking her slow and deep.

Every time with Kinsley is amazing, but when she pushes me onto my back and climbs on top of me, giving me access to her luscious tits while she rides me, I'm pretty sure this is what heaven looks like.

"Fuck, baby," I groan as she swivels her hips, finding the spot she needs to get herself off.

With one hand tweaking her nipple, I reach between us to massage her swollen clit. It's the push she needs, and within seconds, we're both coming as we moan each other's name.

"My God, that was so good," she sighs, her words coming out a bit slurred.

"Damn right it was," I tell her, flipping her onto her back so I'm caging her in. "Because we're good together."

I slide down her body, kissing her rose-dusted nipples, her flat stomach, and each of her hip bones because I can't seem to get enough of her.

I'm about to climb off the bed to go grab her a washrag to clean her up when she lazily parts her thighs and I catch a glimpse of my cum leaking out of her.

"I like this," I say, running my finger along her slit. "You filled with my cum. It's the sexiest thing I've ever seen."

Kinsley lifts onto her elbows, glancing down at me with wide eyes. "Um, Shane," she says, her voice off. "I … I didn't think about it before, but … we haven't been using protection."

It takes me a second to understand what she's trying to say because I'm aware we haven't been using protection. But once my brain wraps around her words, it hits me.

No protection … fuck.

We never even discussed it.

The first time we had sex wasn't planned. We were at Exposed Ink, and one thing led to another, and before we knew it, I was fucking her on the pool table. And every time since then, we're just so busy getting lost in each other that we don't even think to discuss it.

"Are you on birth control?" I ask.

She shakes her head.

"I'm sorry," I tell her, pulling her into my arms so she's straddling my lap. "I didn't even think. It's been a while for me, and I always used protection, but it was never like it is when I'm with you."

"What do you mean?" she asks.

"When I'm with you, it's like all common sense flies out the window."

She smiles softly. "I didn't think about it either," she admits. "Before ... I was on birth control. An implant that lasted three years. And when we decided to get pregnant, I had it removed. I've been so lost in my own head and then lost in you that it didn't cross my mind."

"I mean, that's not necessarily a bad thing," I say with a smirk. "I like that you're lost in me."

"Yeah, but that means we've had sex a bunch of times without using protection, and even though the doctors said that it will most likely be harder to conceive, they didn't say it would be impossible. I don't know my cycles, but from the number of times we've had sex, I could already be pregnant."

The thought of her swollen with my baby has my cock hardening. But we've only just started dating, and Kinsley asked to take things slowly.

"We can't do anything about it now," I tell her, palming her cheek. "But we'll start using protection until you decide if you want to get on birth control. But just know this ..." I lock eyes with her. "I wouldn't be upset if you were pregnant."

Her eyes comically widen. "But ... but ..."

"I know. You're not ready for that, and I respect that. But I know you're the person I want to spend my life with. I've fallen in love with you, Kinsley, and I hope, one day, you'll want a life with me too."

"I don't know if I can do that," she whispers. "I never thought … I didn't consider my future."

"I know, and that's okay. But if at any point you feel like you're ready for more, I need you to know that I want that too. Marriage, babies. I want it all with you."

"But what if I don't want that? Or what if I can't? They said there's a chance …"

"Then, I'm content with you and me and Taylor." I lean in and press my lips to hers. "All I want is you, any way I can have you. Whatever that looks like is completely up to you."

I deepen the kiss, and instead of her pulling away, when my hard cock pokes her ass, she guides me back inside her. With her already full of my cum, she slides down easily, riding me once again.

"Kins," I groan when I'm close, "if you don't want me to come in you, you're gonna have to move now."

Instead of her moving off my lap, she shocks the hell out of me when she pulls my face to hers and fucks me harder, kissing me like I'm the air she needs to breathe as we both find our release.

As we catch our breath, she leans in and nuzzles her face into my neck. "I never thought I'd feel like this again," she murmurs softly.

"Like what?"

"Like I'm not so broken."

"I can't believe it's raining." Kinsley pouts, staring out at the buckets of rain hitting the pool while I make us breakfast.

Yesterday, it was nice out, so we spent some time in the heated pool before we walked down the beach to a local bar and restaurant, where we had dinner and hung out, listening to the band play while we had a few drinks. But today, since the moment we got out of bed, it's been pouring down rain.

"That's New York for you. One minute, it's snowing, and the next, it's ninety degrees. Then, you turn around, and it's pouring outside." I set her bowl of Greek yogurt and iced latte on the island and walk over to her.

"I used to love the rain," she admits, her gaze staying locked on the outside. "Until that night."

I wrap my arms around her from behind, and she sighs into me.

"How can something so beautiful be so devastating?"

I don't answer since I know she's not actually looking for one. She's lost in herself, stuck between the present and past, and all I can do is be there for her until she's back here with me.

"Rain used to make me think of good things, like dancing in the rain, skinny-dipping during a storm."

Through her reflection in the sliding glass door, I can see the silent tears sliding down her cheeks.

"It reminded me of a new day. It's what makes the grass grow and the flowers bloom."

"It can still mean that," I tell her, an idea coming to me.

I reach into my pocket and pull my phone out and find the song I'm looking for. Taylor's played it a million times over the years, and when the words start up, I know I've found the right one.

"Dance with me," I tell Kinsley, pushing the slider open and extending my hand.

She looks at me with confusion etched in her features until her brain wraps around the lyrics of Taylor Swift's "Fearless."

She takes my hand, and even though no words are spoken— both of us letting the lyrics speak for themselves—we can feel the shift in the moment.

I pull her outside, and with the song playing loudly—even over the rain pelting the area—I hold her in my arms and sway to the music.

The rain drenches us, and at first, Kinsley doesn't smile, still lost in her thoughts, but then I spin her around playfully so she glides away from me and then straight back into my arms, and her eyes light up with mirth.

"It's so cold!" she yells, wrapping her arms around my neck as we continue to dance. "But it feels so good."

I bend down and capture her mouth with mine, and she hops into my arms. We dance like this for several minutes, in the cold rain, our bodies and mouths connected, and then I do something she doesn't see coming. I run us toward the pool and jump in.

Kinsley screams as we plunge into the water, and then she's laughing so hard that she can barely catch her breath as she holds on to me for dear life.

Her hair is a mess, and the bit of makeup she put on when she woke up is dripping down her cheeks, yet she's never looked so damn beautiful.

"I can't believe you did that." She shakes her head, her smile still in full force.

"I love you," I tell her, pushing several strands of hair that were sticking to her forehead out of her eyes. "There are going to be good days and bad, but I promise, no matter what happens, I'll be right here, dancing in the rain with you."

I press my lips to hers, and she wraps her arms around me tighter, like I'm her lifeline.

"I want that too," she murmurs against my lips. "I want to dance in the rain with you."

Twenty-Three

Kinsley

"I SHOULD GO," I SAY, MAKING NO MOVE TO LEAVE. We got back to Shane's house a couple of hours ago and have been lounging on his couch, watching reruns of trash TV ever since. He didn't ask if I wanted to be dropped off at home, and I didn't suggest it, not ready for our weekend to be over yet.

Despite the crappy weather, we had an amazing time at the cottage, creating memories that will last a lifetime.

"Or you can stay," Shane says, lifting my chin and kissing me. "Taylor will be home soon, and she'll be excited to see you and tell you all about her competition."

Taylor called us last night to let us know they placed second and would be heading to Nationals, but because everyone was getting ready to go out and celebrate, the conversation was quick.

"Fine," I say, snuggling into his side. "But I'm not spending the night." I glance up and give him the stink eye, making him laugh.

"Whatever you say." He presses a kiss to the top of my head.

His phone goes off, and a few seconds later, he sighs.

"Everything okay?" I ask since Taylor is due to be home any-time now.

"Jamie, Taylor's mom, is coming into town next month to take Taylor on a girls' trip."

"Isn't that a good thing?" I turn slightly so I can look at him while we talk.

"Yeah, it is, as long as she sticks to it. The last time she took her away ended with her working and Taylor begging to come home be-cause she was bored."

"Well, hopefully, she sticks to it. And if she doesn't, we'll get Taylor and have our own fun."

Shane grins, and butterflies erupt in my belly.

When he doesn't say anything, I squirm in my spot.

"What?" I ask, wondering why he's looking at me all funny.

"You said *we*."

"Huh?"

"You said *we'll* go get her and have our own fun. I love that." He cups the back of my head and lifts my face toward his. "I love that you're including yourself."

Before I can say anything, the door swings open, Becky barrels toward the door, barking in excitement, and Taylor stumbles in, dropping her bags on the floor.

"Dad, I'm home!" She glances at us and grins. "Kinsley, you're here!"

"I hope that's okay," I tell her. "I can't wait to hear all about your competition."

"Of course it is," she scoffs. "And based on the cheesy-ass grin my dad's sporting, I have a feeling if you leave, he's going to try to tie you to the bed."

Shane snorts out a laugh, but doesn't deny it.

"Get over here," he says. "Tell us about your weekend."

Taylor scurries over and plops onto the couch with us. "It was so good!" She beams and then proceeds to tell us what seems like every detail from the past three days without taking a breath.

The entire time, Shane holds me, listening intently while rubbing circles on my arm, and I can't help but feel like, for the first time in a long time, I'm right where I belong.

And when the guilt hits, I take a deep breath and push it away.

I can't change the past, but I'm alive, and I deserve to have a future.

Soft kisses flutter against my flesh, forcing me awake. When I pry my eyes open, I find Shane staring at me, a soft smile spread across his handsome face.

"Morning," I croak out, stretching my limbs.

I wasn't planning on spending the night, but I once again fell asleep while we were watching a movie, and instead of insisting Shane take me home, I let him carry me to bed.

"It's a damn good morning," he says with a smirk. "Especially when I get to wake up with you in my bed."

"Don't make a habit of it," I say, trying to give him the best stink eye I can muster up. "Where's Taylor?"

"Already left for school. It's just after ten. You slept in."

Ten? Holy shit, that means I got, like, twelve hours of solid sleep. Maybe I should spend the night more often.

"I should probably get going …"

"Or you could spend the day with me." Shane rolls us over so I'm underneath him. "We're both off today."

"Oh, yeah? And what do you propose we do all day?" I wrap

my legs around his waist and dig my heels into his butt so his body is flush against mine.

"Not sure." He shrugs. "But I think getting naked with you is the perfect thing to do while we figure it out."

He captures my mouth with his, and I nod in agreement since I'm completely on board with starting our day with him inside of me.

And truth be told, I think I would be on board to start every day that way.

"I'm pretty sure days off are supposed to be spent away from the office," Shane says with a chuckle as we walk through the door of Exposed Ink.

I type in the code when the alarm goes off and then lock the door since we're closed.

"This is my sanctuary," I tell him, flipping on the lights and texting my dad so he knows it was me who triggered the alarm. "It was my dream to open my own shop, but after Brandon died, I wasn't even sure I'd be able to tattoo again.

"Thankfully, my dad dragged me out of my depression and insisted we open this place." I glance around at the beautiful shop, proud of what we created.

"Wait, you own this shop?" Shane asks. "I figured you managed it, and I kind of thought your dad might own it …"

"Exposed Ink is all mine. My dad says he's a silent partner, but he never takes a dime from the earnings, and my name is on all the business documents. He only did it because I didn't want him handing me an entire business I hadn't worked for."

"Wow, Sour Patch." He looks at me with awe. "That's incredible."

"Thanks. I always thought I'd open a place in the city, but I've grown to love it here, and I can't imagine inking anywhere else."

We step into my station, and I set my phone on the charger and turn on my playlist. "You ready?" I ask Shane, who looks at me, confused. "To get your tattoo. I canceled on you Friday, so I figured I could do it today."

He groans, sitting in the chair, and I laugh.

"You know, if you don't want to get any more, you don't have to." I step toward him, and he parts his legs, reaching out and gripping the curves of my hips. "You only did this in hope of getting the girl," I taunt playfully.

Shane looks up at me and grins. "And I got the girl."

I lean over and give him a chaste kiss. "You definitely did," I agree. "So, if you don't want to continue …"

"Nah," he says, pulling back. "I do. I was just hoping when we came in here, it was to have some more pool-table sex."

He waggles his brows, and I throw my head back with a laugh.

"Oh, we can still do that … *after* your tattoo."

"Are you bribing me with pool-table sex?" he asks, lifting his sleeve up. "Because if you are, it's totally working."

"What are you doing this weekend?" Shane glances up from his phone as I turn the tattoo gun off and set it on the tray so I can clean it.

"Not sure yet. This guy promised to take me out on a real date, so maybe that will happen."

I smirk, and he chuckles.

"I'm definitely taking you out on a real date," he says. "But

Sunday, the fire station is hosting a family barbecue. Naturally, I'll be manning the grill. Any chance you want to go? Taylor will be there."

I stumble back a bit. "You want me to go?"

"Of course I do."

"But you said it's for families," I say dumbly.

Shane smiles and pulls me into him. "And one day, I hope we will be a family," he murmurs, pressing a kiss to my lips. "But it's not just for families. Plenty of girlfriends and boyfriends will be there. The guys I work with are family. I've been working with some of them since before Taylor was born, and I would love to introduce you to them. They've heard a lot about you and—"

"You talk about me?" I mumble against his mouth.

This has him chuckling. "Kins, I love you. I know you're not on the same page yet, and I'm okay with waiting until you are. I meant what I said about taking it one day at a time. But do you really think guys who I consider family wouldn't know about you? Besides the fact that they've watched me show up to work with new ink"—he smirks—"I talk about you constantly. And they can't wait to meet you."

My heart warms at his words. The truth is, aside from the family I grew up with, I've never been a part of anyone else's family. Brandon's parents sucked, and he was pretty much adopted into our family from the beginning.

The thought of meeting new people is scary, but it's also kind of nice. If they're anything like Shane, I know I'll like them. And I want to be a part of his world.

"Okay," I tell him, dragging my fingers through the back of his hair. "I'll go to the family barbecue with you …"

His face lights up, and he's about to pull back, but I keep him close for what I'm about to say next.

"And Shane …"

My heart pounds in my chest, not because I don't mean the words I'm about to say, but because they haven't been spoken in this context since my husband was alive.

"Yeah?" he asks.

"I love you too."

A beautiful boyish grin spreads across his face. "Day fucking made, Sour Patch. Now, wrap my ink up, so I can eat your pussy on the pool table."

I bark out a laugh. "Such a romantic."

And that's how we spend the rest of the day … with Shane and I showing each other how much we love each other, until we're both sated, and we head home to meet Taylor for dinner.

And it doesn't go over my head that, despite not living with Shane, I refer to his place as home. We agreed to one day at a time, and I thought that would mean taking things slow. But I'm falling for this man, and I have a feeling slow isn't an option.

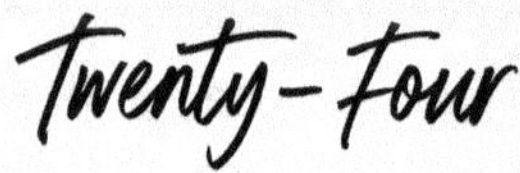

Twenty-Four

Shane

"Nice addition." Eric nods toward the tattoo Kinsley inked on me on Monday when we spent the day together.

"Thanks. The woman is talented. That's for sure."

I can't help the grin that spreads across my face when I think about Kinsley.

Of course, my brother notices. "Judging by the cheesy smile you're sporting, things are going good?"

"Damn good. We're dating."

"Good for you. And Taylor's okay with it?"

"More than okay with it. They bonded over book boyfriends and their favorite authors and never looked back." I chuckle. "Taylor told me straight out that she'd love for Kinsley to be in our life long-term."

"Wait, are you considering asking her to marry you?"

I shake my head. "Kinsley's been through a lot, and she needs for us to take things slow. Don't get me wrong. I'm all in …"

"All in for what?"

I whip my head around and find Kinsley standing there, dressed in her workout gear with her hair up in a high ponytail and her beautiful face free from makeup.

"I'm all in with you," I tell her, grabbing her hand and pulling her toward me so I can give her a kiss. "I was just telling my brother that you've moved me out of the friend zone and into the boyfriend zone."

Kinsley snorts out a laugh. "I don't think you were ever fully in the friend zone," she sasses playfully, making Eric laugh.

"What are you doing here?" I ask, realizing after how dumb my question is. We're standing in my brother's health club, so she's obviously here to work out.

"I signed up for the self-defense class since I don't have any clients until after noon."

"Well, that works out well because I'm teaching that class." I shoot her a wink, and her creamy skin turns a gorgeous shade of pink.

"By the way," she says to my brother, "I'm Kinsley." She extends her hand.

"I'm Eric, this guy's brother and the owner of this place. Well, co-owner. My wife, Katie, owns and runs it with me, but due to the risk of preeclampsia, she's been put on bed rest for the remainder of her pregnancy, which is thankfully only a few weeks away."

"Ugh, that sucks," Kinsley says. "I was anemic while I was pregnant, and it was horrible."

She doesn't realize what she said, and since I haven't told my brother her story, he doesn't know what she's been through. I spot the train wreck before it happens, but I'm not quick enough to prevent it.

"I didn't know you had a baby," he says, glancing from me to her. "How old is he or she?"

Kinsley's eyes widen, her mistake finally hitting her, and she stumbles to figure out how to answer. I don't want to put her business out there, but at the same time, I can't just stand here and leave her to answer him on her own. She's in this position because of me, because I've pushed for her to put herself out there.

"Kinsley—" I begin but stop when she surprises me by placing her hand on my arm and glancing up at me with a soft yet confident smile that tells me she appreciates me saving her, but she's got this.

"Unfortunately, when I was seven months pregnant, I was in an accident and lost my baby girl," she says.

Eric's eyes shine with sympathy. "I'm sorry. I can't even imagine."

"It was hard," she admits as she moves into my side and encircles her arm around my waist. "But your brother has been helping me move forward."

She smiles up at me and then kisses the corner of my jaw, and I swear I fall even deeper in love with this woman.

"I'm glad he could help you," Eric says. "Shane is a good man." He reaches over and squeezes my shoulder. "All right, I have a private session, so I'd better head to the front, but it was nice to meet you," he tells Kinsley. "We should all do dinner at our place one night. Katie's heard a lot about you, and I know she'd love to meet you." He glances back at me. "And Mom and Dad are coming home soon."

"I'd love that," Kinsley says. "It was great to meet you. You have a beautiful health club."

"Thank you."

Once Eric is gone, I pull Kinsley around the corner and into my brother's private office, closing the door behind us.

"Do you know how fucking amazing you are?" I tell her, gently pushing her against the wall.

"What? Why?" she breathes out, her brows furrowed in confusion.

"You're so strong," I say, tipping her chin so she's looking at me. "You've been through hell, yet you keep going, keep fighting."

I capture her mouth with mine in a heated kiss that I'm forced to end far too quickly due to us needing to get to the women's self-defense class I'm instructing and she's participating in.

"Come over tonight. I don't care how late it is. I need to see you." It's been almost two days since I last saw her, and I'm craving everything about her.

"I don't know," she says with a sly grin. "Do you think you deserve for me to come over?"

"Seriously, Sour Patch?" I scoff.

Only instead of her responding, my phone chimes in, "To confirm, you'd like to call Sour Patch."

I pull my phone out of my pocket, confused as to what the hell Siri is going on about, and see that on my screen is the name Sour Patch. Siri—who thought I said, *Siri, call Sour Patch*—is trying to call her.

I press call on my phone, and a second later, Kinsley's phone starts ringing. I glare at her, and she cracks up laughing.

"Are you telling me that I've had your number on my phone this entire time?"

"No, only for a little while."

"Since when?"

She wraps her arms around my neck. "Since I knew I was falling for you."

Fuck, this woman.

"If I didn't have a class to teach …" I shake my head, wondering how pissed my brother would be if I bailed on the class so I could bring Kinsley back to my place and fuck her on every damn surface.

"It will have to wait," she says, stepping away from me. "I've been wanting to take this class. C'mon, boyfriend. You can show me how to fend off an attacker."

She takes my hand in hers, and I follow her to the studio where the class is being held while thinking about two things. One, I would follow this woman anywhere. And two, while I love the fact that she called me her boyfriend, I want to be so much more than that.

"Dad, you home?" Taylor calls out as she slams the front door and stops in the living room.

"You already know I'm home. My truck is in the driveway," I point out, clicking pause on the movie Kinsley and I were watching.

It's Thursday afternoon, and since I'm not working and I got done at the health club earlier and Kinsley's last session ended around the same time, she rode home with me so we could watch a movie and make dinner.

My daughter rolls her eyes like the dramatic teenager she is.

"Dad," Taylor groans. "Focus."

Kinsley laughs, and Taylor grins at her, like she's just noticing that she's sitting next to me.

"Kinsley!" Taylor runs over and throws her arms around Kinsley, making Becky, who was cuddled into Kinsley's side, move to the floor so she can go back to sleep.

"I'm so glad you're here," Taylor says. "This is perfect!"

"That's my daughter's way of saying she's about to con you into whatever idea she's thought up," I note, making Kinsley snort out a laugh and Taylor glare.

"I'm not conning anyone," Taylor says, squishing herself

between Kinsley and the arm of the couch. "You know how we have spring break coming up, right?"

I nod. It's coming up soon. When Taylor was little, she would spend it with my parents, but since she's older, she tends to just work or hang out with her friends that week.

"Mom said her photo shoot is wrapping up earlier than planned, so she's coming into town. And we're going to take a girls' trip to New York City to go shopping and see the museums and stuff. She said we can even go see a Broadway show!"

Taylor's face lights up, and I pray Jamie doesn't fuck this trip up because I'll be the one dealing with a brokenhearted daughter while she's off jet-setting to her next location.

"NYU has opened their college tour dates," she continues, "and one of them is during my spring break, so I was wondering if you could meet us in New York. Mom said she's planning to fly out of JFK anyway, so it would save her the drive back to Brookside, and we could spend a few days in the city, exploring NYU and doing their tour. They said applications will be opening in August, and that's only, like, five months away. Plus, this will mean I won't miss any school."

Her eyes go dramatically wide, and I stifle a laugh that I know she won't appreciate.

"Oh!" she exclaims, glancing at Kinsley, her eyes softening. "The reason why I'm glad you're here is, you have to come. Dad hates the city. He avoids it at all costs. But you said you used to live there, right? And you went to NYU. So, I need you there to show me everything."

"Taylor …" I start, knowing the word *no* isn't in Kinsley's vocabulary when it comes to my daughter.

"I'd love to," Kinsley says before I can finish. "I haven't been there in forever, but, yeah, I know the city like the back of my hand.

I can show you all the great hangouts and places to eat and study. And there are so many cute bookshops. Who knows? Maybe we can make a lover out of your dad." She bumps me playfully, and I shake my head.

"Yes!" Taylor squeals. "That would be awesome! Can we, Dad? Please?"

She flutters her lashes at me, and I chuckle.

"Yeah, let me know the dates you're going with your mom and the date of the college tour, and we'll plan it out."

"Yay!" Taylor throws herself across Kinsley's lap so she can hug me. "Thank you! Thank you! Thank you!"

She clambers off the couch, her phone in her hand. "I'm going to text Mom and let her know. I have to get to work. Thank you! Love you!"

And like the tornado she is, she's out the door as quick as she came.

"Wow," Kinsley says with a light laugh. "She's …"

"A lot?"

"No." She shakes her head. "Passionate. I love that. She's out-going and smart and so … adult. You've done such a good job with her," she says, snuggling into my side. "I know you think she might be affected by her mom being gone, but because of you, she's thriving."

I wrap my arm around her and grab the remote to turn the movie we were watching back on. "You spending the night?" I ask.

"Actually, I think I'm going to go home." She glances up at me apologetically. "I have no clothes, and we both work in the morning."

It's on the tip of my tongue to tell her she should just move in here, and then the problem would be solved, but she'd probably freak out and run. So, instead, I throw the remote to the side and flip her onto her back so I'm hovering above her.

"Then, I'd better make the most of the time I have with you."

Me: What are you wearing?

I hit Send on the text and chuckle, knowing this text is going to go one of two ways—Kinsley will either go along with it or tell me to go fuck myself. Either way, it'll be worth whatever response she gives me because I finally have her number.

Well, technically, I've had her damn number for quite some time. But now, I know I have it and can text or call her anytime I want. I've actually known that I've had it for a couple of days, but since she's been with me, this is my first time using it.

The bubbles appear and then disappear, and for a moment, I second-guess myself because what if she thinks I'm being serious and questions the man she's been spending time with?

Shit. I really didn't think this through.

I click on the text box, ready to backtrack, when the most breathtaking image comes through of Kinsley. She's lying in what looks like her bed, based on her position. Her face looks freshly washed and moisturized—the way it does when she's done using her skin care stuff when she's at my place. She's smiling, and her shiny lips look plump and kissable. I can't see too far down since it's a selfie, but she's sporting a tank top that shows off the swells of her breasts, making my mouth water.

Fuck, I hate being away from this woman. If she were with me, I wouldn't have to settle for a picture of her. I could hold her and touch her and kiss her all I wanted.

My text was initially meant to be flirty, but when I click to respond, my tone has changed.

Me: I miss you.

She insisted on going home to sleep at her own place because we both work in the morning, but I really wish I had pushed her to stay.

Sour Patch: I miss you, too, but I'll see you on Sunday for the BBQ.

Me: What about Saturday?

Sour Patch: I have to work all day, and my cousin Natalia is in town. We're going out for drinks. Hopefully, this time, it doesn't end with me needing to be brought to the hospital. <silly face emoji>

I hate that I won't see her until the barbecue, but I love that she's going out with her cousin. She deserves to get out and have a good time.

Me: Don't make me come over there and spank you.

It's a joke, but when she responds, my cock doesn't find it funny.

Sour Patch: Don't tease me with a good time.

Me: Keep it up, and you'll be getting a knock on your door.

Sour Patch: I know that's not true because you hate leaving Taylor home alone when you don't have to.

Me: I might just need to make an exception.

Sour Patch: I'm falling asleep. This sex-crazed maniac fucked me until I could barely walk earlier. If I disappear, it's because I fell asleep.

I can't help but grin at her message because she's not wrong. But in my defense, Kinsley is just as insatiable as I am when it comes to sex. Before her, I didn't understand why people put such an emphasis on sex. Not that I haven't had my fair share of sex, and plenty of it was good. But there's something different about being intimate with the person you love, the woman you want to spend your life with. Every time with her always feels like more.

Me: Good night, Sour Patch. Sweet dreams.

When she doesn't respond, I laugh, knowing she's already asleep. And then I go to sleep as well, wondering how soon is too soon to ask her to move in with me so I never have to sleep without her again.

Twenty-Five

Kinsley

"Y ou look different," Natalia says, dragging her gaze along my body, scrutinizing every inch of me.

"It's because she got laid," Mom says with a giggle, making my aunts, Celeste and Willow, join her.

I thought I was only meeting Natalia at The Black Cat, but it turned into a girls' night when our moms and Willow crashed.

"Mom," I groan, glaring at her.

"What?" She shrugs. "It's just us girls."

"So, is this thing with you and …"

"Shane," Mom answers Willow. "His name is Shane, and he's a single dad, firefighter." She waggles her brows, and my aunts laugh.

"I'm going to need to get massively drunk to get through tonight," I murmur to Natalia, who laughs.

"Well, to take the heat off Kins, I've met someone," Natalia says, making everyone look at her. "His name is Kevin, and he's—"

"Oh my God!" Celeste cuts in. "Is he one of the attorneys on retainer for Leblanc?"

"Yeah." Natalia blushes. "I've been working with him on a case, and we've gotten close."

"Oh, honey!" Celeste wraps her arms around her. "I can't wait to meet him. He seems very nice over the phone."

"He is," Natalia says.

While she tells us all about Kevin, I think about the fact that for the first time, instead of being jealous or envious of someone finding love, I feel like I can relate to them.

We spend the night drinking and dancing and talking about guys, and when Shane texts me, telling me that he's thinking about me and is hoping I'm having a good night, I'm drunk enough to respond with something flirty.

> Me: I'm having fun, but I think I would be having more fun if I were with you right now.

And because Shane knows me too well, he replies with: How much have you had to drink?

> Me: Enough to make me hot and horny.

"Are you sexting with your boyfriend?" Natalia asks with a knowing smirk.

"What? No." I shake my head, but she just laughs since my translucent skin is no doubt bright red and giving me away.

"I heard he's getting a sleeve done from you," Willow says over the music.

"Yeah." I laugh. "He was a tattoo virgin. It's been fun, getting to create something cool for him."

I pull up the most recent photo to show her, and while I'm

explaining what each piece means, Shane must respond because she snorts out a laugh.

"Oh, to be young again," Willow says. "Speaking of which, I think I'm going to call it a night. It's way past my bedtime."

"Me too," Mom and Celeste agree at the same time.

"What?" Natalia pouts. "It's still early. You wanted to crash, and now, you're bailing early?"

"Sorry, honey," Celeste says, kissing Natalia's cheek and then mine. "You look wonderful, Kins. I'm so glad to see you so happy."

"Thanks," I tell her.

After saying goodbye to my mom and Willow, who I promise to have lunch with soon, I pull up my messaging thread and find the reason for Willow's laughter.

> Shane: Just say the word, and I can have you screaming my name.

With a smirk splayed on my face, I type out my reply.

> Me: Don't make promises you can't keep.

"So, how serious are things with you two?" Natalia asks, leaning over and trying to read my messages.

I close out of it quickly, wondering how Shane will respond.

"He told me he loves me … and I said it back."

Natalia's eyes widen. "Wow, coz, that's pretty serious."

"Yeah," I admit, taking a sip of my drink. "I think I'm going to move out of the pool house."

"Are Aunt Quinn and Uncle Lachlan giving you a hard time?"

"No, not at all. And honestly, we spend most of our time at Shane's since he has Taylor. But I think it's time. I want a real place I can call home. A place with a separate kitchen and a dining room I can decorate. A room for a library …"

"I get it," Natalia says. "I told Mom I want to slow down on the traveling. I think I'm ready to settle down."

"Wow, are you and Kevin talking marriage and babies?"

"Yeah," she says with a soft smile. "What about you? I know after everything, you said you didn't want any of that again, but …"

"I think I'd like another baby one day. Shane and I have talked about it since we haven't been exactly careful. The doctors said it will most likely be harder for me to conceive, so I'm pretty sure we're okay, but I've made an appointment to get on birth control anyway."

"Well, if you need anyone to help you find a place, I love house shopping."

"I might hold you to it. Now …" I tip my drink back and down it in one fell swoop, then drop it onto the table. "What do you say we dance?"

Natalia's eyes light up. "I say, hell yeah!"

She downs her drink, and then we head onto the dance floor. On our way, I spot Shane's friend Trudy, who waves and then walks over.

"I heard we'll be seeing you tomorrow at the station barbecue."

"Yep, should I bring something? I asked Shane, but he just said all I need to bring is myself." I playfully roll my eyes, and Trudy laughs.

"He's probably just so excited that you're going." Trudy grins. "We're all happy he's finally found someone. The man has always been such a recluse when it comes to women. I tried setting him up too many times to count, but everyone was a dud. Now, we know why …"

"Why?" I ask, not really wanting to think about Shane dating other women even if that's ridiculous since we both had lives before each other.

"Because he was waiting on you, sweet girl."

"Damn right I was," a masculine voice says, making me twirl around.

Because of the drinks I've had, I stumble slightly, and Shane catches me.

"What are you doing here?" I breathe.

"Keeping my promises." He winks, and I swear my panties dampen.

Trudy laughs, and Natalia snickers.

"I think that means it's time to call it a night," Natalia says.

"Don't leave on my account," Shane says. "I am one hundred percent on board with watching you dance."

He pulls me into his arms, so my back is flush against his front. In this position, I can feel his hard length pressing up against me, and I can't help but rub my backside against him.

My face heats up, and Natalia laughs.

"Neither of you will make it through a single song without jumping each other's bones. Let's go. Maybe Kevin will be up still, and we can have phone sex." Natalia winks playfully, and I groan at how vocal and open my damn family is.

Shane insists on taking Natalia back to her parents' place, and thankfully, it's a small town because the entire drive, all I can think about is how badly I want Shane.

He's dressed casually in a pair of jeans with a blue shirt that has his station's logo in the corner. The shirt isn't super tight on him, but it showcases his toned arms and shows off the ongoing tattoo I've been working on.

"Like what you see?" Shane smirks when he catches me looking at him.

"I love knowing that I'm the only person who has inked you," I admit despite Natalia being in the back seat. Then, a thought occurs to me. One that has my blood boiling. "You'd better not let anyone but me finish that sleeve."

Shane grins and reaches over, taking my hand in his. "You think I'd let anyone touch me but you?" he scoffs. "Not happening."

"I need to get out of this truck before it combusts with the sexual tension that's filling the space from you guys," Natalia whines.

Shane pulls into her driveway, but before Natalia gets out, she leans into the front between us. "I expect a thank-you in your wedding speech since I'm the reason you two met and fell in love. You're welcome." She leans over and kisses my cheek and then hops out of the truck, slamming the door behind her.

"I like her," Shane says.

"Me too."

"But you know what I like even more?"

"What?"

"Time alone with you," he says, his lust-filled gaze searing into me. "Taylor is spending the night at her friend's, so we have the place to ourselves."

"Mmm." I scoot closer to him. "Looks like I'll be screaming your name after all."

"Damn right you will be," he says, putting the truck into reverse. "Several times."

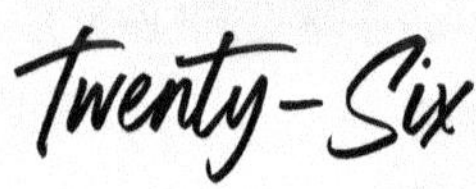

Twenty-Six

Kinsley

"THERE'S A LOT OF PEOPLE HERE," I SAY, NOT REALIZING I said the words out loud until Shane tightens his hold on my hand.

"It's for the entire station," he explains. "I work shift A with four other guys, but there are four shifts at our station, plus everyone's families."

I nod in understanding, keeping quiet since there's a nervous lump in my throat. We live in a small town, and news travels quickly, so the moment I moved into my parents' pool house, everyone knew about the accident. It's one of the reasons why I barely left, aside from going to the shop a couple of years later. Everywhere I went, people, especially moms who were my age, would shoot me sympathetic looks while elderly women would offer me their condolences and bring my mom dishes for me. It was all too much. I never knew what to say, so I stopped leaving so I wouldn't have to say anything.

Honestly, I'm surprised Shane didn't know my story before I told it to him. The only reason I can guess is because he's not one to gossip. He seems to stay in his own lane, focusing on himself and his daughter.

"Hey," Shane says. "Are you okay?" He stops before we make it to where everyone is hanging out and looks at me with concern. "If you don't want to be here …"

"I do," I whisper. "I want to be here."

And that's the truth. I want to be here for him and Taylor, who got home this morning and hugged me tightly, telling me that she got in for the campus tour at NYU and how excited she is to see the city through my eyes. I want to be a part of their family, to make them as happy as they make me.

"Okay," Shane says, the furrow in his brow deepening.

I hate that he feels like he has to worry about me. That, instead of simply enjoying the barbecue, he needs to make sure I'm okay. I know he says I'm strong, but sometimes, I feel really damn weak.

"If anything changes, if you want to leave … just let me know, and we'll go. I'm off today, so I don't have to be here."

He leans in and presses a soft kiss to my lips, and I sigh into his touch.

"Thank you," I whisper against his lips.

He introduces me to several people, whose names I'll sadly never remember because there are too many people, and then he grabs us a drink.

"Evans," a gentleman yells. "You ready to get this grill going?"

"Duty calls," Shane says, giving me a quick kiss on my cheek. "Want to join me?"

"Sure."

I don't know anyone, and Taylor immediately took off to chat with people she knows.

We go inside the station, and Shane gives me a quick tour of the place. It looks more like a house than what I'd imagine a fire station would look like.

When he shows me where he sleeps, I can't help but give him a hard time.

"Is this where you lie in bed and think of me?"

I plop onto the mattress and bounce a little, and Shane groans.

"You know I think of you all the time," he says, pulling me back up and pushing me gently against the wall. "But I try not to think of you like that while I'm here since I'm surrounded by four other guys, and it would suck to get a hard-on and not be able to do anything about it."

He rubs his pelvis against me, and I feel his bulge forming.

"Well, I'm here now." I reach down and cup him through the material of his shorts. Then, after unzipping them, I pull his hard length out.

Dropping to my knees, I give his swollen head an open-mouthed kiss and then slide his velvety-smooth shaft in and out of my mouth.

"Oh fuck," he groans, which spurs me on to take him all the way down my throat.

"What do you say, Evans?" I glance up from giving him head. "Think you can be quick and quiet?"

"Oh, Sour Patch." He chuckles. "You're the one who's going to be screaming my name."

He pulls me to my feet and slants his mouth against mine as he lifts me against the wall, pushes my jean skirt to my hips, and shoves my panties to the side.

A few minutes later, true to his word, we're both moaning

each other's name as Shane fucks me against the wall until we find our release.

"I'm never going to be able to sleep in here again without thinking about fucking you against the wall," he says as he carries me to the bathroom so we can get cleaned up.

"Good." I kiss the corner of his jaw. "I like knowing that you're thinking about me because I'm always thinking about you."

The boyish grin he grants me causes butterflies to attack my chest.

Once we're cleaned up, he finishes showing me around, and then we head to the kitchen. He makes the patties for the burgers and prepares the chicken for the grill while I cut up the veggies. Then, we take everything back outside to where the grill is.

"Shane!" a petite woman says, waddling over, looking like she's ready to pop, with a gentleman who's sporting an identical shirt to the one Shane is wearing, telling me he's a firefighter as well.

"Sandra." Shane gives her a kiss on her cheek. "Kinsley, this is Sandra and David Fowler. David works the same shift as me."

"It's nice to meet you," I tell them.

"Actually," David says, "we already met. I was with Shane when you had that allergic reaction."

"Oh," I breathe, mortified.

Shane chuckles and pulls me into his side. "I hate that you ingested raw fruit, but I'm damn glad you forgot your EpiPen," he says, making everyone laugh.

While Shane grills the burgers and chicken, I help a few other women set up the side dishes on the serving tables.

Once the food is ready, everyone flocks over, making their plates. Since Shane is cleaning the grill, I make us each a plate and then have a seat.

"Hey!" Taylor drops into the seat next to me. "I'm starved."

She bites into her burger and then moans. "So good. Dad is seriously the best cook."

"That he is," I agree, taking a bite of my chicken. "Have you finished the new Evaline Winters book yet?"

"Oh my God, I'm reading it now!" she says, though it comes out muffled since her mouth is full.

"Taylor," Shane chides, sitting across from us. "Don't speak with your mouth full."

Taylor rolls her eyes but waits until she's done chewing before she continues, "That book is making me so mad. How far along are you? I don't want to give you any spoilers."

"I already finished it," I admit sheepishly.

"What? How? It's so freaking long!"

"Yesterday, I had to draw up a few designs for some upcoming appointments, so I was listening while I was drawing."

"I feel like that's totally cheating," Taylor says, "but also kind of brilliant."

"Reading is reading," I tell her with a shrug. "E-book, paperback, audiobook … doesn't matter."

"Fine," she concedes, "I'll give it to you, but that means I get to bitch because seriously, that hero is making me so mad. How does a man so stupid run such a successful business? The miscommunication trope is the worst," she whines in between taking bites of her food. "Like, you run all these businesses, but you can't just talk to her?"

Shane chuckles. "It's a guy thing."

"No." Taylor shakes her head. "That's a lame excuse. Be better."

We both laugh and then continue to eat while Taylor spends the next twenty minutes listing everything that's wrong with the book. And since she's completely right about all of it, all I can do is agree.

"Hey, Evans!" Fred, another firefighter Shane introduced me to earlier, calls out. "Come be on my team, so we can kick these guys' butts."

Shane glances from Fred to me hesitantly, looking like he's unsure if he wants to leave me. While I appreciate him staying by my side all afternoon, I also want him to enjoy himself.

"Go," I insist. "I'm good. I can watch you play and ogle you from here."

Shane chuckles. "All right. I'll be back." With a kiss that promises there's more to come later, he gets up and runs over to join the guys.

I'm watching them play while nursing my lemonade when a woman walks over and introduces herself as Pamela. I recognize her as one of the women who attends the yoga classes Mom and I have been to at the health club.

"I must admit," she says, taking a sip of wine cooler and having a seat next to me, "I was holding out hope that Jamie would pull her head out of her ass and put her family back together, but she's clearly too late."

"Jamie?" I ask in confusion because there's only one Jamie I know and …

"Shane's ex." She shakes her head like she can't believe I don't know who she's talking about. "We were friends in high school."

"Right." I nod, dreading where this conversation is going and wishing Shane would come back to save me, but he's too distracted by trash-talking with the other guys. "Haven't they been broken up for a while though?"

Shane said she took off when Taylor was a baby.

"Technically," she says, lowering her voice, like she's revealing a secret. "But everyone knew they would still hook up when she came into town." She giggles, and her drink sloshes out of her bottle and onto her hand and dress. "Whoops."

She laughs it off like she's not a drunken mess, and I force a smile, feeling sick to my stomach.

"Anyway," she continues, "with Shane never dating, we all thought maybe one day …" She leans in closer, and more of her drink spills. When it almost hits me, I stand, having had enough. "But it looks like he's moved on," she finishes, standing right along with me, clearly not taking the hint.

"Yeah, he did," Taylor says, appearing out of nowhere. "And you saying that stuff is a bitch move, Pamela. Just because your husband is screwing the nanny and you don't want to admit your perfect family isn't so perfect doesn't mean you have to rain on other people's parade. My parents are over—have been for, like, ever—and my dad is happy, so quit your crap."

I shrink back, hating that Taylor has now garnered everyone's attention while also loving her even more for standing up for her dad and me.

"Taylor, if your mother knew how you were speaking to me …" Pamela splutters. "You know I'm just looking out for your family. Did you know this woman killed her husband and baby? Do you really think your mom would want you hanging out with someone like that?"

I gasp at her words, tears blurring my vision, and I wish I could do or say something. But instead, I stay stuck in my spot, unable to speak or move.

"What is wrong with you?" Taylor yells. "My family is right here, and Kinsley didn't kill anyone. It was an accident. And unless you want to say something nice about my dad or Kinsley, you need to keep that shit to yourself."

"What the hell is going on over here?" Shane barks, making me jump.

"You need to teach your daughter how to speak properly to adults," Pamela hisses.

"No, you need to learn when to keep your mouth shut," Taylor argues. "She just accused Kinsley of killing her husband and baby and told her that you and Mom used to hook up and everyone thought you guys were going to get back together."

"What the fuck, Pam?" Shane hisses, just as an older gentleman walks over and steps between Shane and Pamela.

I think he's Shane's boss, the firefighter battalion chief or something.

"I'm so sorry," the gentleman says, glaring at Pamela. "My daughter has been going through some personal stuff, but that's no excuse."

Pamela huffs and stumbles away.

"I love this department, and you know I respect you," Shane says to the man, whose name I can't remember to save my life. "But if I ever see that woman at this station or near Kinsley …"

"It won't happen again," the man says. Then, he looks at me. "I'm truly sorry. I don't know all that was said, but I'm sorry. I'm working on getting her the help she needs, but it's still no excuse."

"No, it's not," Shane says before taking my hand and stomping away from everyone back to his truck with Taylor following behind.

The ride back to their place is quiet, and I consider asking if he can drop me off at home, but I don't, not wanting to be alone.

When we pull into the driveway, Shane glances at Taylor and says, "Can you give us a moment, please?"

Taylor nods and then leans over and kisses my cheek. "Fuck her," she says to me, making me choke up and smile at the same time.

Once she's inside, Shane sighs and turns toward me. When he

sees the silent tears sliding down my cheeks, he reaches out and wipes them away with his thumb.

"While I don't condone the language my daughter used, I agree one hundred percent with what she said." He tips my face to look at him. "I don't even know where to start." He shakes his head.

"There's nothing to say," I tell him, leaning into his hand. "She said things out of spite, and you don't owe me any explanation. We all have pasts, and I wouldn't judge you for yours, especially since you've never judged me for mine."

"There's nothing to judge. And the shit she said was …" He sighs in frustration, trying to find the right words.

"Mean? Vindictive?" I finish for him. "Yeah, I know. And before I spent years in therapy, I probably would've let her get in my head, but I know that what happened was a tragic accident, and all she did was show me once again how amazing you and Taylor are."

"We love you," he says, leaning in and kissing me.

"And I love you both."

Twenty-Seven

Shane

Me: Want to order in Italian for dinner tonight?

Sour Patch: Rain check? I'm meeting with a realtor after work.
But I can come over afterward if that's okay.

I stare at my screen, unsure of how to respond. How is it that I've been spending damn near every minute of my free time with Kinsley, yet she's never once mentioned moving out of her parents' pool house or buying a place of her own?

I start to type a response, but delete it. Then stare at her message.

"Why are you looking at your phone like it just offended you?" Taylor asks, plopping into the seat across from me.

"Kinsley's house-hunting," I grumble, setting my phone down since I have no idea how to reply to her message.

I should probably ask what houses she's looking at or if she needs a second opinion, but I'm kind of annoyed that she didn't bring it up to me in the first place. We've talked about the renovations I've done to this place, so she knows I'm knowledgeable about houses.

"Why?" Taylor asks, scrunching her nose up in confusion. "She should just move in here. She pretty much already has anyway."

She's not wrong. Since Kinsley and I started dating, she spends more nights here than not. Even on the nights when I work my shift, she'll come over and watch movies with Taylor.

"You'd be okay with that?"

I already know she would be. She's made it clear when she told me she'd love for me to marry Kinsley, but this is her home, too, so before I consider asking Kinsley to move in, I want to make sure my daughter is completely on board with it.

"Dad, seriously?" she scoffs. "You already know I love Kinsley."

"I know, but hanging out with someone and talking books is different from her moving in and living here permanently."

"I'm not a kid," she says. "I know how it works, and I'm one hundred percent okay with Kinsley moving in. I'd even share my library with her. She's awesome, and she makes you happy, and if you guys want to move in together and get married and give me a cute little brother or sister, I'm okay with that. But you'd have to do it soon if you want me to babysit because I only have a year until I graduate and move to the city."

"Hey now, slow down," I say, glaring at her. "You can't be saying shit like that. I'm in denial of you growing up and leaving me for college, and I prefer it that way."

Taylor rolls her eyes. "Be in denial all you want, but unless NYU denies me, in sixteen months, I'll be moving into my dorm."

"You'll get in," I tell her as she stands.

"I know." She grins. "I've worked too hard not to."

"Where are you going?"

She just got home from her shift at the coffee shop.

"To pack. My trip with Mom is coming up and I haven't started figuring out my outfits, and then I'm going out with Haley and Jillian.

Is it okay if I spend the night at Haley's? We both work the opening shift tomorrow morning."

"Sure. Just check in with me when you're in for the night."

"Always!" she yells, running up the stairs.

Once I'm alone again, I pull up Kinsley's and my text thread to read what she wrote again. I'm about to respond when an idea forms, and I send her a completely different response from the one I planned to send.

Me: I'll see you when you get here. Love you.

Her response is instant.

Sour Patch: Love you too!

"Hey, Tay!" I yell up to my daughter. "I have an errand to run. You good?"

Instead of responding, she appears on the landing. "Where are you going?"

"To convince Kinsley to move in with us."

"You got this, Dad," she says, a grin spreading across her face. "But in case you need any help, feel free to text me. You know I'm an expert on romance. I mean, my pizza idea worked."

She shrugs, and I chuckle.

"Yeah, it did. But I think I got this one."

And if all goes as planned, Kinsley will be moving her shit in here instead of into an empty house.

Twenty-Eight

Kinsley

"I KNOW THIS IS AN OLDER HOUSE, BUT WITH SOME WORK …" The realtor goes on about the potential the house has, but I tune her out, frustrated that we've seen six houses in Brookside and I couldn't imagine living in a single one. I know it's only our first day of looking, but there aren't many options in this small town, and every one she's shown me felt like a stranger's house.

I mean, obviously, that's what it is, but when Brandon and I moved into our apartment, it was an empty space, yet it still felt right. I could imagine where we'd hang our photos, the color scheme I wanted to go with. And when my parents gifted us their old townhome, it instantly felt like it was where we belonged. Maybe it's because I'm an artist, but I need to be able to feel something, and with every place I've seen, I haven't felt anything.

"I appreciate you showing me these places," I tell Patty, the realtor my mom is friends with. "But none of these feel right."

"That's okay," she says. "There are plenty of options. I'll take a look this week and then call you to schedule some walk-throughs once I have a few worth checking out."

After saying goodbye, I text Shane that I'm on my way, and he lets me know he's home and to just come in when I get there.

The second I open the front door, Becky jumps off the couch, greeting me with a wagging tail, so I kneel in front of her to pet her, and she comes closer, licking the side of my face.

Since I'm here often, I've gotten close with her. I never had any pets growing up since my sister is allergic, but I can see why people get dogs. She's so sweet and cuddly and protective.

When I stand, ready to find Shane, I notice the living room is dark, and there are several tea lights placed on various surfaces, creating a warm glow.

And then my eyes land on the pink rose petals all over the floor.

"Shane?" I call out in confusion.

Becky runs to the back slider, so I let her out into the backyard and then close the door. When I turn around, I find Shane standing in the middle of the room, dressed in a blue button-down shirt with his sleeves rolled to his forearms, showing off his corded muscles and the sexy sleeve I tattooed on him, along with a pair of jeans that mold to his thighs perfectly. His hair is freshly cut, and his beard is trimmed … and he's holding a beautiful bouquet of flowers that match the petals on the floor.

"What's going on?" I ask with a nervous laugh.

"These are for you."

He hands me the flowers, and I lean in, closing my eyes and inhaling the floral scent. When I open my eyes, Shane is staring at me with a mixture of concern and confusion, and I realize there are tears in my eyes.

"I love flowers," I choke out. "And it's been a long time since anyone gave them to me. They remind me of happiness and all that is good in the world."

I smile down at the flowers, bringing my nose back to them so I can smell them again. "Thank you," I whisper, looking back up at him with a smile.

Shane chuckles softly. "I knew it," he says, cupping the side of my face. "I knew that under all that sour would be so much damn sweet." He leans in and presses a soft kiss to my lips that has me craving so much more. "If buying you flowers means seeing you light up like this, I'll buy you flowers every day."

I snort out a laugh. "Maybe it's not just the flowers," I tell him honestly. "Maybe it's partly you."

Shane's smile grows. "I love you, Kinsley, and I was wondering ..."

He reaches into his pocket, pulling out a small box, and my heart starts to pound in my chest.

There's no way he would propose, right?

It's too soon.

But even as that thought crosses my mind, a small part of me can imagine spending my life with Shane as my husband. He's sweet and selfless, and the sex is incredible. He's such a good person, and when I'm around him, the world feels like a better place because he's in it.

But it's too soon, I remind myself. *We only just started dating ...*

My thoughts are cut off when Shane opens the box, exposing a key.

"This is the key to my house," he says softly. "Taylor and I spoke, and we would love for you to move in with us."

As I stare at the key in his hand, it hits me that if I say yes, I would move from my parents' pool house into Shane's house.

Is that the right thing to do?

For some reason, the idea of him proposing felt less intimate.

Maybe it's because engagements take time, whereas moving in together would be right now.

His home would become mine.

Am I ready for that?

"This is all so sweet," I tell him, looking around at the romantic ambiance he's created with the candles and flowers.

"Why do I feel like there's a but coming?" Shane mutters.

"No, not a but." I step closer to him and put my hands on his chest, so we're connected. "I want to move in with you. At least, I think I do."

I shake my head, hating that I kind of suck at all this.

"You're so damn good," I tell him, trying to explain myself. "You give and give and give, and you deserve someone who can reciprocate. And I just don't know if I'm capable of that.

"I want to be. I love you, and in the short time we've been together, it's the happiest I've been in a long time."

"You give me so much," he says, gliding his knuckles down my cheek. "You might not see it, but I promise that being with you makes me so damn happy. The way you are with my daughter and how every time you walk in, you make it a point to give Becky attention. Your passion for your work ... I could watch you tattoo me all day."

He chuckles. "I love going to bed and waking up to you in my arms. And when you mentioned getting your own place, my first thought was if getting to do that with you every day for the rest of my life is an option, I want you to move in here."

"I love spending time with you," I tell him. "I love going to bed and waking up with you. But I don't know if moving in together is the right move."

When he frowns, I reach up and run my finger along the seam of his lips, not wanting him to be anything but happy.

"I'm not saying no," I clarify. "I just need to make sure. A few months ago, I couldn't even imagine moving out of my parents' pool house. And then today, I was looking at houses, and … I just need a little bit of time to make sure whatever decision I make is the best one … for everyone."

Shane nods in understanding.

"Okay," he says, taking my hand in his and placing the box in it. "But the key is yours. Even if it's just so you can come and go as you want. I want you here as much as I can have you."

He grips the back of my neck and captures my mouth with his for a quick yet emotionally charged kiss. "And until then," he murmurs against my lips, "I'm going to do everything in my power to convince you that moving in is the right choice."

He glides his hands down to my ass and lifts me into his arms. Then, he carries me to his room, where he does a damn good job of convincing me that the only place I belong is right here, in his bed, with this man.

"Kinsley, wake up."

I hear Shane's voice, but it's so hard to open my eyes. The number of times he made me come last night left me in an orgasm-induced coma that I wasn't sure I'd ever wake from.

His hand glides down my side and settles on my hip, and I snuggle closer to him, loving how hard yet comforting his body is.

"Sour Patch," he says with a chuckle. "As much as I'd love to stay in bed with you, Katie and Eric had their baby last night, and my parents are on their way, so we can go to the hospital to see them."

At the mention of his parents, I freeze. I knew he had parents. He talks about them all the time. They even live next door to him.

But I've never spoken to or met them because they've been traveling in their RV all over the country.

"Hey," Shane says softly. "If you don't want to go to the hospital, it's okay. Nobody would fault you for not wanting to—"

"It's not that," I tell him, rolling over so I can look at him. "I'm okay with meeting the baby. But I've never met your parents. Do they even know who I am?"

Shane's brows furrow, and then a grin spreads across his face. "Of course they know about you." He shakes his head. "I've told them all about you, and Taylor has, too, and they can't wait to meet you. They texted that after we leave the hospital, they'd love to go to breakfast."

"Oh," I breathe.

"What's wrong?" he asks.

"I've never met anyone's parents before," I admit sheepishly. "Brandon's parents lost custody of him when he was younger, so he didn't have any family, and before him, I'd only dated a few guys, but it was never serious enough to meet the parents. I just hope yours like me."

Shane smiles. "Kins, they're going to love you. How could they not?" He presses a soft kiss to my lips. "They already know their son has fallen in love with you."

His words cause butterflies to swarm in my belly. I turn into him, hooking my leg over his, and he chuckles.

"As much as I would love to be inside you, they're actually due to arrive any minute."

"What?" I shriek, sitting up. "How did they get here so fast?"

"They left their RV with friends, so they can return to it. It would've taken them days to drive back, so they flew. Taylor is getting ready, and they should be here soon, if they haven't already arrived."

Holy shit, I'm meeting his parents today!

I jump out of bed and into the shower. Shane joins me, but I don't try anything, knowing his parents might have to wait on us if we don't hurry up.

Thankfully, I have enough clothes here that I can pick out something nice to wear. While I'm doing my makeup, Taylor yells that her grandparents are here, and Shane says we'll be down soon.

I love that he didn't leave me to walk down alone, proving once again that he's always thinking about me.

Once we're both ready, he takes my hand in his, and we head downstairs. The sound of laughter fills the space, and I can't help but smile when I hear it. The way Taylor and her grandparents are talking and laughing reminds me of my family. They're clearly close.

"Son!" His dad comes over and gives Shane a bear hug when he sees us. "And you must be the infamous Kinsley."

He steps back, and I'm able to take him in. His eyes are brown, like Shane's, and he's about the same height as his son. He's not as muscular and toned as Shane, but it's clear that, even at his age, he's fit. Shane mentioned he used to own a construction company that he sold when they retired.

"That's me," I breathe out, my heart thumping behind my rib cage as I pray his parents like me. I've heard horror stories about parents not liking their child's significant other. One time, Natalia dated this guy whose parents hated her and despite him really liking her, he broke up with her.

"It's nice to meet you, Mr. Evans," I say, trying to be polite while extremely nervous.

"Oh, nonsense." He shakes his head. "Family calls me Pop." He leans in closer, like he's about to tell me a secret. "And I hear you're pretty damn close to being family."

"Kurt," an older woman, who must be Shane's mom, chides. "Don't scare her away."

She steps over to me. "I'm Cathy, but you can call me Grams."

She smiles warmly, and I know immediately where Shane gets his smile from.

"Has my son been courting you properly?" Cathy asks.

"Dad's trying." Taylor laughs. "But he's not very good at it. I told him he should read a couple of my romance books."

Shane groans, and I laugh.

"He's doing a great job," I say, patting his chest. "He's pretty much made it impossible not to fall for him."

"Does that mean you're moving in?" Taylor asks, hopefulness lighting up her face.

"Umm …" I glance at Shane for help.

"She's thinking about it," he says, draping his arm across my shoulders and pulling me into his side. "Moving in with someone is a big deal. Something nobody should go into lightly."

The way he protects me warms my heart and makes me want to go all in. I just need to make sure I've completely thought it through. The last thing I want is to break his—and his daughter's—heart. I already hurt two people I loved, and I refuse to do that again.

"Oh my God," Taylor whisper-yells as she scoops Emma-Lynn into her arms. "She's so precious."

"Don't get any ideas," Shane grumbles, making Taylor glare his way.

"Do you really think I would screw up my entire future by having a baby?" Taylor scoffs. "Besides, not that it's your business, but I still have my V-card."

Shane visibly blanches. "I wasn't talking about you," he murmurs. "I thought you were trying to hint at Kinsley and me having a baby."

"Oh." Taylor cringes. "Guess I misunderstood. But now that you mentioned it, I wouldn't mind having a brother or sister." She glances at me, her face softening, and I know, without her saying anything, that she's remembering what happened to me … to my baby. "But only when or if you want to," she adds softly. "I wouldn't mind being an only child." She shrugs. "Just makes me that much more spoiled."

I can't help but choke up at her sweet words. She's only seventeen, yet she acts so much older and wiser.

"She is precious," I say, looking over Taylor's shoulder. "A beautiful little miracle. Proof that there's good in the world."

Katie and Cathy nod in agreement.

"Would you like to hold her?" Taylor asks, her words slow and careful.

"Sure."

I haven't held a baby since my daughter was born. Because she was stillborn, she was cold and still, but as I take Emma-Lynn into my arms, I note how warm she is. Her chest is moving up and down as she sleeps peacefully, and I realize in this moment how much I want to have this one day.

Not to replace the daughter that I lost—nothing and nobody can replace her—but because I want the chance to love someone the way my mom and dad love me. I want to share that love with my husband, to create a family that laughs and loves and fights. I want the good and the bad.

And as I glance up at Shane, who's watching me hold his niece with love shining in his eyes, I know I want to have that with him.

Twenty-Nine

Kinsley

"JESUS, BABY, DO YOU HAVE ANY IDEA HOW GOOD YOU TASTE?"

I pry an eye open to glance down at Shane, who's currently lying between my legs, licking my center like he's desperate for my taste.

"I think you've made me taste myself a time or two," I say, lifting onto my elbows. "Now, can you please make me come before Taylor wakes up and you're late for work?"

"Don't rush me," he says with a pout. "It's bad enough I'm going to be without this pussy for the next twenty-four hours."

He goes back to licking me, and I drop back down onto the pillow. It's been a little over a week since Shane asked me to move in, and while I haven't agreed yet, I have been sleeping at his house every night—even on the nights he has a shift.

I have an appointment with the realtor today to look at a few more places, and my mom has agreed to go with me, so I can talk to her about everything that's going through my head.

I already know where I stand and what I want, but I feel like this is a life-altering decision, and I just want to make sure I'm doing it because I love Shane and want to live with him and not because I'm using him as a crutch.

A part of me wants to insist I live on my own so I can prove that I can do it, but the other part of me doesn't want to waste time just to prove a point that nobody cares I can make.

"I must not be doing my job well," Shane says, snapping me out of my thoughts.

When I open my eyes, he's hovering above me, and it hits me that I was so lost in my head that I forgot he was going down on me and didn't realize he'd stopped.

"What's going on?" he asks, caging me in with his arms.

"I'm meeting with the realtor this morning," I admit, making his brows furrow.

"Well then, looks like I'll need to work extra hard to convince you that living on your own won't bring you half the pleasure you'd get by living with me."

Before I can respond, his phone makes a weird noise. He grabs it, sighs, and throws it back onto the nightstand. "My damn phone won't stay charged. I'm going to have to have it looked at tomorrow."

"Maybe it's because it's, like, five years old," I joke.

"Hey, it still works!"

I raise a brow.

"Well, it did," he mutters. "Now"—he leans in and traces my upper lip with his tongue—"where was I?"

Before I can answer, his mouth comes down on mine, and his tongue slips past my parted lips as his fingers slide into my pussy, making me groan when he adds another, filling me so good that I have no doubt I'll be coming soon.

The moment my orgasm hits, Shane pulls his fingers out, but

before I can complain, he's spreading my thighs wider and entering me slow and deep, his cock hitting that perfect spot that he knows will have me coming for a second time within minutes.

"Fuck, Kins," he murmurs against my mouth. "You feel this, right?" He pulls back slightly and wraps his fingers around my throat. "The way my cock fits so perfectly in your tight pussy?" He squeezes gently as his thrusts become more chaotic. "I can't get enough of you."

With his eyes locked on mine, he shakes his head as if he can't believe how much he wants and needs me, and I get it because he's quickly come to mean so much to me, and even though I want to look at those houses today to be mature and responsible, to consider all of my options, I already know that I can't live without Shane, nor do I want to. His home has become my home. His bed, mine. And all I want is to spend every day and night with this man.

"I feel it," I breathe as my orgasm begins to work its way out.

Shane must feel that it's closer because he applies the tiniest bit of pressure to my throat as he shifts his hips in a way that has me climaxing once again.

"Fuck yes," he hisses, releasing my throat and connecting his mouth with mine to swallow down my moans of pleasure as he finds his own release.

He doesn't waste any time pulling out and spreading my lips so he can watch his cum seep out of me—something he does often.

"You know, every time we have sex, there's a chance I've gotten you pregnant," he points out with a smirk that tells me he wouldn't mind it at all.

"Then, it's a good thing I have a doctor's appointment this week to get on birth control," I volley, making him frown. "Don't give me that look!" I lift my foot and give his stomach—which feels more like a concrete wall than flesh and muscle—a little shove, sitting up on my elbows. "I'm trying to be a responsible adult."

"Fuck being responsible," he scoffs, grabbing my foot and throwing it to the side so he can situate himself between my legs.

He pushes me onto my back and cages me in his strong arms. "You said it yourself," he murmurs, his mouth so close to mine that I can feel his cool breath. "The doctor said it might be harder to get pregnant, so if you did get pregnant, it'd be like it was meant to be." He hits me with a lopsided grin that causes my insides to tighten.

"You mean that?" I breathe out, suddenly feeling overwhelmed with emotion.

"Yeah," he says softly. "I get it. You're trying to take things slow and do them the right way, but if by some crazy chance you got pregnant, I'd be more than okay with it." He leans in and kisses me. "I know you need to get on birth control because you're not there yet. But that's okay because I'll be right here, waiting for you to catch up. And you will." He kisses me again and then looks into my eyes. "You and I are forever, Kinsley, and I'll wait however long you need for you to see that."

The word *forever* causes a lump of emotion to clog my throat.

"What's wrong?" Shane asks, cupping the side of my face.

"Brandon was supposed to be my forever," I choke out, "but forever only turned out to be a short time. What if it's the same with us? What if I move in and we get married and have babies and I lose you too?"

A panic attack starts to hit me as the possibility of losing Shane flashes before my eyes. He's a firefighter, for God's sake. What if something horrible happens to him? Or to Taylor?

What if—

"Hey," he says, sliding his knuckles down my cheek. "Don't do that, Kinsley. You're right. Anything can happen to any of us at any time. We're all on borrowed time. But I promise that I'll do everything in my power to make forever as long as possible."

I nod in understanding, blinking back my tears that are blurring my vision, and I count back from ten to calm myself down—a technique Julia taught me. Once my heart rate is somewhat normal, I take a deep breath and wrap my arms around Shane's neck.

"I love you," I tell him. "And I want forever with you ... whatever that looks like."

"All right, I gotta go." Shane kisses my cheek as he grabs his travel mug containing the protein shake I made him—his go-to breakfast. "I love you. Have a good day."

"I love you too." I turn around and kiss him on his lips. "Be safe."

"Always. I promised you forever, remember?"

He shoots me a wink, and I shake my head, loving how playful he is. It doesn't matter how emotional or deep I get. He always handles it with such patience.

"Taylor!" he calls out. "I'm leaving. Get down here so I can say goodbye."

"Coming!" she yells, her feet stomping down the stairs.

Becky jumps up at the commotion and trots over to them, wagging her tail excitedly.

"If you need anything while you're with your mom, text or call me," Shane says. "I don't care what time it is, if I'm at work ..."

"I know," she says, bending to scratch behind Becky's ear. "It'll be fine. It's only four days, and then you and Kinsley will be there."

"What time is your mom getting here?" he asks.

"She said around ten." She stands, and Becky comes over to me since she's done getting attention and I'm making eggs.

I glance at the time on the stove—7:50. I normally hang out here when Taylor's home if I'm off, but since she's leaving and I'm not really up for meeting the ex, I make a note to leave once I'm done having coffee and breakfast with Taylor.

"Okay," he tells her. "Text me once she's picked you up and again when you get to the city."

"Will do."

"Have fun. I love you."

"Love you too, Dad." She kisses his cheek, and then he takes off.

"Breakfast will be ready in a few minutes," I tell her.

I finish making our eggs and toast, just as Taylor comes back down with her luggage in tow.

"So, what do you and your mom have planned?" I ask, making small talk while we eat.

"I'm not sure. She loves museums and stuff, so I'm sure we'll go to a few. She's big on history and current events, hence her being a journalist. She mentioned seeing a Broadway show, and I'm hoping we can do some shopping as well, but I figured if we don't, we can go once you and Dad get there. I also found some bookstores for us to check out near campus. They might be the ones you used to frequent."

She pulls her phone out and starts to name the ones she found, and we spend the rest of breakfast talking about which stores I've been to and which ones are new. Since we're doing the guided tour on Friday, we make a game plan to check out the bookstores on Saturday.

When we've finished eating, I offer to do the dishes when Taylor remembers that she forgot to pack her favorite pair of shoes.

I'm standing at the sink, washing the dishes with Becky lounging by my feet, when the front door opens. Becky jumps up in excitement while I turn the sink off, assuming Shane came back for something.

I'm drying my hands when a feminine voice says, "Who are you?" in an accusing tone that has me spinning around.

I know immediately that it's Jamie, Taylor's mom. She has the same red hair, green eyes, pale skin, and freckles as Taylor. They might as well be twins. Hell, if Taylor wants to know what she'll look like in twenty years, she only has to look at her mom.

Who, I just realized, is standing in the kitchen without having been let in.

"Hi," I say, extending my hand. "I'm Kinsley."

Jamie's gaze flits from my face to my hand, making a face as if it's personally offended her. "Is there a reason why you're standing in the kitchen where my daughter eats breakfast, not wearing any pants?" She huffs. "Shane and I are going to have to have a conversation about him allowing his one-night stands to hang out like this in front of our daughter."

Okay, so this is how it's going to go.

I should've expected it based on how her friend behaved at the barbecue, but I was hoping I wouldn't have to find out yet, hence me planning to leave before she got here.

"One, I have pants"—I lift Shane's T-shirt to show her I'm wearing a pair of cotton shorts underneath—"and two, I'm—"

"Mom!" Taylor appears, wrapping her arms around her mom while her mom continues to glare daggers my way, and I briefly thank God that Shane was the one who raised Taylor because she clearly has his personality.

"Have you met Kinsley?" Taylor asks when she pulls back.

"I have," Jamie says, plastering on a fake smile for her daughter's sake.

"I actually need to go," I tell Taylor. "Have a good trip with your mom."

I give her a quick hug and pet Becky, who's wagging her tail and demanding attention, and then, after grabbing my phone and keys, I leave without bothering to get changed, just wanting to escape as fast as possible.

Once I'm home and dressed, I have a seat on my couch, grabbing my current read. But I'm only a few pages in when the quiet gets to me. There's no Taylor talking my ear off and stomping up and down the stairs. No dog wagging her tail and begging for attention. Usually, when I'm reading while at Shane's, he's watching a sports game on the TV while touching me in some way.

But here, it's just me and the quiet.

Missing Shane, I shoot him a text even though he just left for work not too long ago.

Me: Miss you.

He texts back within seconds.

Shane: Miss you more, baby. I'm counting down the minutes until I get you to myself for the next four days. I expect you to be in my bed, waiting for me, tomorrow morning.

Since we're going to be heading into the city to meet with Taylor on Friday, Shane took the rest of the week off. I still have to work the next few days, but I don't have to be in until later, so waiting for him in his bed is definitely going to be happening.

But I still have to mess with him, so instead of agreeing, I respond with: And what's in it for me?

Instead of the message showing delivered, after several minutes, it turns green, and I roll my eyes because his phone probably went dead again. We will definitely be getting him a new phone this week.

Since I'm clearly not in the mood to read—or be in this quiet house by myself—I head over to my parents' place. My mom is in her library, reading a book, but my dad is nowhere to be found.

"Where's Dad?" I ask, making my presence known.

"With your uncles. They're on a mission to find a new poker table since the one in Jase's man cave needs to be replaced."

She closes her book and stands. "You ready to go see some houses?"

I nod even though looking at houses is the last thing I want to do.

Seven houses, two condos, and one townhome later, and Mom and I are sitting at the coffee shop, drinking our iced lattes.

"The second home we saw was nice," Mom says. "The yellow was a bit much, but that can be painted."

"Yeah, but you can't see the kitchen from the living room."

Mom smirks.

"What?" I shrug. "I like when the living room can be seen from the kitchen. It feels more open. When Taylor and I are watching TV and Shane is cooking …"

Her smirk widens, and I huff in annoyance.

"What?"

"Nothing." She shrugs nonchalantly. "I'm just wondering when you're going to admit that the only house you want to live in is the one where Shane and Taylor live."

"It is," I admit, "but it's too soon. Right? I mean, Brandon and I didn't move in together for years and—"

"Don't do that," Mom says, losing her smirk. "Don't compare. It's not fair. Shane isn't Brandon, and the love you share with him isn't the same." She leans in and takes my hand in hers. "The accident changed your life, and you aren't the same person you were when you were with Brandon."

When I frown at her words, she adds, "That's not a bad thing, Kins. It just means that you, of all people, know how short life can be. You have to go by what you feel in here." She gently taps the area above my heart. "What is your heart telling you?"

I don't even have to think about it when I say, "It feels like being with Shane and Taylor is where I'm meant to be. I don't want to waste time questioning things. I just want to live, and when I'm with Shane, that's exactly what I'm doing."

"Then, I think you already have your answer," Mom says, squeezing my hand.

"I'm sorry for dragging you to see houses."

"Nonsense." She waves me off. "I already told Patty you wouldn't be buying anything, but you needed to see for yourself that what you want is to live with Shane and Taylor."

"Is that why she took off after giving us the codes to all the houses?" I laugh. "I thought she was flaking."

Mom shrugs, taking a sip of her coffee. "So, when are you going to move in?"

"I was thinking I'd tell Shane in the morning, and then we could figure it out together. He surprised me with this romantic night and a key to his house when he asked me to move in, so maybe I'll do something similar since Taylor is out of town with her mom and we have the place to ourselves."

Speaking of which … I shoot Shane a text, letting him know I'm done looking at houses and to call me later if he's bored. Sometimes during his shift, when it's slow, he'll FaceTime me, and we'll talk while I'm in bed. It's quiet and nice, and it feels like he's with me even though he's not.

The text once again turns green.

"What's wrong?" Mom asks.

"Shane's phone is dead. It's, like, a hundred years old, and it won't keep a charge. Thankfully, he said he'll have it looked at tomorrow. But I'm hoping it's done for and he'll get a new one."

After we finish our coffee, I head to the lingerie shop to pick up something sexy and then stop at the store to grab the items I need for my surprise.

When I get to Shane's house, the dog walker is just coming out, and I make a note to let Shane know there's no reason to pay someone to walk Becky when I'm here all the time anyway. He did it for the days and nights Taylor wasn't around and he was on shift, but between the three of us, someone is always around.

I send him another text, but when it turns green, I wonder if maybe he's having an issue with his messages, so I try to call him, only it goes to voice mail. I consider calling him at the station, but what if he's busy?

I put away the lingerie I bought since I won't need it until tomorrow morning. And then I go about placing sticky notes all over the room—Kinsley's toothbrush goes here, Kinsley's shampoo here, Kinsley's clothes here, Kinsley's pajamas here, Shane and Kinsley sleep here—so when he reads them, he'll know that I'm planning to move in.

Once I'm done, I grab my book and settle in on the couch to read. Becky joins me, so I pet her while she cuddles into my side, snoring softly.

Eventually, I get bored of reading, so I make myself a sandwich for dinner, and then I work on some tattoo designs for clients until my eyes can barely stay open. I go to bed, falling asleep almost instantly, excited at the thought that if all goes well, I'll officially be sleeping here, in Shane's arms, every night.

"Kinsley, I need you to wake up."

Shane's gravelly voice has me waking with a sudden jolt. I must sit up too quickly because the room spins.

"What's wrong?" I ask, shaking the dizziness away.

Even if I didn't hear it in Shane's tone, I see the black circles under his eyes and the stress lines in his furrowed brows. Something is wrong … very wrong.

"I need you to stay calm," he says, his words causing me to be anything but. "Taylor and her mom were in a car accident. I tried to call you, but my damn phone went to shit, and I didn't know your number by heart. I called the shop, but of course, nobody was in yesterday …"

He continues to speak, but the only detail I can absorb is that Taylor was in a car accident.

Like Brandon.

Like me.

Like my unborn baby.

And just like that, everything around me goes black.

Thirty

Shane
Twenty-Four Hours Earlier

"SHANE, MY MAN." LUKE GRINS UP AT ME WHEN I WALK INTO the station, and I already know what's coming next. "I'm craving a steak and baked potato. What do you say? Want to go by the store and pick up dinner?"

Chuckling, I shake my head as we go about doing an equipment check.

Luke and I have been working together for too many years to count, and before that, we went to school and played baseball on the same team. He's been married for about six months now, and he doesn't have the heart to tell his wife, who loves to cook, that she can't cook for shit. So, instead, he pretends to love it, barely eats, throws it away when she's not looking, and then begs me to cook on our shifts since he can't cook either.

"I'm going to buy you and your wife cooking lessons for whatever holiday is next," I tell him, pulling my phone out of my pocket when it beeps, indicating that it's dying, so I can try to charge it.

I connect it to the charger, but after a few seconds, it disconnects and blinks red, letting me know it's almost dead and not charging.

"Fucking phone," I grumble, accepting the fact that I'm going to have to buy a new one. It's not that I'm cheap, but phones are expensive, and I literally use it for nothing except to text and call my friends and family. Hell, half the time, I can't even keep track of where the thing is.

Once the trucks have been checked, Luke says, "Store?"

"Yeah, yeah." I wave him off. "Let me get a workout in, and then we'll go."

"I'll join you," David says.

We're just finishing up our run on the treadmill when my phone goes off with a text from Taylor, letting me know that she's with her mom and they're on their way to the city.

But before I can respond, my phone dies.

"Fucking hell!" I throw my phone on the table. "Can I borrow your phone?" I ask David. "Mine's dead, so I need to let Taylor know to call the station if she needs me."

"Sure."

He hands it over, and luckily, I know her number by heart. It rings once, twice, a third time, then goes to voice mail.

"Hey, Tay, my phone is dead. When you get to the city, call me at—"

My words are cut off by the sound of the emergency tone ringing out through the station, followed by the details of the incident—two females in a car accident, both injured and in need of medical help.

Since we're the only fire station in town, our engine fits two patients, so we jump into emergency mode, heading straight to the scene of the accident.

Because we've done this too many times over the years, my brothers and I work like a well-oiled machine. So, when David gets to the victims before I do since I'm grabbing the gear with Luke and yells for me in a tone that indicates he's freaking out, I'm confused … until I get over to him and see why.

"Taylor!" I yell, racing over to my little girl, who's lying on the ground, unconscious.

There's metal and glass shards poking out of her skin in various places, and her arm is in an awkward position. I glance at the other woman, who's still in the car, and even from here, I can see it's Jamie.

"Shane," David says. "Snap out of it, man. We need to get them to the hospital."

His words kick my ass into gear, and like the professionally trained paramedic I am, I work with my guys to get my daughter and her mother stable and to the hospital, the entire time praying that my little girl will be okay.

Shane
Present

"Fuck, Sour Patch."

I pick her up and carry her over to the couch while Becky follows, sensing that something is wrong. When I sit on the couch with her in my lap, Becky sniffs and then licks her face.

"It's okay, girl," I tell her, patting her head. "Kinsley just needs a moment."

The entire way here, I was worried about telling her what had happened because of how her late husband and baby had died, but I thought by telling her to stay calm, she'd listen. In hindsight, that probably wasn't the best approach.

I move several strands of hair out of her eyes as she stirs slightly, blinking several times in confusion. I know the moment she remembers what I told her because her face pales, and she scrambles to climb out of my lap.

"Where is she?" she chokes out when I try to hold her so she won't freak out. "Please tell me she's okay."

Tears fill her lids, and I tighten my hold on her. The past twenty-four hours have been hard enough, and the last thing we need is Kinsley in the hospital as well.

"She's okay. I wanted to call you, but I didn't know your number, and I didn't want to leave her yesterday. Her phone got smashed in the accident, and mine's fucked. I'm so sorry I couldn't reach you sooner."

The first thing I'll be doing when this is all over is getting a new phone, and then I'll be writing down Kinsley's number. Not being able to get ahold of her was fucking hell. I just kept thinking she thought I was blowing her off.

My parents were already at the hospital with Eric and Katie when we brought them in, and I asked my dad to go by my place to see if Kinsley was there, but she wasn't. And when he went back last night to check again, he found her and Becky asleep in my bed. He asked if I wanted him to wake her, but since visiting hours were over, I didn't want to stress her out when there was nothing she could do, so I told him to let her sleep and that I would tell her myself in the morning.

Thankfully, my parents have cell phones, so I've been able to use my mom's phone to communicate with everyone.

"It doesn't matter," Kinsley cries. "I just need to know she's okay. I need to see her."

"We can go see her," I tell her, standing and setting her on her feet. "But you need to be prepared. She broke her wrist in numerous places, and the glass caused several gashes that needed to be glued. When she hit the concrete—"

"What do you mean, she hit the concrete?" She gasps, covering her mouth as tears slide down her cheeks.

"Her seat belt wasn't on."

"Why the fuck wasn't her seat belt on?" she demands.

"It was bad luck," I say, pulling her into my arms. She's shaking like a leaf in the middle of a damn storm. "Her mom had a benign tumor pressing on her brain that no one knew about. It caused her vision to blur, and she crashed the car while Taylor was unbuckled, reaching in the back seat to grab her iPad so she could go over the list of things she wanted to do in the city. She flew out, landed on her wrist, breaking it, and cracked her head on the concrete. She suffered from a concussion and had to have surgery on her wrist to fix it."

"Can I see her?" she asks, her eyes glassy and her face blotchy.

"Yeah, but if you want to wait until she's home …"

"No." She shakes her head. "I need to see her for myself. To know she's okay."

"Okay. We can go see her. They've put her and Jamie in the same room."

"Is Jamie okay?" Kinsley asks.

"Yeah, the tumor wasn't cancerous, but between her shoulder getting dislocated in the accident and needing to have emergency surgery to have the tumor removed, she's going to need some time to recover."

Kinsley nods in understanding. "When can Taylor come home?"

"They're hoping tomorrow. Because of the concussion, they want to keep her another night to monitor her and check to make sure there's no swelling in her brain. I told her I needed to find you, and she asked me to grab some stuff for her since she doesn't have any working electronics."

"I'll grab her favorite books," she says with a forced smile. "Just give me a few minutes to get ready."

"Thanks." I reach out and wipe a few tears that are resting on her cheeks and then give her a quick kiss. "I'm going to grab some clothes and toiletries she asked for. I'll meet you back down here."

She nods, and as she starts to walk away, I can't help the ominous feeling that comes over me, like everything is about to change—and not in a good way.

So, I grip the curve of her hip and pull her back toward me. "Everything is going to be okay," I tell her, palming her cheek and looking into her eyes. "You know that, right?"

"I know," she says. "Everything will be okay."

Thirty-One

Kinsley

As I walk to the master bedroom, I keep repeating to myself that Taylor's okay, hoping if I repeat it enough times, I'll believe it. Shane might've said everything will be okay, but until I see her for myself, I won't believe it.

I don't understand why her mom would let her take her seat belt off. And what was Taylor thinking? It only takes a split second. What if the accident were worse and she flew farther? Hit her head harder? We could've lost her, and for what? So she could have her damn iPad? The second I see her—after I confirm she's okay—I'm going to make sure she never does that shit again.

When I step inside the room, I'm hit with all the sticky notes I put everywhere. I quickly remove them all since now isn't the time to be cute—and Shane obviously didn't notice them when he was in here, waking me up—and shove them into my makeup bag, knowing he won't look in there. After I get ready, I locate a few of Taylor's favorite books and then meet Shane by the front door.

On the way to the hospital, a thought hits me. "How did you know about the accident if your phone was dead?"

Shane glances at me and then back to the road. "It's a small town. There's only one fire station, and the accident was on Main Street."

"Oh my God." I gasp. "You …"

"Yeah," he says, not needing me to finish my question. "We got the call, and I didn't know it was them until we arrived. I freaked, but David helped me get my shit together. We only had five men on the scene with two victims. Luckily, she veered off the road and hit a bench so nobody else was injured. We're not usually supposed to treat family, but we needed all hands on deck, so David and I treated Taylor while Luke and Brian treated Jamie. Billy was driving the engine."

"I'm so sorry," I say to him, threading our fingers together. "I can't even imagine. When Brandon and I got into the accident, I blacked out. I used to wish I had stayed awake, wondering if maybe I could've saved him, but the doctors said there was nothing I could have done, so at least I don't have the horrible memories of seeing him hurt and watching him die."

"It was the worst call I've ever had," he admits. "I'm just so damn thankful that Taylor's okay. That they're both okay."

A few minutes later, we arrive and head in through the main entrance. After going through security, the scent of antiseptic hits me in the gut like a horrible reminder that while hospitals help people, not everyone who comes in has the luxury of leaving.

I take a deep breath as I try to slow my racing heart, but when I glance down, I find my hands shaking, and I worry that I'm about to have a panic attack.

"Can I meet you there?" I ask Shane, spotting a little store that has balloons and candy. "I want to grab a few things for Taylor." And have a chance to calm myself down before I end up in a full-blown panic attack.

"Yeah. They're on the third floor, room 302." He kisses my temple. "I know this is hard for you, so if you can't stay …"

"I'm okay," I tell him. "Taylor is worth the discomfort. I'm just glad she's okay."

I spend a few minutes picking out a cute stuffed dog and her favorite candy, and when I know my emotions and nerves are in check, I head up to their floor.

I find their room number, and I'm about to walk in when I hear voices that halt me in place.

"Dad!" Taylor giggles. "I can't wear this gown. It's so ugly. Tell him, Mom."

"She's right, Shane," Jamie chides playfully. "What if that cute doctor comes back?"

"That doctor is too old for you to even be looking at," Shane growls, making Taylor and her mom laugh.

I step closer, peeking in, and find Shane sitting on the edge of Taylor's bed with her mom lying in a bed next to her.

I watch them for a few minutes, and I can't help the way my gut churns at how much they look like a family.

When Jamie groans, Shane gets up and goes to her side.

"You okay?" he asks, concern laced in his tone.

"Yeah." She smiles warmly at him. "But would you mind fluffing my pillows? I feel like I'm sinking."

"Sure." He goes about fixing her pillows, and once he's done, she threads her fingers through his, making me want to rip her hand off and cry at the same time.

"Thank you, Shane," she says. "This whole ordeal has been horrible, but I really appreciate everything you've done for us."

"It comes with the job," he says, removing his hand from hers and taking a step back. "Both as a paramedic and Taylor's dad."

When he turns around, his eyes lock with mine, so I step inside.

"Hey," he says, walking over and giving me a kiss.

"Hey," I say back.

"Kinsley, I'm so glad you're here," Taylor says with a soft smile.

I glance over at her, and it's then I notice all the tiny cuts on her face and arms. Her wrist is covered in a bright pink cast, and her forehead looks like it's been glued together.

But she's alive. Her heart is beating behind her rib cage, her eyes are a bright green, and she's smiling.

I try to keep my tears at bay, but they still come. "I brought you some stuff," I say, setting her books and items I bought at the gift shop on the table. "But first, I need to hug you." I lean over and give her a gentle hug, kissing the top of her head and inhaling her scent. "I was so worried," I tell her, sitting on the edge of her bed. "When your dad told me what happened …"

"I know," she says, "but I'm okay. A bit banged up but okay. I promise. Though Casey is going to be super pissed when she finds out that I won't be going to Nationals or Worlds since I'll be stuck in this cast for the next few months. She's going to have to rework the entire routine."

I want to tell her that none of that matters and the only thing that does is that she's alive, but I know cheerleading is important to her, so instead, I say, "You have next year, right?"

"Yeah." She shrugs. "If we make it that far."

"You will," I assure her. "It won't help with cheerleading, but I brought your favorite books." I grab one of the books from the bag. "Figured you could get lost in Marco and Bella."

She told me they're her go-to couple when she's feeling down.

"Thank you." Taylor grins, taking the paperback from me. "What else is in there?" She eyes the bag playfully.

"I saw this, and it reminded me of Becky." I hand her the stuffed dog. "And your favorite candy." I grab them out of the bag and set them in her lap. "When you get out of here, we're going to need to—"

"Shane," Jamie says, cutting me off, "I hate to cut this visit short, but my head is pounding, and the noise is making it worse." Her words come out sugary sweet, but someone would have to be an idiot not to see what her intention is.

"Jamie," Shane starts, but I stand, not wanting to cause anyone stress, least of all Taylor.

"It's okay," I tell him. "I actually have a doctor's appointment I need to get to."

With everything going on, I forgot about it, until the calendar alert on my phone went off and reminded me while I was in the gift shop.

"Everything okay?" he asks, clearly having forgotten that I mentioned going to the doctor this week to get checked and get on birth control.

"Yeah, just a routine checkup."

"Okay, I can drive you there …"

"No need." I plaster a smile on my face. "It's actually in the west wing of the hospital."

"Oh, okay. Do you want me to go with you?" He glances from me to Taylor, torn between staying with her and coming with me, and I shake my head.

I didn't plan on him going, but even if I did, I wouldn't pull him away from his daughter.

"Nope." I lean on my tiptoes and kiss his cheek. "Stay here. Taylor needs you."

"All right, well, when you're done, if you want to come back here—oh!" He pulls out a phone. "Before I forget, give me your number. I'm using my mom's phone until I can get mine replaced."

I relay my number to him and then walk over to Taylor. "I love you, kiddo."

"Love you too," she says. "When I'm better, do you think we can still go see NYU?"

"Of course." I squeeze her hand. "Just focus on healing."

I turn to leave, and as I walk by Jamie, I'd like to glare at her, but instead, I shoot for the higher road and say, "I'm glad you're okay."

"Thank you," Jamie murmurs. "If you could turn down the lights on your way out, I think that will help with my headache."

When I get to the doctor's office, I fill out the paperwork, give them a urine sample, and then head back with the nurse so she can get my weight and blood pressure.

She hands me a paper gown since I'm due for a full checkup today, and after getting undressed and putting it on, I hop up onto the medical bed to wait for Dr. Greenburg.

"Kinsley," the doctor greets me a few minutes later. "How are you, dear?"

"I'm good," I tell her as she takes a seat and opens her laptop.

"And how's your mom?" she asks, looking up at me.

The thing about living in a small town is that everyone knows everyone, and since there are only a few gynecologists in Brookside, all of whom are part of the same practice, the women in my family—who live in town—come here.

"She's good. I think my dad is close to retiring for a second time," I say with a laugh. "She mentioned them doing some traveling since all of us are grown and out of the house."

She told me this after I told her I was moving in with Shane. I think she's been wanting to travel, but she was afraid to leave me. I'm glad they'll finally get to enjoy their retirement. They deserve it.

"That sounds like fun," she says, "but I expect she won't be going too far since she'll be a grandmother soon."

She smiles warmly, and I look at her in confusion.

Did my sister get pregnant and not mention it? I didn't even know she was serious with anyone.

Oh my God, did my brother knock someone up? No way. Mom would've told me.

"I'm sorry," I say. "I think you're confusing my mom with someone else because nobody in my family is pregnant."

Dr. Greenburg's brow furrows. She looks at her laptop, types something, and then murmurs, "Oh, dear."

"Everything okay?" I ask, getting a little antsy.

"Yes, I thought you were here for a new pregnancy appointment, but I misunderstood."

"Oh, no," I say with a laugh. "The opposite actually. I'm planning to get on birth control."

Dr. Greenburg stands and walks over to me. "The reason I thought it was a new pregnancy appointment was because the urine sample you gave tested positive for pregnancy."

It takes me a moment to wrap my brain around what she's saying, but once I do, I shake my head. "That doesn't make sense," I tell her. "I was told that due to the accident and the placental abruption, it would make it harder for me to get pregnant."

Dr. Greenburg nods in understanding. "How about we do an ultrasound, and that way, we can know for sure and go from there?"

She pushes the ultrasound cart over to the side of the examination bed, and suddenly, I really wish Shane were here with me.

"Since you didn't know there was a chance you were pregnant, I'm going to assume you wouldn't know how far along you are?"

I try to do the math in my head, but Shane and I have never used protection—despite saying we would start—and my periods have always been irregular. I was on birth control for it when I was younger, but after I lost Brenna and Brandon, I wasn't in the right state of mind to deal with it.

"No, I have no clue. It couldn't be more than a few weeks … maybe a couple of months? I'm sorry." I sigh. "I sound so irresponsible."

"No, you don't," she says. "You sound like most women who aren't keeping track. Since you aren't sure, I'm going to do a transvaginal ultrasound. Let me just grab the nurse."

While she's gone, I lie on my back and stare at the ceiling, refusing to believe that I'm pregnant. There's no way. I mean, sure, we never used protection, but to get pregnant that quickly … no, there has to be something wrong.

A few minutes later, Dr. Greenburg returns with a nurse. She goes about checking me and then grabs the probe to do the ultrasound.

The screen is gray and fuzzy at first. I have no clue what I'm looking at, but I try to stay focused on what she's doing, not wanting to think about the last time I was in this position. I was married, and we were so excited. Brandon held my hand while we both held our breaths, waiting for the doctor to confirm I was in fact pregnant.

"And that's the heartbeat," Dr. Greenburg says, snapping me out of my thoughts.

"Wh-what?" I stammer, blinking back the tears that are filling my lids. "Say that again."

"Based on the size, you're roughly seven weeks pregnant with a due date of December 16. Looks like you'll be getting the best Christmas gift."

"Are you sure?" I ask even though I can tell she's not messing with me. No doctor would be that cruel.

"I am," she says. "I know this is a shock to you, but you're only seven weeks, so you do have options."

Oh my God, she thinks …

"No," I breathe out, my hand going to my belly. "I don't want any options. I want this baby. It's just … I don't feel sick at all, and I was told it would be hard to conceive."

"I read your chart, so I understand your concern. But right now, everything looks good. I'm going to recommend you get started on a prenatal vitamin and avoid as much stress as possible. I'm going to have the nurse run a panel of blood, and we'll see you back in two weeks."

"I thought it was every four weeks."

"It is, but because of your history, I want to see you every two weeks, just so we can monitor you closely." She pulls the probe out, sets it down, and removes her gloves. Then, she walks back over to me. "Congratulations, Kinsley. Despite the odds and what you were told, you're carrying a little miracle. Some would say it was meant to be."

Thirty-Two

Kinsley

I'M PREGNANT. I CAN'T BELIEVE IT.

I mean, I can since Shane and I never used protection, but I always thought it would be harder to conceive—which, up until recently, I didn't plan to ever do. I'm scared since I'm only seven weeks and anything could go wrong, but I'm also excited, and I'll do everything in my power to protect this baby.

I head back to where I know I'll find Shane, so I can tell him the crazy good news, but when I get there, I walk in on what looks like a serious conversation.

"She doesn't have anywhere to go," Taylor says. "And the doctor said she needs to be looked after while she recovers."

"I heard the doctor," Shane says with a sigh.

"Is everything okay?" I ask, stepping into the room without knocking since the door was open.

"Yeah," he says, standing and coming over to me. "Can I talk to you for a minute outside?"

I glance from him to Jamie, whose features are expressionless, and then to Taylor, who looks concerned.

"Yeah," I say, my stomach tightening in worry.

"Dad," Taylor says, "you don't have to go outside to talk. Kinsley will understand."

"Understand what?" I ask in confusion.

"My mom lives in the city, but she doesn't have anyone, and the doctors don't want her to be alone while she recovers from brain surgery, so she mentioned staying with us, and I told Dad that we have the guest room that never gets used. We can't leave her to go back to the city on her own. She's family."

"Taylor," Shane says, his tone serious. "I need to speak to Kinsley outside."

He takes my hand and guides us over to an empty waiting room and has a seat. "I'm sorry about all this. Taylor is worried about her mom since she doesn't have any other living family."

Family.

My thoughts go back to what Pamela said at the family barbecue …

"Everyone knew they would still hook up when she came into town."

"With Shane never dating, we all thought maybe one day …"

"When's the last time you slept with her?" I blurt out.

Shane flinches, and I already have my answer.

"Taylor was about two years old, and Jamie came back into town to visit for a few days in between jobs. I was young and dumb," he says. "She said she missed me, and I believed her. But then she left, and I told myself it would never happen again, and it never did."

I nod in understanding, feeling slightly better since that means it's been fifteen years since they were together.

"If you aren't comfortable with her staying with us …"

"It's fine," I say, refusing to be the bad guy. "Like you said, you're her only family, and anyway," I choke out, "you don't need my permission. I don't even live there."

I pull out the key to his house from my purse and hand it to him. "In case she needs it."

Shane shakes his head. "That's your key, Kins. Besides, she won't be there for long. Only until she's recovered and the doctor has given her the green light to travel on her own."

We head back inside, and Shane lets Taylor and Jamie know that Jamie is welcome to stay to recover. Jamie smiles warmly at Shane, and Taylor cheers.

"This is going to be so fun!" Taylor exclaims. "We can watch movies, and I can show you all my favorite books. It sucks we didn't get to go away, but at least we'll get to spend time together."

My stomach sinks as I imagine the three of them in Shane's house. Will he cook breakfast for her the way he does for me? Will they lounge on the couch together and watch movies as a family?

What will happen when Taylor finds out about this baby? She said she was on board with it before, but how will she react now? Will she think I'm trying to encroach on her family? Will she resent me and the baby? This will be the first time Taylor's ever had her parents under the same roof. How could she not want that? Doesn't every child want their parents to be together?

My hand goes to my belly, and I wonder for a moment if this is punishment for what I did to my husband and baby. I fucked up my chance at a family, and now, here I am, pregnant with Shane's baby, thinking about us becoming a family when the fact is, he already has one. And who the hell am I to make him choose? What makes me and this baby more important than Taylor?

"Kins," Shane says softly. "Everything okay?"

"I need to go," I murmur, plastering on a fake smile. "I forgot I have an appointment."

It's not a complete lie … at least it won't be once I text my therapist, requesting an emergency therapy session because of my intrusive thoughts that I know aren't realistic but still feel real anyway.

"Okay." And then as if he just remembered, he adds, "How did your doctor's appointment go?"

"Fine," I say vaguely since now isn't the time to tell him that I'm pregnant.

He has enough going on, and the last thing he needs is to add the stress of me being pregnant to the equation.

He looks at me for several seconds, and I can tell he's trying to figure out what I'm hiding, but then he sighs and says, "I love you, Kins."

I say the words back, but for some reason, as the words leave my lips, instead of us sharing how we feel about each other, it feels like we're saying goodbye.

Thirty-Three

Kinsley

Shane: I need to see you.

Shane: I miss you.

It's been a week since Taylor and her mom were discharged.
Since I found out I was pregnant.

Since I thought I would be moving in with Shane and Taylor,
but instead, Jamie moved in.

Because we were supposed to be out of town, I didn't have any
work scheduled, so I've been spending time in the pool house.

Shane has reached out several times, but I couldn't bring myself
to see him, to force him to choose between his recovering daughter
and baby mama and me. So, I've been avoiding him. And in doing
so, I've sunk into a weird sort of depressive state. My therapist says
it's self-sabotage.

Instead of speaking to Shane about my feelings, I'm letting my
mind wander to crazy worst-case scenarios. I know it's not healthy,
but I've allowed myself to go down that dark road.

Shane: I'm coming over.

When his text comes through, I consider telling him not to, but the truth is, I really miss him. Being here, alone, without him and Taylor and Becky, has been hard. I used to crave the quiet, and now, I resent it. I got used to sleeping with Shane's body wrapped around mine, and now, my bed feels cold and lonely.

A few minutes later, Shane's knocking on my door, and it hits me that I haven't showered in a few days. My hair is a mess, and I'm wearing ratty pajamas.

Another knock, and I get up, resigned to him seeing me like this because it's too late to do anything about it now.

I quickly fix my hair the best I can in the mirror, plaster on a fake smile, and open the door, hoping he won't see right through me.

But one look at me, and his face drops. "What the hell is going on?"

"I'm not feeling well."

It's not a lie since morning sickness has crept up on me, and I've spent more time than I'd like with my arms around the toilet seat, praying to the porcelain god.

"Why didn't you tell me?" he says, stepping inside. "What's wrong? Are you taking medication? Fuck, Kins. I thought you were avoiding me. You should've told me that you were sick."

I swallow thickly at the assumptions he's making, but don't correct him. "I'm sorry. I know you have a lot going on," I mutter, sitting on the couch. "How's Taylor … and Jamie?"

"Taylor is fine. Jamie is Jamie. Right now, I'm concerned about you." He pulls me into his arms. "Are you taking meds?"

"I'm okay," I tell him, avoiding his question.

He looks at me for several seconds, like he wants to call bullshit, but instead, he nods and nuzzles his face into my neck. "Fuck,

I've missed you so much. I thought you were staying away because Jamie is there."

"Just sick," I tell him even though he's right.

"I was thinking—" he begins, but he's cut off by the sound of his phone ringing.

Since he was too busy with Taylor and Jamie, he ordered a new phone online and had it shipped the next day.

"Give me a second." He kisses my temple and then pulls out his phone, the name *Jamie* appearing on the screen.

His gaze flits between the phone and me like he's trying to choose between us. The phone stops ringing, and then a moment later, it starts up again.

"You should answer it. It could be important."

With a sigh, he nods in agreement and then hits Accept, putting it on speaker.

"Shane, is everything okay?"

"You called me," he says.

"And you didn't answer."

"I'm fine," he tells her. "Is everything okay?"

"Yes. I was just wondering what time you'd be home. Taylor and I are making dinner."

Home. She's calling his place home.

A ball of emotion gets lodged in my throat as I fight back tears.

"You're both supposed to be resting," he says.

"And we have been. You know this. We just thought we'd do something nice for you since you've been waiting on us hand and foot for days."

"Dad! We made your favorite," Taylor calls out through the phone.

"You should go," I murmur.

But he shakes his head. "I'm with Kinsley. Let me see if she wants to come over for dinner."

"Oh, yes! Tell her to come," Taylor says. "I feel like I haven't seen her in forever."

Shane says he'll talk to me and then hangs up.

"Come over for dinner, please."

"With your ex?" I cringe. "Won't that be awkward?"

"Maybe," he admits. "But that doesn't mean I don't want you there. She's just that … my ex. But you're everything, Kins. You're my present and my future. Besides, you heard Taylor. She wants you there. It's been too long since we've gotten our Kinsley fix, and we both know you can't say no to her."

Because he's right, I agree to go. After I shower, we head over to his place despite knowing this is going to be a disaster.

The moment I walk in the door, Becky comes running over, begging to be pet, so I reach down and give her some love before I follow Shane into the kitchen, where Taylor and her mom are cooking.

"Kinsley!" Taylor shrieks. "You're here." She wraps her arm that isn't in the cast around me. "Where have you been?"

"I've been a bit under the weather," I tell her.

"If you're sick, should you be here?" Jamie asks, her words sickly sweet, but her gaze is anything but.

"Jamie," Shane says, a warning clear in his tone.

"What?" she asks. "I'm still recovering, and getting sick could possibly set me back."

"This smells delicious," Shane says, looking at Taylor with a smile as he lifts the lid of the pot that seems to contain some kind of soup while ignoring Jamie's comment. "I have my shift tomorrow. If there are any leftovers, I'll be bringing it with me."

"*If,*" Taylor says with a laugh. "We both know you're going to eat it all in one sitting."

Shane shrugs. "Probably."

"What is it?" I ask.

"Broccoli cheddar soup," Taylor says, grabbing a spoon and scooping a little out. "And we serve it in bread bowls. Grams taught me how to make it. When I was little, she would cook with me. Since my mom sucks at cooking, I was showing her how to make it."

"I do not suck," Jamie mumbles. "I just prefer to focus my attention on more important things, like the poverty in Madagascar."

Shane's phone goes off, and his brows furrow in concern. "It's the station. I'm going to take this and then wash up for dinner." He leans in and kisses me. "I'll be right back."

Once he's gone, the veil hiding Jamie's cattiness seems to disappear. "So, Kinsley, Taylor tells me you tattoo people for a living. That must be fun."

"She's so talented," Taylor gushes, missing her mom's condescending tone. "She's doing Dad's arm, and she re-created a picture I drew for him when I was little."

"That's cute," Jamie says. "Hey, Taylor, would you mind grabbing my migraine meds from the bathroom? I feel one coming on."

"Sure." Taylor rushes out of the kitchen, and the second that Jamie and I are alone, she steps over to me, her eyes narrowed.

"I'm just going to cut to the chase," she says. "I messed up. I was so busy chasing the next story that I didn't consider what I had here. But now that I'm back, I'm not going anywhere."

"I think that's great," I tell her. "Taylor's mentioned that she misses you when you're gone, and she only has a year left until she leaves for college."

It will suck, having to deal with this woman on a daily basis, but it will be worth it for Taylor to have her mom in her life—

"I think you're misunderstanding," Jamie says, her voice low. "I want my family back."

She steps closer, and that ball of emotion that was already lodged in my throat damn near chokes me, making it hard to breathe.

She wants her family back. Not just Taylor. She wants Shane.

"I'm sure you can understand where I'm coming from," she continues. "Had you not been the reason your family is dead, you'd still be with them. But they are because you killed them. But I didn't kill mine, and after spending this past week with Shane and Taylor, I want a second chance, and since my family is still alive, I can have that."

Her words cause my heart to clench and tears to prick my eyes, but I blink them away, refusing to let her see that she's affecting me.

"I know you care about Taylor," she says, "so I'm hoping you'll care enough to walk away and let her have what she's always wanted—a family. It might be too late for you, but it's not for us. So, I'm asking you, as one mother to another, to walk away and let me put my family back together."

"Are these them?" Taylor asks, walking back into the kitchen and shaking a pill bottle.

"Yes, thank you." Jamie kisses her forehead. "I don't know what I would do without you."

"Well, lucky for you, you'll never have to find out," Taylor says with a giggle.

I stand in the corner, watching them go about putting the finishing touches on dinner as Jamie's words run on replay in my head.

I hate her for what she said, but at the same time, I can't blame her because she's not wrong. If Brandon and Brenna were still here, I would be living in the city with them, and there wouldn't be anybody or anything that could stand in between them and me.

"Have you thought about moving here?" Taylor asks her mom.

"I have," she says. "And I think I'm going to look at some places."

"Oh my God! Yay!" Taylor jumps up and down. "I'm going to tell Dad!"

She runs out of the room, and Jamie glances at me.

"Do you see how happy she is? Do you really want to be the one to destroy her happiness?"

"She's happy because her mom is staying for once," I choke out, finally having found my voice. "But you're missing one important detail—Shane. He loves me, not you."

Jamie scoffs and sets the ladle down. "And you're missing one important detail—Shane loved me first, and he would be with me again. The only reason why he won't consider it is because of you. Because you're fragile and weak and he feels bad for you."

"That's not true," I whisper, swallowing down my insecurity. "He loves me."

I know he does. I see it in the way he looks at me and holds me … the little things he does for me, the way he makes love to me. He can't even go too many days without seeing me.

"He'd get over you." She shrugs. "I can't make you do anything, but for the sake of my family, I hope you'll do the right thing and walk away."

I hate this bitch so much, but what if she's telling the truth? Taylor deserves to have her family back together, and Shane did say that it was Jamie who walked away, not him. If I wasn't in the picture and she stayed, would he take her back?

My stomach roils at the thought of not being with Shane, of raising our baby without him, but she's right. I had my chance at a family, and even though it was an accident, I lost it. Can I be the reason another family isn't together? Do I deserve another chance at having a family at the risk of another family not being together?

A few months ago, my answer would've been no, I didn't deserve it. But now, Shane has shown me that I'm worthy of love, of second chances, and as much as I hate that it might mean potentially keeping a family apart, I can't just walk away.

"I'm sorry," I tell Jamie, the tears I was trying to keep at bay falling. "But I love Shane and Taylor, and I'm not going to walk away until they send me away. I love them so damn much, and maybe that makes me selfish, but I want a life with them."

"That's exactly what it makes you," Jamie hisses. "Selfish. And when my daughter finds out that you're the reason why her mom and dad can't live under the same roof, she'll hate you."

"She's wrong," Taylor says, making me jump. "Mom, you're wrong," she says. "I love you, and you'll always be my mom, but Kinsley is our family too. While you've been gone, she's been here every day, loving Dad and me."

"That's going to change," Jamie tells her. "I'm going to stay, and we can be a family."

"Then, stay," Taylor says. "Stay because I'm your daughter and you barely know me. But if you're doing it because you think Dad is going to take you back, that's pathetic. He loves Kinsley, and she loves him, and they deserve to be together. I told her that if she got together with my dad, there wouldn't be any other woman drama, but you've made me a liar. And honestly, the way you're acting is embarrassing."

Taylor's hands go to her hips, and her chin juts out as she glares at her mom.

Jamie's eyes widen in shock. "Taylor …"

"No, Mom. I've seen the way you've been batting your lashes at Dad all week, and I didn't want to think the worst of you, but you've just confirmed it."

"Confirmed what?" Shane says, walking into the room.

"Mom told Kinsley to walk away so she could get her family back together," Taylor says, making Shane's eyes bug out.

"What?" he hisses, glancing from Taylor to me and lastly Jamie.

"Shane, please," Jamie begs. "Can we talk *alone*?"

"Fuck no, we can't," he barks. "I let you into my home, and you pull a stunt like this? You've clearly recovered enough if you have time to plot against me and try to ruin my relationship with the only woman I've ever loved."

"You loved me too," Jamie points out.

"No, I didn't," he scoffs. "I liked you. I was a teenager, and you were cute. We had fun together, but it wasn't love. I love my family, I love our daughter, and I love that woman right there." He nods toward me, and butterflies attack my chest.

"You need to leave," he tells Jamie. "If you're not up for going back to the city, there's a bed-and-breakfast in town. I'll have my dad take you there."

Jamie glances at Taylor—I think hoping she'll argue for her mom to stay—but Taylor says, "I agree. You should go."

With a huff, Jamie storms out of the kitchen.

Shane calls his dad, who agrees to take her to the town's bed-and-breakfast, and within a few minutes, she's gone without so much as a goodbye.

"I'm so damn sorry," Shane says, pulling me into his arms. "I never should've left you alone with her. I knew she was hinting at wanting to get back together, but I ignored it, thinking once she was healed, she'd leave again, and then we'd go about our life."

"It's my fault," Taylor says. "I asked you to let her stay with us, and you only said yes for me."

"It's not your fault," he corrects. "She's your mom, and you were trying to do a good thing. She took advantage of the situation." He looks at me and notices my hands shaking. "Are you okay?"

"Yeah, I think I'm just hungry."

"Fuck, the food," Shane says. "Three of the guys have caught the same bug, and they're short a man. I agreed to go in tonight. I can call them …"

"No," I tell him. "Go. They need you. We can talk about all this once you're done with your shift."

"I can pack your soup for you to bring to the station," Taylor offers. "And I'll make sure Kinsley is still here when you get back."

"Okay, thanks." Shane chuckles.

"Come here," he says, pulling me into his arms. "I don't know what was said, but I know Jamie can be brutal with her words. I want to know what happened, what all was said, so we can discuss it and move forward, but until then, I need you to know that even if you weren't in the picture, I wouldn't be with her. You're not keeping our family from being together—you *are* my family."

"And mine," Taylor says, those two words helping to piece back together my heart.

"Well, that's good," I choke out. "Because you both are mine too."

"What are these?" Taylor asks, holding up the dozens of sticky notes.

"They're mine." I snatch them from her. "It was my way of telling your dad I wanted to move in with you guys."

"Okay. Then, why were they in your makeup bag?"

"Why were you in my makeup bag?" I mock glare.

"I'm out of finishing spray, so I was borrowing yours."

"You're not even going anywhere," I say with a laugh.

"I don't need to be going anywhere to put on makeup," she sasses. "I put on makeup for me, not for anyone else," she scoffs, making me laugh harder.

God, I love this girl so much.

"Now, back to these." She waves the sticky notes in the air. "Are you serious about moving in?"

"Yeah, I was planning to surprise him, but then …"

"The accident," she finishes.

"Yeah."

And then, after the Jamie drama, Shane had to leave for work. We've been texting while he's been gone—in between the movies Taylor and I have binged and the reading marathon we had last night—but telling him that I want to move in with him in a text message doesn't feel right.

"Well, what are you waiting for then?" she asks. "These are cute, but if you want to show him that you want to move in, why don't you just do it?"

"What?"

"You already know my dad and I want you here. So, why don't you just move in? He'll like that way more than sticky notes." She shrugs.

"And you're definitely okay with that?"

I was little when my mom and dad moved in together, but I still remember when she sat down with me to make sure it was okay. I loved Lachlan, so it wasn't even a question, but Taylor is older, and having another woman move in, after spending all these years with just having her dad to herself, will be a big change.

"I'm more than okay with it," she says. "And you won't have to worry about my mom causing problems. She texted me this morning that she accepted an assignment and took off."

"I'm sorry." I extend my arms, and Taylor slides in next to me so I can hug her.

"I hate that she couldn't stay for me," she says, laying her head on my shoulder. "But it's for the best. She's not made for this kind of life, and it's better that she left now instead of later."

She pops her head back up. "So, what do you think? Want to surprise my dad?"

"I don't know how we'd pull it off. He's due to get off his shift in the next hour."

"That's easy!" She grins. "Just distract him. The guy will go anywhere you go. And while you're keeping him busy, I can find some friends who will help me move your stuff in. And I know my grandpa will help for sure."

Her idea is sound, but I'm not sure how I could distract him. And then an idea hits me.

I pull out my phone and send Shane a text.

> Me: Can you meet me at Exposed Ink when you get off work?
>
> Shane: Of course. Everything okay?

We had a session scheduled for today, but it wasn't until later.

> Me: Yeah, I have a scheduling conflict, so I need to move our session to earlier.
>
> Shane: Okay, see you soon.

"Done," I tell Taylor.

"Perfect. Now, give me your key and leave the rest up to me."

Thirty-Four

Shane

Fuck, it's been a long couple of days. Usually, I don't mind being at work, but having to leave after the bullshit drama Jamie tried to cause nearly killed me.

All I wanted was to spend the night with Kinsley, reassuring her that she was all I wanted. But I couldn't leave my brothers in a lurch. If something had happened and they didn't have enough guys, I would have had to live with that. So, begrudgingly, I left.

But that didn't stop me from texting Kinsley damn near every hour. Especially after Taylor relayed what she'd overheard when she was eavesdropping on her mom and Kinsley.

I'll never forgive Jamie for the shit she spewed, and while she might be Taylor's mom, after the crap she pulled, she's no longer welcome in my home, and I told her as much.

All I want is to go home and spend time with Kinsley and my daughter, but going to the shop is the next best thing since it means hanging out with Kinsley and watching her do what she loves.

"Shane," Lachlan says when I walk in, extending his fist to bump mine. "How's it going?"

"Good," I tell him, glancing around to make sure Kinsley isn't near us. "I need to speak to you, but not here. Could we meet up for a drink one day this week?"

After nearly losing my daughter, I'm reminded of how delicate life is, and I'm done wasting time with Kinsley. I love her, and I want her in my home, in my life, as my wife.

Lachlan stares at me for several seconds before a knowing grin spreads across his face. "We can meet up for a drink anytime you want." He leans in so nobody else can hear his next words. "But if you're going to ask me for permission to marry my daughter, you already got it."

I chuckle and nod. "Am I that obvious?"

"You remind me of myself," he says with a shrug. "A man who's in love and wants everything with the woman who's captured his heart."

"Dad, what are you going on about?" Kinsley asks, appearing out of nowhere. "Shane, let's go," she says. "We need to get started."

"Yes, ma'am," I tell her, following her back.

"I was thinking for today's session, we'd do something a little different," she says, closing the door behind her, but it's been nearly forty-eight hours since I've seen her, and the only thing I want to do is kiss her.

So, I do just that.

Spinning her around, I gently press her against the counter, and holding her face, I press my lips to hers. She tastes like the perfect mixture of sweet and sour, and I realize she's chewing on a Sour Patch Kid.

"You stealing my favorite candy?" I ask when I pull back.

"You left them here, and I had a craving." She shrugs. "I missed you," she says, wrapping her arms around me.

I lift her onto the counter and step between her legs. "I missed you so much fucking more."

I trail my tongue along the seam of her lips, loving that she tastes like my favorite snack, and then run my tongue along her neck.

She tilts her head to the side, giving me better access to kiss my way up to her ear.

"I think we should forget the tattoo and go back to your place so I can spend the next couple of hours inside of you," I tell her.

"Not happening," she says, pushing me back. "Sit. I have a cool design, but since it's not one you suggested, I'm going to draw it with a marker first, and then if you like it, I'll tattoo it."

"Okay." I sit in the chair. "But you know I trust you, right? Anything you want to draw on me, I'm going to be good with it."

Kinsley grins, her eyes twinkling with happiness. "I love you, Shane."

"I love you." I grip her hips and pull her into my lap because I can't help myself. "One more kiss, and then you can draw on me."

I reach around and fist her hair, pulling her face toward mine, and kiss her with everything in me, hoping like hell she knows just how damn much I love and want and need her in my life.

When we break apart, her eyes are glassed over, and I'd bet anything, if I reached into her pants, she'd be wet. But I don't because if I did that, there would definitely be no drawing on me today.

She climbs off me and sits on the rolling seat and then gets to work. While she draws on my arm, she's quiet, concentrating on whatever it is she's creating. It doesn't take long, and once she's done, she steps back and smiles at me, looking almost nervous.

"Okay," she says, handing me a mirror. "Take a look."

But before I can look, she snatches the mirror back. "Actually, I'm going to take a picture of it, so it's not backward."

She pulls her phone out and takes a picture, then hands it to me. The first thing I notice is that she drew Sour Patch Kids.

"That's you and me and Taylor," she says, pointing to each one.

"That's cute. I love it." But then I notice that there's a fourth one. It's smaller than the others, making it look like a Sour Patch Baby instead of a kid.

I look at the image she drew, trying to wrap my head around what it means.

And then it hits me—a Sour Patch Baby.

"Are you pregnant?"

I glance up at her, and she nods, the most beautiful smile lighting up her face.

"I am," she admits, taking my hand and placing it on her belly. It's still flat, but the thought that there's a baby growing in there has me wanting to never let go.

"I had it confirmed when I went to the doctor to get on birth control." She smirks. "Looks like you have some kind of super sperm," she says with a watery laugh as she pulls a piece of paper out of her back pocket and hands it to me. It's a sonogram photo. "And our little Sour Patch is due December 16."

Holy shit, she's pregnant. Against all odds, we created a miracle.

"I wish I had been there," I tell her, looking at the photo. It's just a grainy gray-and-white image with a tiny speckle in the middle since she's not that far along, but she's fucking pregnant with my baby.

"You know what this means, right?" I say, setting the photo aside and standing.

"That we're going to have a baby?" she smarts.

"That you're moving in with me." I grip the curves of her hips and pull her toward me. "And I'm not taking no for an answer."

"We'll discuss it," she says, her gaze filled with mirth. "Now, do you want the tattoo as is, or are there any changes you want me to make?"

"It's perfect," I tell her, kissing her soft lips. "But make sure you leave room."

"For what?"

"For when we need to add more babies because we both know this won't be the last time that I knock you up." I smirk, the thought of Kinsley growing my babies in her filling me with pride. "I have plans to fill you with as many Sour Patch Babies as you'll give me."

"I still think we should go to your place," I say a few hours later as I drive us back to my house.

After she finished my tattoo, she mentioned she was hungry and asked if we could go to lunch. After we ate, she insisted we go by the bookstore, saying she needed to pick up the latest book in the series she loves—and grabbed a copy for Taylor as well.

When I suggested we go back to her place—since the only thing I want to do is get her naked, and going to my place means having to wait until Taylor either leaves or goes to bed—she said she'd rather go to my place.

"We'll have plenty of time for that," she says, raising a brow that tells me she knows right where my mind is at. "I want to get back to Taylor. She's still recovering."

"She's going to school tomorrow," I point out. "She's doing just fine."

"Then, we'll have all day tomorrow to get naked."

"I'm not waiting until tomorrow," I scoff. "Tonight, the second she goes to bed, I'll be inside you. It's been too long since you were avoiding me." I shoot her a look, and she smiles sheepishly.

"I'm sorry. It was just so much at once. With Taylor and Jamie getting into the accident and then finding out I was pregnant. I think I needed a minute to wrap my head around it all."

"I get it," I tell her, taking her hand and threading my fingers through hers. "But you're not in this alone, so in the future, when you need to wrap your head around shit, come to me, and we'll do it together."

She's quiet for a few minutes, until we pull into my driveway, and she turns toward me. "I want to wait until I'm twelve weeks to tell anyone outside of our immediate family about the baby, just in case something happens. We can have dinner with my parents and yours to tell them, but I want to tell Taylor first."

Fuck, this woman. She has no idea how special she is, but I'm going to spend every day for the rest of our lives reminding her.

When we get inside, Taylor's sitting on the couch, reading a book. She looks up and grins at Kinsley like she knows a secret, and when Kinsley smiles back, it confirms they're definitely up to no good.

"What's going on?" I ask.

"Nothing," Taylor says in a tone that tells me she's full of shit.

"I got you a new book." Kinsley reaches into her bag and pulls out the one she got her at the bookshop. "And they're signed."

"Oh my God, thank you!" Taylor jumps up and grabs the book, giving Kinsley a hug. "I wanted to get one before they sold out, and I completely forgot to ask Jillian to get it for me. We're going to buddy-read it, right?"

"Of course." Kinsley pulls out her copy of the book and waves it around before setting it down. "After we finish our current read."

"Cool. I'm going to put it in my room."

"Okay, and then afterward, can you come back down?" I ask her. "Kinsley and I want to talk to you."

Taylor looks between us suspiciously, nods, and then heads upstairs.

"You know," I say, pulling Kinsley into my arms, "we never discussed you moving in here. With a baby on the way …"

"A baby that won't be here for several months," she notes. "I need to go pee, and then I'm going to freshen up."

I follow her into my room, and the second we enter, something feels different. The first thing I notice is a candle on the dresser. One I haven't seen before.

"Did you buy this?" I ask, picking it up. It's white, and it reads, *We love sex in the first chapter.*

"No." She laughs. "My cousin Natalia gave that to me a few years ago for my birthday."

She takes it from me and sets it down, then heads to the bathroom, but I stay where I am, looking around. There's a picture frame on the dresser that wasn't there before. It's of Kinsley and her parents in a whitewash wooden frame. I've only been to her place a few times since we usually come here, but I remember it being on her end table in her living room.

I glance around and notice several more items that weren't here before—Kinsley's pink silk pillow, a HomePod that I saw on her nightstand, another picture of her and her cousin Natalia.

I walk toward the bathroom to ask when she brought this stuff over—I mean, I don't care because I want all her shit here, but I'm confused as to when she brought it all over since she hasn't been here—when my eye catches on the clothes in the walk-in closet.

I step inside and find that my clothes have been moved to one side while the other side contains hundreds of pieces of women's clothing. I look down and find several pairs of women's shoes next to my sneakers.

"Sour Patch," I call out.

"Yeah?" she says, popping her head out.

When I meet her eyes, I can see the humor in them, and it clicks—why she and my daughter were smiling at each other.

"Tell me this isn't some kind of joke," I warn. "Did you move all your stuff in?"

"I didn't," she replies in a serious tone, making my heart sink.

Did I somehow misunderstand?

"But Taylor did while I kept you busy all day," she adds, a smile spreading across her face.

"You moved in?" I ask, just to make sure.

"I did. Taylor apparently knows a lot of guys with big trucks, and they helped her move all my stuff in."

"Taylor," I call out.

"Yeah?"

"I owe you big time!"

"I know," she shouts back, making Kinsley giggle.

"This is for real?" I ask, scooping her up into my arms and making her squeal.

She wraps her legs around me and nods. "This is for real."

"No take-backs?" I joke.

"No take-backs," she says through her laughter as I carry her over to the dresser and set her on it.

"Fuck, do you have any idea how happy you've made me?"

"Hopefully as happy as you've made me," she says. "And I'm hoping as happy as Taylor will be when we tell her that she's going to be a big sister."

Oh shit. That's right. Taylor's waiting for us out in the living room.

"She's going to be thrilled," I tell her, giving her a quick kiss. "Let's go share the good news." I lift her off the dresser and set her on the floor. "And then, tonight, after she's asleep, we'll be celebrating," I say as we walk out of our room in search of Taylor. "Not only is my woman pregnant with my baby, but she's living here for good. Can life get any better than that?"

"Can life get any better than what?" Taylor asks, having caught the tail end of what I was saying.

"There's something we need to tell you," Kinsley says.

"Kinsley's pregnant," I finish.

Taylor grins and then laughs. "I knew it!" she exclaims, hugging Kinsley and then me. "When we were moving your stuff, I found the prenatal vitamins, but I didn't want to assume. This is so awesome! When are you due?"

"December 16," Kinsley tells her.

"Wow," Taylor breathes. "I'll be graduating, and you'll have a new baby in the house."

"Speaking of which, we never got to go on that tour," Kinsley points out. "You should check when the next one is so we can go."

Taylor nods, but doesn't look very excited.

"Hey, what's wrong?" I ask her.

Taylor shakes her head, but her glassy eyes tell a different story.

"Tay, talk to me," I insist.

"It's nothing," she says as tears fill her lids and fall. "I guess it's just hitting me that this time next year, I'll be graduating." She sniffles. "It's going to be hard to leave you, and now, with Kinsley living here and a baby on the way, it's going to be even harder."

"Yeah," Kinsley agrees, "it will be hard, but you won't be far at NYU, and we'll come visit."

"I'm going to hold you to that," Taylor says, enveloping Kinsley in a hug.

"Trust me, we'll be there so often that you'll get sick of us," Kinsley tells her. "Want to see a picture of your baby brother or sister?"

"Yes!" Taylor pulls back, and Kinsley pulls out the sonogram image.

"Check it out," I say, pointing at the speckle on the paper. "That's our Sour Patch Baby."

Taylor laughs. "You guys are so adorable. Meet-cute, single dad, small town. I seriously hope, one day, I find love that's fit for a romance novel."

"You will," Kinsley tells her. "Because you've seen firsthand what a good man looks like." She glances at me. "And you won't settle for anything less."

"Damn right I won't," Taylor says. "Now, I just have one question. Because everyone knows that a good romance book has to have a happily ever after … when are you guys getting married?"

Thirty-Five

Kinsley
Two Months Later

"**S**OUR PATCH!" SHANE CALLS OUT, SLAMMING THE FRONT door.

"In the bathroom!" I yell back.

I swipe some lip gloss on my lips, fluff my hair, and then head out, meeting Shane in the bedroom.

"You look fucking gorgeous," he says, palming my cheek and planting a soft kiss on my lips. "How are you feeling?"

"Good."

Since I entered my second trimester, the nausea has almost completely subsided, and I've gained most of my energy back. Thankfully, it was never horrible to begin with.

"Give me a few minutes to shower, and then we'll get going."

Shane was teaching a class at the health club. Usually, when I'm not working, I'll join him to get my exercise on. But since we're meeting our family for dinner, I came straight home from work to get ready. With me being almost four months pregnant, we've decided it's time to tell everyone that we're expecting a baby.

"I'm going to let Becky out for a few minutes before we go."

"Sounds good," Shane says. "Is Taylor coming with us?"

"No, she's meeting us there with Logan."

Shane grimaces, and I hold back my laugh. It's not that he doesn't like Logan. He just doesn't like the fact that his little girl is dating.

When we arrive at the restaurant, everyone is already there. I give hugs to my aunts and uncles and cousins, stopping to give Natalia an extra-long hug.

"You look so beautiful," she says, scanning her eyes down my body. "Happy and in love suits you." Her gaze lands on my belly, but she doesn't mention me being pregnant since nobody else but her, Taylor, and our parents know.

"Thank you. It feels good to be happy. Speaking of which …" I grab her hand so I can admire her engagement ring. She and Kevin got engaged last month when they were in London, so I haven't gotten to see the ring or congratulate her in person. "It's beautiful."

"Thank you. Kevin definitely did good."

After we talk for a few more minutes, promising to do a girls' day soon to properly catch up, I move on to Shane's parents, who have decided to stick around since their granddaughter was born and they found out we're expecting.

I wasn't sure how it would be with them living next door, but they're great about respecting our space while spoiling us. Kurt is constantly making sure I don't need anything from the store, and Cathy makes me so many delicious, healthy meals. I've also gotten closer to Katie, and I'm learning a lot from her since she has a newborn.

Once we have a seat and the waiter takes our drink orders, I stand to get everyone's attention. "As you know, Shane and I asked everyone to come to dinner tonight because we have news that we'd like to share with you."

Shane stands and threads his fingers through mine. "Kinsley and I are expecting a baby. She'll be sixteen weeks next week, and she's due on December 16. It was unexpected," he says with a smirk that has me blushing, "but we're very excited."

Everyone cheers and gets up to congratulate us. When my aunt Celeste calls dibs on organizing the baby shower and I stiffen, remembering the last baby shower that took place just before I lost my husband and baby, Shane pulls me into his side and kisses my temple.

"Actually," Shane says, "we've decided to do something a little different. After the baby is born, we're going to have a celebration and invite everyone to come and meet him or her."

We've talked about it, and I told him that while I feel like I'm mentally doing well, I don't think having a baby shower is something I want to do. I would be so worried of history repeating itself that I wouldn't enjoy myself. And thankfully, Shane understood.

"Oh, that will be lovely," Celeste says. "And I stand by my offer to organize it."

"Thank you." I give her a hug, and then we have a seat since the waiter has returned with our drinks.

Dinner is a blast, and as I laugh and talk with everyone, I think about how blessed we are to have so many friends and family who love and support us.

When the waiter asks if we'd like to do dessert, my pregnancy craving kicks in, and I order two desserts since I can't pick one.

I'm eating my way through both when Shane turns to me and says, "I got this for you."

He hands me a book, and I glance at him, puzzled.

"I already have this book," I say with a laugh. "You were there when I met the author and got it signed. Thank you though," I tell him, not wanting to sound unappreciative.

"It's different," he insists. "Open it."

I set my fork down and open the book despite knowing it's the same copy I have. The author only made one edition. It's a hardback with sprayed edges and …

When I flip the cover over, I'm met with a square hole in all the pages.

"What the heck did you do?" I gasp, wondering why the hell he cut out the pages. It's then I notice that inside the hole is a small black velvet box.

"Shane," I say slowly as he plucks the box out of the pages.

"Kinsley," he says, pushing his chair back and kneeling in front of me. "I've learned a lot about romance from living with two bookworms."

I hear Taylor laugh, but I can't take my eyes off Shane.

"In every book, there are trials and tribulations that the main characters go through before they get their happily ever after. When Taylor told me about some of the things the authors put their characters through, I didn't understand why they would be so cruel, and I didn't understand why she would read books like that. Until I met you."

He smiles warmly at me, and I blink back my tears.

"You are strong and resilient, loving and warm," he continues. "You care with your entire heart, and even when life knocks you down, you get back up.

"I learned that for a book to be considered romance, the

characters must get a happily ever after. Otherwise, it's called a love story."

He palms the side of my face, and my heart races behind my rib cage as I take in his words. He's not only pouring his heart out to me in front of our family and friends, but he's once again showing me how much he understands.

"Your love story was with Brandon," he says, "and it sadly ended in tragedy. If I could give you him back, I would, but since I can't, my hope is that I can give you the next best thing—the reason why you love romances."

He lets go of my face and pops the box open, exposing a beautiful diamond ring.

"I want to write our own story," he tells me. "One that ends with the happily ever after that you deserve. Chapter one was the allergic reaction—or as Taylor would say, our meet-cute."

Everyone laughs while I start to cry.

"Chapter two was convincing you to go on a date with me."

"You worked damn hard for that date," my dad says, making Shane chuckle.

"Chapters three, four, and five were getting you pregnant." Shane leans in and lowers his voice. "I gave it three chapters because we spent a lot of time unknowingly working on that one." He playfully winks.

Despite him whispering, everyone heard, and Taylor gags while my face heats up as I remember all the amazing sex we've had.

"You're thinking about that time on the pool table, aren't you?" he whispers.

"Shane!" I gasp, praying no one heard.

"Sorry." He chuckles. "But that was a damn good scene. Am I right?"

"You're not wrong," I admit.

"I love every chapter that we've written so far," he says, loud enough for everyone to hear, "and now, I'm asking to write many more, starting with you marrying me."

He takes the ring out of the box and looks into my eyes, and it's like everyone around us disappears. "I know you thought your last book would end differently, and we both know that there are no guarantees in life, but my hope is that we'll get our happily ever after.

"So, Kinsley Elizabeth Bryson, will you marry me and continue to write this romance with me for the rest of our lives?"

Sure, there's a chance tragedy could strike again. As he pointed out, there are no guarantees in this life. But I'll never regret any moment that's spent being happy and in love. Even knowing the way my story with Brandon ended, I could never regret it. Just like I'll never regret letting Shane into my heart.

Which is why there's only one answer I can give him.

"Yes," I tell him, throwing my arms around his neck. "I'll marry you and continue to write this romance with you."

Shane captures my mouth with his and kisses me with such passion that I feel it throughout my entire body.

When he pulls back, he rests his forehead on mine and says, "Thank you, Sour Patch. You have no idea how happy you just made me."

"Yes, I do," I tell him. "Because you make me just as happy every day."

Shane came into my life when I wasn't in a place to let love in. But little by little, with every appointment, he chipped away at the wall guarding my heart, until it was exposed and vulnerable and ready to love once again. And now, I'll spend the rest of my life loving him—for however long that might be.

Epilogue

Shane

A Little over a Year Later

"**W**ELL, THIS MIGHT JUST BE THE PERFECT WAY TO wake up," Kinsley rasps, still half asleep.

I glance up at my wife with her sleepy eyes, messy hair, and makeup-free face and think, not for the first time, how lucky I am that she not only fell in love with me, but also agreed to spend her life with me.

I go back to licking her clit, knowing the perfect spot to focus on that will send her over the edge, and sure enough, less than thirty seconds later, she's moaning my name as she comes all over my fingers and tongue.

I don't give her a chance to catch her breath before I'm pulling my cock out and entering her in one solid movement.

"Shane," she gasps as I fill her. "Condom."

"Don't want to," I grunt, caging her in and kissing her the way I'm fucking her—hard and deep.

"Oh God, Shane, I'm close," Kinsley groans.

"Tell me I can come in you," I say, continuing to fuck her raw.

Sure, I might sound like a damn caveman, but in my defense, I'm addicted to my wife, and it doesn't matter how much time I spend with her, how many times I make love to her. I can't get enough. If it wasn't for the eight-month-old and eighteen-year-old in the rooms upstairs, I'd probably live inside her. And I have every intention of getting her pregnant a couple of more times if she'll allow it.

Her eyes pop open, and she stares at me for several seconds, knowing what that means. Without protection, there's a chance she can get pregnant. We've been using condoms since our son was born, but we've talked about starting to try again. And right now, I'm straight-up telling her I want to start. If she tells me to pull out, I will. My wife calls the shots, but I'm really hoping she's going to give me the green light.

"Yes," she breathes. "Come in me, Shane."

My mouth connects with hers, and Kinsley lets go, her pussy tightening around my shaft like a vise and pulling every drop of cum out of me, no doubt coating her inner walls. The thought of getting her pregnant has my cock staying semi-hard.

"I can't believe you," she says once she's come down from her orgasm high. "Is this because of what today is?"

"No," I scoff, but she glares, knowing I'm full of shit. "You said okay," I point out.

"Only because my logic was replaced by my need to come!" She playfully smacks my chest. "Admit it. Your baby girl is leaving for college, and you're freaking out, so you're trying to fill the damn house with more babies."

Because I can't argue her logic, I simply shrug, and she cracks up laughing.

"Hey," she says, pulling my face down to hers. "You want to have another baby? You already know I'm fine with that. But you can't replace Taylor, and she's not leaving us for good. She's going to college a few hours away. She'll visit. We'll visit. It will be fine."

"I know," I say, nuzzling my face into her neck so I can inhale her scent for a few seconds.

There's just something calming about my wife. Her smell, her touch, the way she's so damn sour on the outside but sweet on the inside. I can't get enough.

After I've gotten my fill of her, I look up at her, knowing she'll get it because she's not just my wife and mother of my child—she's my best friend.

"I woke up this morning, and it hit me that she's about to be gone, and I love our chaotic house. It's full of love and laughter, and, fuck, Kins, Colton is almost one already. Soon enough, he'll be going to kindergarten, and then he'll be off to college, and it'll just be me and you and—oh fuck! Becky's already ten years old. Who knows how long she's got left?"

Kinsley snorts out a laugh, and I glare, which only makes her laugh harder.

"Colton's only eight months old, Shane. And he has many years until he starts school and even more until he goes off to college. And true, Becky is getting older, but you can't think like that. If you want to start trying for another baby, I'm okay with that." She pulls my face down to hers, and her lips caress my own as her warmth rubs against my once-again-hard length. "And since this chaotic house is still quiet, I think we have time to try again."

And that right there is one of the many reasons why I love my wife.

We're always on the same damn page.

"This is why I said I should get an apartment instead of a dorm,"

Taylor whines as she and Kinsley attempt to sort through her books, trying to decide which ones she's taking with her and leaving here. "There's not enough room in that tiny place for all the things I need."

"A book is hardly a necessity," I point out, earning a glare from Kinsley and Taylor.

"We'll get you a bookshelf," Kinsley suggests. "And you can swap them out when we visit or you come home. Living in a dorm is like a rite of passage. Everyone should do it once."

Taylor nods and sighs, and once again, I'm so thankful for Kinsley. Jamie was supposed to be here to help Taylor move, but she texted that she's stuck somewhere and won't make it. It didn't shock any of us since Taylor's only seen her once this past year.

"Tay Tay!" Colton yells, crawling toward Taylor.

He lifts his arms, and she places him into her lap, giving him a hug.

"I'm going to miss you, little man," she chokes out. "I'm going to miss everything," she says, looking from Kinsley to me. "His first real words, his first steps. Maybe I should stay home. I can take classes online …"

"Not happening," Kinsley says. "We'll take pictures and videos and FaceTime anytime you want. You've wanted this for too long and too badly to not go."

"Plus, we're gonna need your bedroom for the next baby," I joke.

"What?" Taylor screeches, her head whipping around to look at Kinsley. "You're pregnant?"

"Oh my God, no!" Kinsley glares at me. "I'm not. And we're not touching your room."

"I mean, I wouldn't mind sharing if she's a girl," Taylor offers, which makes Kinsley start to cry.

I swear it's been like this for the past couple of months since Taylor graduated. They're fine until someone says something regarding Taylor leaving, which triggers them, and then they turn into a crying mess.

"I was just kidding," I tell Taylor, taking Colton from her so she can finish packing up the last of her books and we can get going.

After loading the truck up with her stuff and her saying good-bye to my parents—who are back to traveling but came in to wish their granddaughter well on her college journey—and stopping by Kinsley's parents' place because Taylor has grown close with Quinn, we're on our way to NYU.

The drive is long, thanks to the traffic, and we have to pull over once so Kinsley can breastfeed Colton, but once we arrive, moving Taylor in doesn't take long. And before I know it, we're standing on the sidewalk, saying goodbye.

And as I look at my daughter, who somehow went from a tiny little newborn to an eighteen-year-old college student in the blink of an eye, I wish I could turn back time.

"So, this is it," Taylor says, looking at me.

"You're going to be amazing," I choke out.

The emotion in my voice sets her off, and the next thing I know, we're both crying.

"If you need anything, Tay, I'm here, always."

"I know, Dad," she murmurs. "Thank you for everything. For being the best dad ever. For raising me to be strong and independent. I love you."

"I love you," I tell her before I take a step back.

Kinsley hugs her for what feels like the millionth time, and then we stand there and watch as Taylor walks into her dorm building.

"This is really hard," I say to Kinsley as we continue to stare at the building despite Taylor having already gone inside.

"Yeah, it is," she agrees. "But I look at it like this: To get that happily ever after, you have to keep reading the book. So, while this chapter is hard, it means we get to look forward to the next chapter. And I have no doubt that Taylor is going to rock the next chapter in her life."

I slide my arm around my wife. "And what about our next chapter?" I ask, leaning over and giving her a kiss. "What does it look like?"

"I don't know," she murmurs against my lips. "I guess we'll have to keep living to find out."

I hope you enjoyed Kinsley and Shane's story. If you want more of them, you can head over to my website to read a bonus scene that takes place six months after the epilogue. And if Quinn and Lachlan intrigued you, you can read their story *in Through His Eyes*: a standalone, single mom romance.

About the Author

Nikki Ash is a *USA Today* Bestselling author of contemporary romance, focusing on single parent, secret baby, and surprise pregnancy romances. She spends her days and nights getting lost in words. When she's not writing, she's reading. From the Boxcar Children, to Wuthering Heights, to the latest single parent romance, she has lived and breathed every type of book.

Nikki resides in South Florida with her husband, two children, and dog that she considers to be one of her kids. When she's not reading or writing, she's traveling the world with her family—in search of inspiration.